OF CROWNS AND LEGENDS

CHELSEA BANNING

D1531308

TEMENOS PRODUCTIONS

This is a work of fiction. Names, characters, places, and incidents either are the product of the author's imagination or are used fictitiously. Any resemblance to actual persons, living or dead, events, or locales is entirely coincidental.

Copyright ©2022 by Chelsea Banning

All rights reserved. No portion of this book may be reproduced in any form without written permission from the publisher or author, except as permitted by U.S. copyright law.

First Paperback Edition

Published by: Temenos Productions

Cover Design by: Seventhstar Art

Copyediting Services provided by: Enchanted Ink Publishing

CONTENTS

Nimue

PRONUNCIATION GUIDE

- Anwil - ahn-wil

- Ariadne - ar-ee-ahd-nee

- Blanchefleur - blan-sh-fler

- Caradoc - care-ah-dok

- Caewlin - cow-lin

- Cerdic - ser-dik

- Dindrane - din-drayn

- Dumnonia - dum-no-nee-ah

- Elyion - ehl-ee-ohn

- Eudocia - you-doh-sha

-

OF CROWNS AND LEGENDS

Gawaine - gah-wayne

- Gingalain - gin-gah-lain (hard g's)

- Gwenc'hlan - gwen-klahn

- Gwynedd - gwen-eth

- Hywell - high-well

- Ilsa - ill-sah

- Leontius - lee-ohn-tee-us

- Lohengrin - low-en-grin

- Melara - meh-lar-ah

- Nimue- nim-o-way

- Uira - your-ah

- Ulrich - uhl-rick

- Xiang - zh-ang

CHELSEA BANNING

To those who read because this world is not enough...

OF CROWNS AND LEGENDS

CHELSEA BANNING

TEMENOS PRODUCTIONS

PROLOGUE

The abbess snorted herself awake. She blinked and looked around, clearing her throat. She had fallen asleep over her desk, quill still in hand. Ink had smeared over the scroll of parchment, and the letter she'd been writing was now illegible. She grumbled and scolded herself for ruining a good piece of parchment and wasting ink. Both were expensive, and with the limited funds in the abbey, she had to be careful. Still muttering to herself, she cleaned the mess and packed the writing tools away on the shabby desk. She could rewrite the letter in the morning. It was late, judging by the moon and the smoldering coals in her small hearth. Yawning, she shuffled across the room to her bed, and it groaned as she lowered herself to sit on the edge.

As she bent to slip off her thin leather shoes, a gust of wind blew the shutters open with a bang, and a shiver ran down her spine. She hugged her shawl tighter around her shoulders and hoisted herself back up. Summer was leaving, and the nights had grown cold. When she was younger, she loved the cool breeze of late summer nights, but as she strained to stand from her bed, the ache in her bones made her feel otherwise. She wrestled with the broken shutters and made a mental note to ask Father Wymund to fix them in the morning. As she did, a sound from outside caught her attention. She peered out at the garden, her eyes straining to see even under the bright light of the full moon. The garden and south corner of the horse pasture were empty, but just near the main path, she could barely make out a horse with a rider. It was far too dark to make out anything other than a silhouette, but the abbess could see they were approaching the abbey's main gate.

They must be looking for shelter, she surmised.

The hour was late for travelers, but as the royal wedding was soon, they were likely headed to Camelot. Since she was up, she decided she might as well greet them herself. She and the other nuns had quite enough soup leftover from dinner, and she could heat it up over the fire if they were hungry. The abbess finally managed to close the shutters and made her way out of her room and down the narrow hallway, careful to not make much noise. The wooden floor creaked under her footsteps. It took her a moment to get down the small set of steps and into the main foyer. She had to steady herself against the wall to cross to the door. She took a breath in and used all her strength to pull the heavy curved door open to reveal a tall figure in a hooded cloak with their hands raised as if they had been pushing on the door.

"Oh! Good evening, Mother." The surprised voice that came from under the hood echoed through the abbess's ears. "I did not expect anyone to be awake. I hope I have not frightened you."

The abbess froze, unable to move. Her thoughts swam around in her head, jumping away from her when she tried to make sense of them. She found herself staring at the deep blue fabric of the robe. It was fine, with small silver thistle embroidery running around the edge. A noblewoman, by any account. After a moment, she shook herself, and her head cleared as if from a fog. She beckoned the woman inside.

"No, no, not at all. Come in, come in." The abbess stepped aside to let the woman in. "I was already awake and heard your horse. I'm Mother Alba."

"Thank you." The woman stepped inside, and as she moved, her cloak glimmered in the moonlight like the stars in the night sky. Alba stared. The movement of the fabric was like water rippling in a smooth pond. The woman removed her hood and revealed straight black hair and bright violet eyes that shone as if light came from inside them. There was something about purple eyes that Alba should have remembered, but she couldn't quite grasp it.

"I do hope I'm not intruding." The woman smiled softly at her, and Alba felt her shoulders relax, forgetting all about the woman's eyes.

"All travelers are welcome here. Our Lord says, 'Forget not to show love unto strangers.'" Alba closed the door behind her as a sense of calm washed over her body.

"You are very kind," the woman said, clasping her gloved hands in front of her.

"Are you traveling far?" Alba took a torch off the wall and crossed back along the foyer to the main hearth, where the coals were still glowing. Her elbow creaked as she stuck the torch into the embers.

"Not too far," the woman answered as Alba poked at the coals. "I'm headed to Camelot for the prince's wedding."

"Oh!" Alba straightened and turned to the woman with a grin. "Such wonderful news, isn't it? I would go myself, but I am far too old to be traveling nowadays. Have you been to the city before?"

"Many times." The woman followed Alba toward the back of the convent. She looked around, her eyes darting to the corners and roof. She even slid her hand across the wooden walls, as if looking for an opening. Alba wanted to question her, but when she opened her mouth, she forgot what she was going to ask. She waved for the woman to follow her to the guest wing. Alba used the wall to steady herself as they made their way down the corridors. Her knees weren't what they used to be, and she really should've just knuckled down and used a cane. But she was admittedly too proud.

"I've only been to the city once myself," said Alba, her breathing labored. "Nearly twenty years ago, I think now."

Alba pushed open another curved door, and they entered the kitchen—one of the few fully stone rooms in the convent. It was cramped and piled high with jars, wheat, dried meat, and various herbs and vegetation. Despite their meager allowance, Alba made sure they were always prepared to feed anyone in need.

"Are you hungry, dear?" Alba headed toward the large cauldron over the now cold hearth. "We have plenty of soup left over. It'd be no bother to heat some up for you." Alba peeked under the lid of the soup, and the spiced scent filled her nose. Perhaps she would even heat some up for herself.

"No, thank you," said the woman, who took it upon herself to look through the various jars and bowls. She studied the hearth, then eventually crossed the kitchen to stand right next to Alba. "I am not hungry, and I'm sure you have many mouths to feed already."

Alba gave a slight chuckle, already forgetting what the woman had done. "Oh, only a few of us here. We're a humble lot. And as you can see, we have plenty of food."

The woman glanced over at the kitchen once more, an unreadable expression on her face. She put her hand on the wall and froze. Her gaze darted to Alba, the soft expression now twisted by an animalistic snarl. Alba started, but the woman no longer stood at the wall glaring. Rather, she stood in front of her, hands crossed in front of her belly, the polite smile back on her face.

"So if you're hungry," Alba was surprised to find herself saying, "don't hesitate to wander in here for some food. And don't be surprised if you see Sister Hunna digging about. She's always coming in for a midnight snack."

Alba led the woman through the kitchen and down another hallway that ended with a curved door. She handed the torch to the woman and pulled a key ring from her belt. She fumbled through the keys, muttering to herself, "So many keys . . . I can hardly remember what they're all for. Ah, here we are." She unlocked the door and let it swing open, revealing the guest chambers. A row of slim cots lined the left wall, with a plain blanket folded on each. A pile of wood sat next to the small hearth, and shutters in the two windows rumbled in the wind.

"It's not much, but the beds are always clean," said Alba, stepping down into the room. "We haven't had many travelers lately, so you may need to shake the dust off the blankets a bit." She reached for the torch, but the woman pulled it away from her.

"Thank you, Mother." The woman smiled again, and her straight white teeth flashed in the firelight. "But I'm afraid you won't be needing this anymore."

"What?"

The woman tossed the torch aside, and Alba's stomach dropped. "What are you—"

The last thing Alba saw was the flames.

CHAPTER ONE

ARIADNE

Ariadne groaned in pain as her leather cuirass dug into her back. She let her head fall back into the sand and groaned again. A shadow passed over her, and Ariadne opened her eyes to see a tall muscular woman with dark braids standing over her.

"That was good!" she said, her Grecian accent thick. "Much better than last time."

Ariadne shot her a look. "How was that good? You flipped me over your shoulder!"

"Because you almost managed to get free." Dame Brionna, Ariadne's personal guard, held out her arm. Ariadne took it, and Brionna hoisted her to her feet. Ariadne slapped the sand off herself, mentally grumbling. Almost wasn't good enough. If she wanted to prove herself and be a Knight of the Round Table, she had to be better.

Most people—the men especially—believed she shouldn't be training at all, that it wasn't right for a woman. They certainly hadn't liked it when Brionna was made a knight. But Ariadne would prove them wrong. She could be just as good as they were. Women were just as, if not more, capable of being warriors.

Ariadne squared up and growled, "Again!" through clenched teeth. Brionna met her halfway, and they grappled, but Ariadne landed on her back once more.

"That is a hard hold to break out of," Brionna said, pulling Ariadne to her feet. "You're improving."

"Doesn't feel like it." Ariadne pushed a loose red curl out of her face.

"No one masters fighting overnight." Brionna handed Ariadne a waterskin. "Patience, Ari. Drink."

Ariadne glared at her over the waterskin, but Brionna sent her a teasing wink. Ariadne wiped her mouth and handed the skin back to Brionna and picked up her sword. It was short and light, blunted for practice. She had been attending lessons with Brionna nearly every morning for the past two years after finally getting her mother, Queen Guinevere, to let her train to be a Knight of the Round Table. Ariadne had begged her mother for years, ever since Brionna had arrived in Camelot with Merlin a decade ago. Brionna had been a warrior in her village back in Greece, and ten-year-old Ariadne had instantly been smitten when the woman in golden armor with two swords on

9

her back had been knighted. Ariadne started carrying two sticks around, "fighting" in the gardens when she thought no one was looking, and had Lady Dindrane braid her hair like Brionna's.

"Let's try again. Slower this time." Brionna picked up her own practice sword and walked Ariadne through the movements. Ariadne still ended up on her back, but when they tried for a third time, Ariadne broke free. Though, she suspected Brionna had let her.

"Good!" Brionna said when Ariadne scrambled away from her. "See? I told you it was all about patience."

"Ari, patient? Does such a thing exist?"

Ariadne whirled around to find her elder cousin smirking as he leaned on the gate. Sir Gawaine and his family, a son and younger brother, were the only other blood relatives Ariadne and Anwil had in Camelot. Gawaine was the same age as her mother, and he acted more like a father figure than cousin. His black hair was freshly cut and slicked back, showcasing the white and gray streaks the women in court liked to swoon over. His goatee was neat as usual, but instead of the leathers Ariadne was used to seeing him in, he wore a green tunic over a shining mail hauberk and a matching velvet cloak. Ariadne could hear the women now. It didn't matter that Gawaine was happily married to Lady Reya.

"Where's the party?" Ariadne asked her older cousin, taking in his clothes.

"Here." Gawaine opened the gate and stepped onto the training field with shining black boots. "Guests are arriving. Thought I'd actually look the part of general."

"Already?" exclaimed Ariadne, a panic rising in her stomach. Her mother would be very upset if she was not out and about in the courtyard to greet their guests. "Anwil's wedding isn't until next week!"

"Aye, already," said Gawaine, taking her sword. He studied the nicks in the blade. "Hmm, this needs to be replaced."

"Is Mother expecting me somewhere?" Ariadne asked, already pulling her gloves off. She would have to bathe quickly and toss a crown or something over her hair. She wouldn't have time to style it, and Lady Mirah, her closest friend and lady-in-waiting, wasn't due to arrive home for another few days.

"No, no," Gawaine said, handing the sword back to her. "You're all right. I came to see how you were progressing."

Ariadne breathed a sigh of relief and put her glove back on. Gawaine was one of the few who fully supported Ariadne in her training. Since he was general, his opinions held weight, and while pushback had died down, Ariadne was still subjected to snide remarks and jeers every once in a while on the fields. "Same as yesterday," she said, turning the sword in circles with her wrist.

"Show me that shoulder throw." Gawaine nodded at Brionna.

11

Ariadne dropped into her stance, facing Brionna.

"Your stance is too narrow." Gawaine pointed down at her feet. "Feet should be shoulder width apart."

"They are! Oh." Ariadne looked down at her boots and realized Gawaine was right. She adjusted her feet.

"Good," said Gawaine, dropping into a stance next to her. "Strong foot forward when attacking, strong foot back when defending. Keep your hips squared and your eye on the opponent, but keep your ears open for anyone behind you."

Ariadne knew this already—both Brionna and Gawaine had already taught her—but she matched Gawaine's form, knowing he liked to make sure. When he backed away, she nodded at Brionna to let her know she was ready. Ariadne lunged, and Brionna was ready and countered, but Ariadne reacted quickly and met Brionna with her left side, locking them both in place. Ariadne struggled, and Brionna let herself get thrown. At least she had gotten the movement.

"Not bad!" Gawaine said with approval as Brionna jumped back to her feet. "Good, in fact. I told you you're a natural fighter, just as your father was."

Ariadne stiffened at Gawaine's words. Could she do anything without being compared to a dead father? A father she'd never even known. He had died a few short months before she and her brother, Anwil, were born. And yet, nearly every day of her life, someone brought up Arthur's name every time she did or said anything. Ariadne understood he had been a good and

12

beloved leader, but people acted as if he were a god. It didn't help that the castle was crawling with artwork of Arthur's various achievements, adventures, and quests. Statues lined the courtyard and gardens; tapestries covered the walls of the castle, along with paintings and woodwork. Arthur was everywhere in Camelot, even in the city proper, where the streets were named after him: *Arthur's Way, Pendragon Street, Excalibur Corners.* There was no escaping.

"Ari has many talents." Brionna folded her arms across her chest and smiled at Ariadne. "She is my best student."

"I'm your only student," said Ariadne, and Brionna laughed.

"Go wash up." Brionna took the sword from her. "It's getting late."

"Thank you," said Ariadne, relieved to get away from Gawaine before he started another trip down memory lane. Ariadne bid her and Gawaine goodbye. She passed through the other fighting rings, where knights were practicing or training squires. The echoing of swords clanging slowed as she passed, but she ignored the stares. After all this time, they should've been used to her on the fields. She pushed another fallen red curl from her face as someone called out her name.

A flutter erupted in her stomach as Lyrion, youngest son of Sir Percival, hurried toward her from the stables. He was a few years older than her, and his light brown hair was tousled from the wind, but that's how Ariadne liked it best. He was her height but leaner, with angular features and not a single freckle on his face, which made Ariadne jealous. Her freckles covered her entire body, and sometimes she wished she could get rid of them.

"Good morrow, Lyrion," she said and slowed her pace.

"How were your lessons?" he asked, stepping in stride with her.

Ariadne shrugged. "Same as usual. I hear you're up for the Trials."

The Trials, the last set of tests a squire must pass in order to be considered for knighthood, included a very difficult obstacle course and various tests run by the Knights of the Round Table every spring. It was Ariadne's goal to not only be considered for the Trials, but to pass them and make her way all the way to the top, as a Knight of the Round Table.

"Word spreads quick," said Lyrion, shaking his head. "I only just found out myself. They're recruiting more and more every day. These attacks on the abbeys are disturbing."

"Yes, they are," said Ariadne. They were part of the reason she was pushing herself so hard. Although she was princess, she had no real power. Sure, she sat in on council meetings and participated in the discussions, but she couldn't *do* anything. She couldn't even delegate festivity orders without permission from her mother or brother. She wasn't in line to the throne. Not really. While there was a succession for the High King of Briton, it was only passed to direct male heirs. If something happened to Anwil before he had any boys, the High

Throne would not pass to her. It would be up to the petty kings of Briton to vote in a new High King. A seat at the Round Table, however, would allow her to do something . . . to become someone.

"But congratulations are in order anyway." Ariadne brushed her hand against his, pulling herself from her thoughts.

A flush spread on Lyrion's cheeks. "To be honest, I'm downright terrified." He glanced over his shoulder as if to make sure no one was listening. The fighters had gone back to their lessons or training, their eyes thankfully no longer on Ariadne. The dirt turned to grass as she and Lyrion walked through the gardens, and the noise from the training fields faded into the background. Lush flowers and hedges swayed in the gentle wind, and the mix of various scents of flora was a welcome difference from the sweat and leather of the training grounds. The trickling of the fountain grew louder the deeper they walked into the maze of the gardens.

"Why? Do you think Lohengrin is going to sabotage you?" Ariadne gave him a nudge and a teasing smirk. Lyrion's older brother, one of the youngest knights to be granted a seat at the Round Table, was also a well-known prankster.

"I'm afraid I'll fail in front of him and Father." His face fell, and Ariadne stopped in her tracks and grabbed his wrist.

"You'll be fine," she said, squeezing his hand. "You're a good fighter."

Lyrion shook his head. "But the Trials are more than that. What if I can't pass them?"

Lyrion had never been so open with her before. She leaned toward him, their chests almost touching. The smell of the stables wafted into her nose, along with a hint of musk. "Well," she whispered, trailing a finger up his arm, "then I'll take your place at the Trials and obtain the knighthood."

"Oh, will you now?" His face softened, and he lifted a hand to brush some wild curls behind her ears.

"Yes." She leaned into his hand. "And then you can squire for *me* while I win all the tournaments."

Lyrion laughed but shook his head. "I'm sorry to lay this on you. I'm sure you have plenty of other things to worry about with Anwil's wedding."

"Everyone needs someone to talk to," Ariadne whispered. They were so close she could see the small flecks of green and gold amongst the brown in his eyes. His lips twitched into a soft smile, and his hand slid around her neck to pull her—

"Your Grace!" Lyrion jumped back from her, his eyes wide and face pale, staring at something—or someone, rather—over Ariadne's shoulder. She closed her eyes and clenched her jaw. She couldn't go anywhere without everyone knowing where she was or what she was doing. Privacy was unfortunately not part of normal life as royalty.

"Hello, Mother." Ariadne put on a pleasant smile as she turned around to face her mother.

Queen Guinevere stood in one of the hedge archways speck-led with roses. She wore a dark brown dress with an apron and held a small shovel in her gloved hands. One day a week, the queen hid away in the gardens, planting and pruning her beloved flowers. No one was to bother her with royal duties except for emergencies. It had been that way for as long as Ariadne could remember. Many noble women hated that Guinevere got on her knees with the servants and wasn't afraid to dig her hands into the soil, but it made her beloved by the castle staff and the people of the city. They thought it humble.

Guinevere folded her arms across her chest, and a sly smile spread across her face. "I seem to be interrupting something," she said. "I do apologize, but may I have a moment with my daughter?"

"Of course, Your Grace." Lyrion bowed and scurried off.

Ariadne watched him go with a frustrated sigh. "Mother!" She whirled around. "Was that necessary?"

"I was going to sneak away," said her mother, an apologetic look on her face, "but Lyrion had already seen me. I didn't mean to pry, I promise. I was only heading back inside."

Ariadne sighed again and took a quick moment to calm herself. "What did you need, Mother?" she asked in a gentler tone.

"Well." Guinevere switched the small shovel to her other hand and linked arms with Ariadne. "Nothing urgent. I received a letter from the king of Gaul sending us well wishes, but he cannot make the trip for Anwil's wedding, so we have a room in the guest wing open."

"He had the double-wide room near the fountains, yes?" said Ariadne, straining to remember the list she'd helped her mother with.

"Yes," said Guinevere. "So I was thinking of moving Lady Laudine there."

"Oh, that's good. Now she won't complain about her room being too small. But that isn't what you really wanted to ask me, was it?

"Am I that obvious?" Her mother sighed. "Well, I have a rather enormous pile of letters on my desk, all asking permission for a marriage arrangement—"

Ariadne groaned. "No! Not now." She had already been bombarded with courtships and marriage proposals from the noblemen of court on her own. She had hoped her mother wouldn't concern her with it as well.

"Ari, you are nearly twenty."

"If I marry a foreign royal, I cannot be a knight," said Ariadne. "Mother, this is all I want."

"Ari." Her mother took her by the shoulders. "You are destined for more than this. You were born to rule. To be a queen."

"I wasn't born to be queen at all," said Ariadne, brushing her mother's hands away. "Let alone queen of a foreign land. I'm not in line to the High Throne. My place is here, in Camelot, by my brother's side. That is my destiny."

Guinevere frowned, causing the wrinkles around her mouth to become more prominent. After a moment, she let out a soft laugh and shook her head, her wimple falling over her shoulders. "You are a Pendragon through and through," she said. "All right. I'll send them away."

Ariadne's eyes widened. She wasn't sure she'd heard her mother correctly. "What? Truly?"

Guinevere nodded. "For now. I do admit, I'm not so fond of you being far away. Call me selfish, but I am your mother first and foremost."

Ariadne threw her arms around her mother, causing her to stumble.

"Oh! Careful!" Guinevere chuckled and returned the embrace.

"Thank you," Ariadne said, relief washing through her.

"Of course, darling." Her mother pulled away and brushed a hair from Ariadne's face. "But . . . what about Lyrion?"

"Mother!"

CHAPTER TWO

ANWIL

The city streets were far busier than usual, and the roar of the crowd was so loud Anwil could barely hear himself think. He wove his way through the people. Some bowed if they recognized him, while others ignored him completely. He was grateful for the latter, especially as he had a trail of knights behind him. It was only recently that more than one guard accompanied him into the city. Briton was facing a string of attacks on abbeys and monasteries, and the culprits had not yet been caught or even identified. And with guests arriving for his wedding, security had doubled in and out of the castle. Anwil knew the guards that followed him were doing their job on his orders, but it agitated him to be so closely surrounded nearly all hours of the day.

He preferred being unnoticed. If he had a choice of his own, he would spend all his days in the library poring over books and scrolls. But as crown prince (well, technically, he was king, but as he had never officially been crowned, he was referred to as prince), his duties to the country came first. Even if that meant sacrificing his own comfort.

"Melon?" A large green melon was shoved into his face as he passed through the food market. A small plump woman with a brown scarf wrapped around her head smiled up at him. She wore brightly mismatched colors and pulled a cart full of the green melons behind her.

"No, thank you," Anwil mumbled, trying to get around her, but she stepped in front of him.

A snicker sounded in his ear as his personal guard and closest friend, Sir Lohengrin, hid a laugh behind his hand. He and Anwil were quite the opposite. When they were younger, Lohengrin and his brother, Lyrion, had roped nearly half the castle into a prank war for a summer, much to the dismay of their parents and the Knights of the Round Table. It had taken them an entire month to find out that Lohengrin was the culprit of many of them, as he had convinced Anwil to bribe the guards not to say anything.

"It's exotic!" the woman cried, shaking the melon. This only caused Lohengrin to laugh harder.

Anwil pushed the melon away from his face. "Thank you, mistress," he said. "But I am in a hurry."

Before she could reply, Anwil got around her and picked up his pace, nearly knocking into a man in green silken robes. He mumbled an apology and hopped off the cobbled street and onto the sidewalk to take a breath. Lohengrin joined him and leaned on the corner of the bakery building. He folded his arms across his chest as the guards hovered around them, keeping distance to give them some space but remaining close enough should they need to step in.

"Quite the crowd," Lohengrin said, turning a smirk on Anwil. "Can't believe they're here for the wanker prince, though. Who would want to see him get married?"

"Hilarious," Anwil said, glancing up at the bakery sign. It was broken, hanging only by one side. "Oy, give me a boost."

Lohengrin followed his gaze and furrowed his eyebrows. "What happened to being in a hurry?"

Anwil didn't answer him, and Lohengrin sighed and pushed his brown hair from his face. He knelt and hoisted Anwil onto his shoulders. Anwil carefully sat on Lohengrin's broad shoulders and fixed the chain, and as he straightened the chipped wooden sign, a yell startled Lohengrin, and he almost lost his balance. Anwil hung on to the planks that the sign dangled from as a small woman dove out of the store with a broom and smacked Lohengrin in the stomach and then the chest.

"Thieves! I'll have your hands for this! You loister sack sots! I'll not have you ransacking my shop again, you cumber-worlds!"

"Ow!" Lohengrin covered his face with his hands as Sir Xiang put a hand on the woman's shoulder. She whirled around on him too but froze. Sir Xiang was nearly twice her size. She looked him up and down, taking in his cord and plaque armor over the Camelot red-and-gold tunic and the weapons on his belt. She turned back to Lohengrin and Anwil with wide eyes as Anwil let himself down, landing on his feet with a soft grunt. She dropped the broom and tumbled onto her knees, bowing low to the ground.

"Forgive me, Your Highness," she said, her voice trembling. "We've had thieves and—"

"It is all right, mistress," said Anwil, holding back a laugh. To see Lohengrin, Camelot's youngest Knight of the Round Table and last tournament's champion, get pommeled by a small woman with a broom was just plain hilarious. He'd never let him live this down. "No harm done. I should apologize to you. I should have said something."

He offered a hand down to her. She stared at his hand a moment before taking it and letting Anwil pull her to her feet. Her hand was rough and covered in patches of flour. Sir Xiang picked up the broom and handed it to her. She mumbled a sheepish thank-you and clutched it to her chest.

"My lord," she said to Lohengrin. "A thousand apologies."

Lohengrin chuckled, and her eyes went wide. "No harm done, mistress," he said. "Your, er, your sign is fixed." He pointed, and her cheeks flushed.

"Thank you," she breathed. "Again, I—"

"Are you the new baker?" Anwil asked, not wanting the conversation to get anymore awkward than it already was. "The one whose scones were the talk of the summer solstice?"

The woman stammered, looking from Anwil to Lohengrin to Sir Xiang, still hovering behind her. "I—er—yes," she said. "Yes, my apple cinnamon scones are my best sells. I can barely keep them in stock."

"Do you have any now?" Anwil clutched his hands behind his back.

"Yes, I just made some," she said, her voice breathless.

"Wondrous," said Anwil. "I would like to purchase a dozen if you have that many."

The woman's mouth dropped. "Of—Of *mine?* I mean, yes, sire. Yes, of course!" And without another word, she ran into her shop, the skirts of her dress whipping about behind her as she turned the corner through the door.

Sir Xiang looked Lohengrin up and down, a smirk pulling at his lips. "Are you hurt, Sir Lohengrin?"

The other knights snickered, and Lohengrin rolled his eyes. "Laugh it up," he said.

"Just wait," said Sir Ulrich, crossing his arms across his broad chest. "This will be the talk of the city in less than an hour."

"Especially His Highness hanging from the sign." Xiang chuckled.

"That image will live in my mind forever." Lohengrin laughed, clapping Anwil on the shoulder.

Anwil shook his head but said nothing. He wasn't offended—perhaps embarrassed, but it wasn't anything he couldn't handle. "As will your loss to the mighty broom?"

The knights sniggered again, but before Lohengrin could respond, the baker returned.

"Here we are." She carried a white bag tied at the top. "Fresh out of the oven." There were more patches of flour on her face, and she'd donned an apron over her dress.

Anwil reached into the pouch on his belt and pulled out a few gold coins. Her eyes widened as he held them out. "Oh, sire, that is far too much."

"Nonsense," he said, taking the bag from her and placing the coins in her palm. "For the trouble. What is your name, mistress?"

"Mathilde, sire." She dropped into another curtsy.

"Thank you, Mistress Mathilde." Anwil bowed. "I hope you have a lovely rest of your day."

"Poor girl," Lohengrin mumbled as they made their way down the street. He took the bag of scones from Anwil, pulled one out, and took a large bite. "Now her shop will be flooded with even more orders. All because"—Lohengrin pressed the back of his hand to his forehead and pretended to swoon—"*His Highness* shops there!"

Anwil shook his head and ignored him as he finally came upon his initial destination: the mapmaker's. It was one of Anwil's favorites. Travelers from all over came and went, giving descriptions and sketches of their homelands to the artists. Anwil could spend all day with them learning about other countries and cultures. He pulled open the door, and the smell of parchment and ink filled his nose. Light poured in from the multiple windows and sconces on the walls. Scrolls of blank parchment filled a shelf on one wall, with drying racks covered in new maps in the far back. Desks lined the right side, occupied by scribes and artists working, the scratching of their quills the only sound in the shop.

"Ah, Your Highness!" A balding man in a brown-and-dark russet tunic hurried over from his desk and bowed. "And Sir Lohengrin, my lord. I have everything ready for you. Come, come!"

As they passed, the other artists continued with their work, ignoring Anwil and Lohengrin, just as Anwil had requested a few years ago when he had made a habit of visiting. He did not want special treatment all the time and didn't want to interrupt their work. The man, Wyot, owned the shop and carefully lifted a large map from one of the drying racks.

"Here we are." He smoothed it out on the table against the wall. "An updated map of Gaul, just as you requested. Merlin was a tremendous help. I sent five men to different cities in Gaul, and they returned with a dozen maps each! There and back in a single day, when the journey would normally take over three months! Those mirrors of his are genius. Absolute genius."

Anwil chuckled. "That they are."

Merlin, the wizard who had tutored and advised King Arthur, now advised Anwil's mother, Guinevere. He had a hobby of dabbling in inventions and when Anwil was young, created mirrors one could step through and exit out of its twin mirror at another destination. Merlin, who could travel by magic himself, had placed mirrors in the foreign cities they had already established trade with, and it didn't take long for Camelot to become a hub of trade, culture, and learning. It had become Briton's version of Rome. Although Camelot was not nearly as large as Rome, it was now a diverse city with shops, libraries, schools, temples, and homes.

Anwil paid Wyot, and although he wanted to stay and see what the others were working on, he had to return to the castle library and deliver the new map to Sir Gawaine. They'd had a falling-out with Gaul a few years before, and they were looking to see if anyone from Gaul could be behind the attacks on the abbeys. And if they wished to send scouts, they would need the best maps.

"What do you say we pop into the Crown and Dragon for a bit?" Lohengrin asked as they passed by Camelot's famous pub. Bards from all over traveled to play in the two-story pub and inn that encompassed half the street. The cook was part fae and made the best ales and food around.

"It's barely midmorning!" Anwil shot a wide-eyed look at Lohengrin after glancing at the sun.

"And we have the entire day ahead of us!" Lohengrin opened his arms wide and gestured around. "No training, no meetings. Come on, Anwil! We need to have some fun."

"You can go," Anwil said, carefully slipping the map into his bag. "I'm headed—"

"To the library," Lohengrin grumbled. "All right, fine. At least meet me in the pond later for a swim? Something?"

Anwil thought about it for a moment. He did like a swim now and then. And he knew his sister, Ariadne, and Lohengrin's fiancée would jump at the thought. "All right. I'll invite the girls too."

Lohengrin's face lit up with a grin. "Excellent."

Anwil sighed in relief at the silence of the library. Like at the mapmaker's, the only sounds were the scratching of quills from the scribes and the rustle of pages. It was Anwil's favorite ambience. He took a moment, hovering near the threshold to the tower to ease away the tension from the bustling city and savor the quiet. The smell of ink and parchment wafted over him as he breathed in. He almost regretted agreeing to go for a swim later. He could spend all day in here amongst the shelves.

"Your Highness." The deep accented voice pulled Anwil from his thoughts. A tall man with brown skin and a silver-flecked beard smiled down at him through tiny spectacles positioned at the end of his nose.

"Master Umar." Anwil greeted the master librarian and pulled the rolled-up map from his bag. "Updated map of Gaul."

Master Umar's face brightened, and his eyebrows shot up, nearly disappearing under his blue turban. "Ah, wonderful!" He carefully took the map from Anwil and unrolled it, then held it up toward the streaming sunlight. "Fantastic. I will have my scribes make copies right away. And I have something for you as well."

Anwil followed Master Umar through the stacks filled with scrolls and mismatched books, past scribes at their desks, and to a corner of the library where Master Umar had a desk set up in front of the hearth. His desk was more like a large table covered with piles of books, parchment, and scrolls. Master Umar set the map down and plucked a small scroll from the pile on his desk.

"A poem," he said. "From Ireland. I think you might like it. It is a love story and very fitting, I think." Umar winked at Anwil, who tensed. His wedding was only a few days away, and to say he was nervous was an understatement. Even though he had known Lady Yvanne since they were young, marriage was much different than friendship. Although he was grateful

29

he wasn't marrying a foreign princess he didn't know, Anwil still wasn't sure he was ready for married life. He had one year to adjust before he was officially crowned, his mother stepped down as regent, and all power transferred to him. It was a lot of change very fast. Just thinking about it made his heart race.

"Thank you." Anwil slipped the Irish poem into his bag, not wanting to be in the library anymore. "Perhaps Lady Yvanne and I can read it together."

A grin spread on Master Umar's face. "A lovely thought, Your Highness."

Before Umar could say anything else, Anwil bid him farewell and hurried out of the library. He needed to be somewhere he was not constantly reminded of his duties. The library was normally a sanctuary for him, but with the wedding so close, it was on everyone's mind. He headed through the south corridors, which were darker and quieter than the others. Old tapestries lined the walls—ones that were fading or unraveling.

Anwil slowed down and leaned against the cool stone of the wall. It was so quiet he could hear the hammering of his heart against his chest. He hated this feeling, the sense of impending doom that had plagued him since he was a child. He slid down the wall until he sat on the floor and rested his elbows on his knees, taking deep breaths. The musty air made him cough, but at least no one would find him for a while. He just needed a bit of solitude before having to face the world again.

CHAPTER THREE

GUINEVERE

"No, no, you daft boy! That is not the right banner. Are you blind? It's too small! Fetch the correct one!"

The poor servant boy on the receiving end of Lady Dindrane's wrath scurried out of the great hall, the too-small red-and-gold banner billowing out behind him. Guinevere did not wish to entice her friend's anger either, so she kept to the opposite corner of the hall, where servants were bringing in small round tables and setting them up. Dindrane was the most organized and efficient person Guinevere had ever met, but she had a temper. The servants would be rewarded when the wedding was done for all their hard work and the stress of the occasion. Many monarchs wouldn't think twice about their

31

castle staff, but Guinevere honored all her subjects, not just the ones with titles.

Guinevere fiddled with the ledger in her hands that contained the budget and lists for the wedding. The flowers they had grown over the spring for the wedding hadn't done well in the light drought, and therefore, they had to make do with only the roses. Guinevere was disappointed, but she was more worried about the food budget. Because of the drought, they'd had to import more herbs and spices than the budget allotted for. It would have to be a frugal winter.

"How many tables do we need?" Lady Blanchefleur asked in awe as table after table was rolled or carried in. Servants wearing red tunics over their clothing ran about, carrying chairs, tables, or other decorations and hanging them throughout the hall. The shields bearing Briton's kings' sigils had been polished and placed high on the inner wall above the doors. Below, the great Pendragon shield gleamed with fresh paint, and underneath hung the twelve shields of Arthur's original Knights of the Round Table.

Guinevere checked the book in her hand. "Fifty-three," she said. "Not counting the head tables. There will be three of those set up over there." Guinevere pointed to where Dindrane stood on the dais. The throne had been removed, and the wooden dais was now bare, except for the wall behind it where Dindrane was overseeing the hanging of the Pendragon and Dumnonia banners. The blue-and-gold Dumnonia banner hung proudly to the left, flanked by red roses from the castle gardens.

"What are we to do with them after this?" said Blanchefleur, watching as three more tables were carried in. Blanchefleur was Guinevere's other lady-in-waiting and one of her longest friends. She was much quieter and gentler than Dindrane. It was a wonder how the sisters-in-law got along at all, but they were inseparable.

"Well, the hope is to use them for Ari's wedding." Guinevere rolled the quill between her fingers. "And perhaps after that, any other celebrations." Guinevere did not wish to even think about other celebrations at the moment. Once this wedding was over, she would have to jump right into planning Anwil and Yvanne's joint coronation. Perhaps they should have had them together as she'd suggested in the first place, but Anwil had panicked when she brought that up and nearly begged her to give him time to adjust in between. She hadn't had the heart to say no when her son held so much anxiety in his eyes.

"Grandchildren?" Blanchefleur suggested, a twinkle in her eye.

"Hopefully not too long now," said Guinevere. She caught sight of a serving girl entering the hall carrying what looked to be a small lion statue. "Darling, where did you get that?"

The girl, who couldn't have been but five and ten, looked around to see who was addressing her and tried to sink into a curtsy when she realized it was Guinevere but almost toppled over. Blanchefleur was to her in an instant, helping to steady her.

"Thank you, my lady," the girl mumbled. "Er, Lady Dindrane said to have it brought in, Your Grace."

Guinevere sighed. "All right." She waved the girl along.

"Perhaps we should just let Dindrane be," Blanchefleur said with a chuckle, her bright blue eyes glimmering.

"And leave the servants alone with her?" Guinevere laughed. "The poor things—Oh, Alyn! The seats for the minstrels go over there."

Guinevere glanced at the sun through the tall windows. It was just past midday, and there was still so much work to do. The musicians were due to arrive later that day and provide the music and acrobats. It was perhaps a silly thing to hire such entertainment, but with so many guests traveling from other countries, she wanted to make it worthwhile. Even if they were using Merlin's mirrors and travel was instantaneous with the magical artifacts, they would still be a far from home. Guinevere remembered traveling to Camelot herself as a young girl, only five and ten, to be married to the High King, a man nearly twice her age who had already been married and widowed. She had been terrified, but Arthur was kind and patient. Guinevere hoped the same for Anwil and his soon to be wife, Lady Yvanne.

"Your Grace."

Guinevere turned to see Lord Roland, her chancellor, and Sir Percival making their way toward her. Roland looked as dashing as ever in brocade fabrics of cream with green threading. His shoes were polished and clicked on the stone floor. They matched the green feather in his green hat. His blond beard was neatly trimmed, and he wore a new pair of circular gold spectacles. Guinevere envied his fashion sense.

Sir Percival, however, barely saw Guinevere as he went straight to his wife. Guinevere smiled as he kissed her cheek, and Blanchefleur giggled like a young girl. She remembered when Percival was a young knight, shy and nervous, squiring under Sir Lancelot, and had taken an eye for her lady-in-waiting. It took him years to work up the courage to ask Guinevere permission to court Blanchefleur, and when he finally had, she was more than happy to say yes, as was Blanchefleur. Percival grew to become one of Arthur's best knights. He'd helped find the Holy Grail, fought in the Battle of Camlann, and now, he was captain of the guard and ran the castle security like a tight ship. He trained the best guards in the country and was one of few Guinevere could trust absolutely.

Guinevere pulled herself from her thoughts as Roland bowed to her. She had told him many times he needn't do that anymore, but he insisted on propriety.

"Lord Roland," she said to her friend with a warm smile. "Welcome back. How is your wife?"

35

"Fully recovered, my lady," he said, straightening. "No more fever and she is back to her old self. She will indeed be here for the wedding."

"Oh, wonderful," said Guinevere, relief washing over her. "I am so glad to hear that. But I am also relieved to have my right-hand man back."

Roland laughed. "I am sure we have much still to do." He reached for the ledger. Guinevere handed it over, along with her quill, and he looked through it.

"Guin," said Percival as Roland mumbled to himself. "Do you mind if I steal my wife away for a bit?"

"Of course not. Best be quick, though, before your sister sees you and puts you to work."

Percival glanced over to Dindrane, who was helping to hang the larger red-and-gold banner upon the wall. He tugged on Blanchefleur's hand, and she followed him out of the hall, her giggles echoing. Guinevere smiled at them. It was nice to see them still so in love after all these years. Though a tug of jealousy swept through her. She was quite used to being alone, Arthur having died two decades ago, but every once in a while, she yearned for that companionship again.

"Aha!" Lord Roland startled her. "Have we begun moving Anwil to the king's chambers and you to—oh, forgive me, my lady." Lord Roland's face fell as he looked at her. "That was insensitive."

"No, no," Guinevere said, clutching her hands together. "It is high time he have the king's chambers. I shall have my maids move my things into the empty queen's chambers first thing in the morning."

The queen's chambers had been empty for nearly as long as Guinevere had been queen. She'd spent the first five years there, but when she and Arthur grew closer, she moved to his room and had been there ever since. But as much as it was sad for her to move from the chambers she had known for more than half her life, it was the right thing to do. Anwil deserved the king's chambers, especially now that he would have a wife soon. And Guinevere was now grateful a door had not been installed to connect the two rooms.

Roland bowed and stuck his nose in the ledger again, moving on to the group of servants bringing in fresh rushes. With Roland there now, Guinevere snuck out to get some fresh air. It was a rare sunny day, and she wanted to feel the sun on her skin, at least for a moment. She found her familiar way to the gardens and sat down on one of the stone benches near the willow tree. She untied her wimple and let her hair unwind, shaking it out and lifted her face to the sun. She closed her eyes, enjoying the warmth on her skin. The floral scents of the flowers and freshly cut grass wafted around her. She could even smell the freshly turned dirt from the other side of the gardens, where the gardeners were planting juniper trees.

"Days like today make it seem as if all is right in the world, do they not?"

Guinevere blinked her eyes open and found Merlin standing in front of her, leaning on his staff. He bore a wide grin on his freshly shaven face, and his hair had recently been cut. The last time she'd seen him, his sandy-colored hair had reached just past his shoulders. Now it was neat and tidy, falling just below his ears. He wore his usual earthen tones but had forgone his famous (or infamous, if you ask Dindrane) cloak of mixed fabrics with a feathered collar.

"You will not ruin it with bad news, will you?" Guinevere made room on the bench for the wizard to sit next to her.

"Well, I have both good and bad news." He laid his staff down next to him. The blue crystal that sat atop, entombed within gnarled woven branches, glinted in the sunlight. "Which would you like first?"

"You know I hate it when you do that," Guinevere mumbled, and Merlin laughed.

"I'll just get right to it, then." His expression sobered. "It was Redshire Abbey. The most recent attack."

Guinevere squeezed her eyes shut. "Any survivors?" she asked through stiff lips.

"No," said Merlin. "The entire abbey was burned to the ground. The stones that did not burn in the fire were crumbled."

"God's bones," Guinevere cursed. It was the fourth abbey to be destroyed within two months, and they had yet to find out who or what was doing it. "Gwenyth?"

"I am sorry, Guinevere," Merlin said softly, laying a hand on her shoulder.

"I sent her there," said Guinevere, tears falling. She wiped them away. "I left her there. Despite all she did to me, she was still my sister. I couldn't carry out her execution, and yet she still died because of me."

"Family is a funny thing," said Merlin. "You cannot choose them, but your heart always does, doesn't it? No matter how they wrong us. Her death is not your fault. She chose her own path."

Merlin handed her a clean handkerchief, and she wiped at her eyes again. Guinevere had long grieved her sister already, but the news of her death still stung. When Gwenyth betrayed Guinevere, she had mourned the loss of their relationship. Perhaps Guinevere had too soft a heart, but how could a woman set her own sister up for treason? Their father had always said family was most important, that they should do all they could to protect their family. But Gwenyth must not have listened or cared when she convinced Lancelot she was the queen and took him to bed. Guinevere cleared her throat and blinked back more tears. No. She would not cry over Gwenyth anymore.

"There is another thing, unfortunately," Merlin said. "At first, I thought it coincidence, but now I see it may be more. They took the Whetstone of Tudwal."

"*If it be a brave man that sharpens his sword*," Guinevere recited, "*any blood drawn from his sword would mean death.*"

"Yes," said Merlin, staring out over the irises. "We have had three abbeys attacked in the last two months. All three protecting most ancient and magical relics. The Knife of Llawfrodedd, the Coat of Padarn, and now the Whetstone."

Guinevere shook her head and pressed her fingers to her forehead. "The Treasures of Briton. It is not a coincidence. But what do they need of them? Surely someone isn't murdering my people just for a few relics?"

"They are more than that, Guinevere," Merlin said, giving her a stern look. "They are tied to the land, tied to the old magics. My guess is some sort of spell." Merlin's voice was grave. "If they wanted to use an object's specific power, they would've only taken whichever one they needed. But to gather all of them—and I am assuming they will look for the others—they must need great power for a great spell."

"A dark spell?"

Merlin shrugged. "Perhaps. Or if they wish for a common spell to be *more* powerful. Once we find out who this is, we can most likely guess what they want. Whoever they are, they are powerful. They have evaded even me. Not a trace left behind. It reminds me of . . ."

"Who, Merlin?"

Merlin frowned. "Nimue."

Guinevere clenched her fists. She had hoped to never again hear that name again. "Nimue is dead," she said through gritted teeth.

"Yes, she is." Merlin looked off, his eyes distant. "When I looked to see who this could be, the patterns were familiar. The absence of a trace of magic . . . It might be someone who knew Nimue. Someone who used to be close to her."

"Who do you think that could be?" Guinevere asked.

"There were a few priestesses that followed Nimue after her banishment from Avalon. And of course, she had many fae friends. I have asked one of Vivienne's priestesses to travel to the fae lands. See what she can find." Merlin's eyes glazed over, lost in his own memories.

Guinevere didn't comment. No matter her feelings for Nimue, she had been like a daughter to Merlin. But Guinevere would never forgive Nimue's betrayal. Not when she and Sir Mordred, Arthur's own nephew and Nimue's lover, had waged war against them and killed Arthur in the Battle of Camlann. Not to mention thousands of soldiers and civilians.

"You said you had good news?" said Guinevere, hoping to bring Merlin out of his own head. He carried so much guilt with him, from Arthur's birth to Nimue's fall from grace and Mordred's betrayal.

"Ah, yes." Merlin blinked and turned back to her. "Vivienne has agreed to stay for a few days after officiating the wedding to meet with the council. She has agreed to aid Camelot herself in the search for the assailant."

Guinevere was torn between a sigh of relief and nervousness. The petty kings of Briton were either terrified of the Lady of the Lake or hated her. Guinevere was closer to terrified. The Lady of the Lake was one of the most powerful of all the fae. Not only was she an ellyll, but a high priestess, blessed by the fae gods. She was made to protect the veil between the fae and human worlds. The Isle of Avalon was the halfway point where realm met realm.

"Can she find whoever this is and put a stop to them?"

"She will try," said Merlin. "But her powers fade the longer she is in the human world. There is not enough magic here for her."

Guinevere blinked. "I did not know that."

"Few do."

"Is that why she rarely leaves Avalon?"

Merlin nodded.

Guinevere took in a deep breath. "Well," she said. "I appreciate all the help we can get."

CHAPTER FOUR

ARIADNE

A riadne had just made it to the market with what felt like a thousand errands when a crack boomed overhead and the skies opened up into a hard downpour. Gray clouds, almost black, rolled over what was left of the sun, and lightning lit up the sky. The market had turned into a frenzy, with vendors gathering their things and closing up before the rain ruined any of their products. Ariadne, who had been caught in the middle of the street when the rain started, tried to duck inside a shop, but ended up helping an old woman pack up her wagon full of melons, and now her linen dress was heavy as it clung to her skin. Water from her hair dripped down her back. She was freezing. The old woman had run away without a word, leaving Ariadne a bit perplexed, but she shrugged it off, wanting nothing more than to make her way back to the castle and curl up next to a fire. She found Brionna, and together they splashed through the puddles of the cobbled street as they hurried back to the castle.

They were ushered under the iron gate that separated the city from the castle courtyard by disgruntled guards, and Ariadne nearly slid on the smooth stone pathway that wound its way through the neat green grass that now looked more like a swamp. The flags that normally waved at the top of the towers were gone, taken down to be protected from the storm, and the normally bright and colorful castle blended into the gloomy sky behind it.

Ariadne groaned as soon as they stepped under the cover of the threshold at the top of the stairs. She wrung out her hair, creating a puddle on the stone floor. "I feel like I'll never be dry again."

"Take a hot bath," Brionna said, brushing her own hair from her face. "Warm yourself up. I must attend to a few other things."

Ariadne heeded her instructions, not bothering to wait for a maidservant. She sighed at the warmth enveloping her skin and sank deeper into the tub. The rain and thunder echoed outside her window, the shutters gently rumbling with the wind. That, paired with the cracking fire behind her, was all she needed to relax. She had been up and running from dawn until late into the night for the past month helping with last-minute preparations for her brother's wedding, and she was feeling the exhaustion. Brionna had even put a stop to their training sessions for the time being.

Only a couple more days and then Ariadne could sleep forever, and the castle would be back to normal life. She couldn't wait for the visiting nobles to leave, especially the men. Her unwed status made up just as much of the talk as her brother's wedding, and if she received one more bouquet, the gardeners would soon be out of flowers. Perhaps she should take her mother's advice after all and wed just to stop all the nonsense. She could marry a lower noble so she needn't leave Camelot and could still continue on as a knight. Brionna was married to Sir Xiang, and they were both Knights of the Round Table.

She was only the spare after all, but her mother had fought hard to ensure Ariadne would not only be looked upon for an alliance. Her mother also already approved of Lyrion, and although he wasn't considered a lower noble, as his mother and father were Lady Blanchefleur and Sir Percival, she wouldn't need to leave Camelot.

Yes, perhaps her mother was right. She should marry soon.

When the bathwater turned cold, Ariadne finished up and dried her hair as best she could by the fire before throwing it into a simple braid over her shoulder. She had picked a warmer dress, not wool—it was still too warm for that—but a nice blue brocade with silver thread. It was fancier than her normal daily wear, but as there were guests in the castle, they expected her to be at her best. So she threw on a plain but thick gold circlet and the dragon crest necklace her father had left for her as a baby. She hated rings, so she left those alone in her jewelry box, even though she had enough for two sets of hands, and checked herself in the mirror before leaving the comfort of her bedroom.

"Good day, Your Highness," said her guard as she closed her door behind her. Brom was one of her day guards and only a few years older than her.

"Hello, Brom," she said, smiling at him. "Did Mother send you?"

"She did." He fell into step beside her. The north wing of the castle was the private royal family quarters and could have been a castle on its own. It was the oldest part of the castle, one that Arthur had helped build himself, but was cozier than the rest of the estate. Tapestries lined the halls, and the rooms were full of rugs and furniture that had seen better days, but it was home.

"You are to meet her in the throne room for supper," Brom said, gesturing for her to go first down the tight winding staircase. "A few more guests have arrived, and Her Grace has invited them for supper as well."

"Do you know who?" Ariadne asked, holding on to the wall because the winding stars were dark.

"I believe they are from the Byzantine Empire."

"Byzantium?" said Ariadne, looking back at him, but all she could see was a dark silhouette. "I didn't know Merlin put any mirrors there."

Brom shrugged, and Ariadne continued on her way, stepping into the light of the main floor corridor and passing a marble statue of Arthur and Guinevere in their wedding attire. The throne room was once the old great hall, but when additions were added and the city grew, a new larger hall was built, and the old hall was now used for council meetings and intimate suppers.

When Ariadne entered, the first thing she noticed was that the Round Table was already full of not only people, but food as well. The scent of pork and vegetable soup wafted to her nose, and her stomach grumbled. She hadn't realized how hungry she was. Guards lined the wall behind the table, where guests in colorful clothing she didn't recognize stared up at her. Her mother, dressed in a maroon dress with navy blue accents, stood as Ariadne made her way to the table. The foreign guests did as well, and the Camelot nobles exchanged glances and then did the same. Arthur hadn't been one for deference or propriety in informal occasions, and Guinevere had carried on the tradition. Respect was earned, not forced.

Guinevere reached her arms out to her daughter, and Ariadne clasped her hands before kissing her mother on both cheeks. Ariadne did not see her brother at the table.

"Darling," said Guinevere. "This is Lord Leontius and his family."

Her mother gestured to a bald man in green Roman-style robes and the woman in a matching dress beside him. Next to her were two boys, perhaps around ten. The man and his family bowed, and Ariadne returned with a curtsy.

"Welcome to Camelot, my lord," she said. "We are glad to have you."

A man Ariadne hadn't noticed whispered in Lord Leontius's ear, and the lord spoke in Greek. Before the translator could reply, Ariadne repeated herself in Greek. Lord Leontius's eyes lit up.

"You speak Greek?" he asked.

"My brother and I are fluent," said Ariadne, taking her seat. Her mother and the other guests followed. "My mother is a master of a few languages—French, Latin, and of course, Breton and Welsh—and wished for us to know a few as well."

"Your mother's Greek is good," said Lord Leontius. "I can tell she has a knack for languages."

Ariadne smiled. "She is a passionate supporter of education. She funded the first universities built in Briton. When did you arrive?"

"Late this morning," he answered. "We rested before being invited for supper here."

"Well, I do hope you enjoy your time in Camelot," said Ariadne with a polite smile. "And you must tell me of your home sometime."

Lord Leontius bowed his head, and Guinevere gave the signal to eat. Servants came around to pour drinks, and Ariadne leaned toward her mother.

"Where is Anwil?" she whispered in Breton.

"Out with Gawaine." Guinevere unfolded a white linen hand cloth. "They are overseeing the new guard posts on the King's Road."

It wasn't like Anwil to skip out on duties, especially with new guests.

"Shouldn't he be here?" Ariadne said, scooping soup into her bowl.

"He greeted them earlier. And he did say he may be late. Now stop fussing over your brother and eat. I can hear your stomach growling."

Ariadne narrowed her eyes at her mother as Lohengrin and Ellyn sniggered. Ariadne shot a look at her friends down the table. Lohengrin sent her a wink and went back to talking with his parents.

Ariadne pulled the small bowl of soup in front of her closer. It was still steaming. The scent of rosemary and oregano made her even hungrier, and Ariadne sipped at it carefully, savoring the broth. It was a perfect choice for such a rainy day. Small talk consumed the first course, and Ariadne learned that Lord

Leontius was from Constantinople and worked under Emperor Justin II as an ambassador. She also realized why her mother had invited them. Constantinople's economy was booming with trade and growing to be another Rome. While the Britons were happy not to be under Roman control anymore, they were genius in their military and ruling. Guinevere had taken inspiration from Roman manuscripts and books and applied them to expanding Camelot. While most of the kings were not happy with the Roman adaptions, they were happy with the money and trade Camelot was bringing in.

Lord Leontius had brought over plants and seeds as gifts of fruits, vegetables, and other foods they didn't have in Briton but would grow in the isle's climate. Ariadne was rather excited to try the olives.

The second course, a honey-glazed pork, was Ariadne's favorite. She had to keep herself from shoveling the food into her mouth as Sir Gaheris, Sir Gawaine's brother, recounted the tale of hunting for the Questing Beast with Arthur and the Knights of the Round Table when they were young. Ariadne had heard it a hundred times, either during drunken retellings at feasts (when the details were always different) or in books, sewn into tapestries, or a bard putting it to song. Gaheris had just finished the tale when the doors opened and Anwil strode in. His hair was slightly damp, and he wore a dark green tunic and brown trousers.

"Apologies for my rudeness by being so late," he said, rounding the table. "But the final post on the King's Road is complete."

"Oh, that's wonderful news!" Guinevere stood to kiss his cheek. "Congratulations, darling. I know you worked so hard on this project."

Ariadne grinned at her brother as he sat down across from her and greeted Lord Leontius before his gaze shifted to her.

"What?" he asked, his eyes narrowing.

Ariadne shrugged, but her grin stayed put. "Nothing. Hang from any signs today?"

Anwil glared at her. "Hasn't that gotten old yet?"

"Absolutely not," said Ariadne, but their mother sent her a look, and she went back to finishing her pork.

Anwil engaged the ambassador in conversation about economics, and Ariadne spoke to his wife, who had been quiet the entire time. Her name was Eudocia, and their sons were Alexander and Julius. They looked like their mother, both with deep brown hair and dark eyes. Eudocia's hair was streaked with gray and curled in a pile on top of her head with gold pins that looked like vines.

"Your name, Your Highness," said Lady Eudocia, delicately moving the food around on her plate. She hadn't eaten much. "It is Greek, not Briton. Was your name chosen for a reason?"

"Oh," said Ariadne, giving a wave of her hand. "No other reason than my mother came across it reading a Greek story and thought it was pretty." She was asked this question all the time. Some sneered at her, saying she should have a good strong Briton name, but Ariadne liked her name. It was unique.

Eudocia nodded. "The Minotaur. That Ariadne was a princess as well, daughter of King Minos. You have Greek stories in Camelot?"

"We have a vast library, with many scribes writing stories and tales every day," Ariadne answered, and from the corner of her eye, she saw that Anwil perked up at the mention of the library. "We have books from all over the world, thanks to Master Merlin."

Lady Eudocia's face went dark. "The wizard," she said in a stiff voice. "We have met him. It is how we arrived, through his . . . contraption."

"His mirrors," said Ariadne brightly, hoping to keep the conversation light. She knew that look on Lady Eudocia's face. She had seen it before from people who hated Merlin and magic. "Aren't they wonderful? You can go nearly anywhere in the world!"

"Where we are from," said Eudocia, picking up her goblet, "magic is something to be feared."

"I can assure you, you have nothing to fear from Merlin. Unless, of course, you ask him about wood carvings. Then you'll never hear the end of it."

Lady Eudocia did not laugh at her joke, and Ariadne thought it best to turn her attention to her mother, who gave her a smile that Ariadne recognized as her forced smile. Ariadne took a long drink from her own goblet of wine. She couldn't wait until Anwil's wedding was over.

CHAPTER FIVE

A woman made her way into the great hall of a small castle, her footsteps echoing on the stone floor. Although it was filled with the humans of the court, it was quiet. It smelled of mead and sweat, and the rushes on the floor needed to be changed. The heat from the fire in the center of the hall was stifling, and the windows at the top of the walls barely did much to keep the smoke out or the air fresh in. They should've had a thatched roof instead of a wooden one with small windows lining the upper wall, but humans never did the smart thing when they wanted to impress each other—although there was nothing impressive about this castle at all. It was falling apart and constantly damp. The king had grown old, and his mind was forgetful. His son was squandering what little money they had with the other courtiers right from under his nose. But that was not a problem she needed or wanted to fix. Let them bury themselves. She only needed them temporarily anyway.

She made her way to the king, who sat at the High Table, picking at his food. He sat at the head of the table with a large crown over his white wispy hair and fox skins wrapped around his shoulders. His frail body was permanently cold, even in the warmth of summer. The men closest to him tried to engage in conversation, but he mostly ignored them and concentrated on his food. Gravy dribbled down his chin, and she had to keep herself from gagging. Humans were disgusting creatures. Heads turned as she passed the table. Even with her human glamour, they knew she was something else. They believed she was some human witch who prophesized for the old king. They had no idea she had once been a high priestess of Avalon.

As she approached the old king, she put a hand on the back of the chair to the king's left. The man sitting in it suddenly found himself in much need to relieve himself and ran from the table. The woman took his seat, and a servant was at her side in an instant, filling a new goblet full of wine.

"Your son has left for Camelot, I see," she said, picking up the goblet. She sniffed the wine and found it tolerable enough to take a sip, though faerie wine was so much better.

"Yes," the king mumbled in a raspy voice. He licked at his fingers. "He's to tell them I am ill. Which isn't too far from the truth." He took a drink from his own goblet, his gnarled hands shaking. His shoulder-length hair was pure white, and his face sagged with wrinkles.

She raised an eyebrow at him. She had hoped this visit would be short and sweet. "What haven't you told me?"

"I developed a nasty cough that won't go away," he muttered, giving a wave of his hand. "The Druids worry." He nodded to the group of men in matching hooded robes to his right, who were conversing with one another. They each sported long beards and pendants, and observed her cautiously. They were men who had been turned away from the Druid High Council for one reason or another. Oath breakers, zealots, no true magic. She doubted they could see through her glamour, but she would be careful anyway.

"The Druids always worry," she said, but would keep that information tucked away for a later time. If the king died before she could carry out her plans, it would prove detrimental. His hot-headed son was unpredictable, but he stayed in line as long as the father was alive. Perhaps she needed to give the king something to live longer, as he was easier to control.

"I hear you were successful," said the king, tearing a strip of meat from the slab on his plate. "Seems dramatic to burn the monastery, don't you think?"

"The fewer monasteries, the better," she said before taking another sip of wine. "But yes, I got what I needed."

"Anything to eat, my lady?" a servant asked her quietly. She nearly jumped at the close contact. The girl had leaned right next to her ear. It surprised her to see the servants behaving so. Weren't they not to speak unless spoken to?

"No." She waved her hand in dismissal, and the girl curtsied and hurried away. She glanced at the food on the table and curled her lip. A pig's head stared back at her. Poor thing.

"While I agree," said the king, "the more eyes you catch, the more swords to follow. Camelot won't like you killing those Christians, especially the nuns. Guinevere has a soft spot for them."

"Everything is working exactly how I wanted," she snapped. "Besides, I'm only looking out for my own. The fewer the monasteries, the less my people are captured and killed."

The king made a hum of agreement, then went on eating, his lips smacking together as he chewed. "Well, we'll know more of how Camelot will answer when my son arrives at the city. I am surprised you are not with him."

"I cannot step foot in the city with that wizard there. You know that," she hissed.

That wizard was Merlin. Her old tutor. A man she had looked up to as a father figure. She'd thought he held the same affection for her, but when he told her sister, the Lady of the Lake, that she had broken her vows and was exacting revenge for the fae who had been hurt and slaughtered by the humans, she was banished from Avalon. And it was Merlin who had nearly succeeded in killing her on the battlefield. She would get her revenge on him too, soon enough.

"Now, what news do you have? It must be important if you asked me to come in person." She took another sip of the bland wine.

The king glanced at her, his bright green eyes the only things unchanged from his youth. He shifted in his chair and wiped his hands on a cloth. He coughed and pressed the cloth to his face. It was a moment before his coughing subsided, and she spotted blood on the rag. Her stomach twisted. He had little time.

"The Lady of the Lake shall indeed officiate the boy's wedding," the king rasped and cleared his throat. The man on his other side handed him a mug of water. "She travels for Camelot the day of the wedding."

She leaned back in her chair and tapped her nails on the armrest, contemplating this new information. If Vivienne was leaving Avalon, it would be vulnerable. Of course, the priestesses left behind would guard it, as well as the faeries, but she could handle them. The isle should recognize her; she was born of it. It would let her in if Vivienne was not there. And she could take Excalibur. If she had Excalibur for her spell, it would amplify the power she needed beyond what she'd imagined.

But why officiate the prince's wedding? She didn't even attend either of Arthur's weddings. Had Merlin convinced Vivienne to take part in Camelot's search for her? Vivienne always had had a soft spot for humans, and she could never understand why. They were all stupid power-hungry creatures with far too much thirst for war. She couldn't wait to be rid of all of them.

She rose from the chair and placed her hand on the king's shoulder. A tingling sensation traveled down her arm and into the old man. She felt the tension leave his body, and the rattling breath in his lungs eased. Hopefully, it would buy him a little more time.

"Thank you for the information. Inform me at once if you hear anything else." She swept away from the table, her dark blue cloak billowing behind her. She slowed her pace. The spell had drained a bit of her energy, but she dared not let that show. The Druids watched her every move.

Nimue glanced over her shoulder at them and winked before leaving the hall.

CHAPTER SIX

ANWIL

The faint scratch of the quill and rustle of the paper relaxed Anwil's mind and put him at ease. The library was his place of refuge, especially this past month, when life had been chaotic with wedding preparations. Extra staff had even been hired to help, and the castle had never been so crowded. He dreaded to think what it would be like once all the guests arrived. The rest were due later in the day. Mostly the petty kings of Briton were left, likely not wanting to arrive too early. They preferred to make an entrance, and of course, Camelot would welcome them with a grand feast.

Anwil felt for the castle staff. Two large feasts in a row had to be stressful. At least they had a day between the welcome feast and the wedding, but still. And he hated to think about what they spent on it. Of course, King Constantine, Yvanne's father, had provided a dowry, and they used that to help pay for food, but Anwil thought it a waste of funds. They could use that to repair buildings, streets, or invest it into the farmlands.

Anwil looked up from the book he was reading and stretched his back. He peered out of the window he was sitting under and could see part of the courtyard, where guests flooded in through the gates. They were met with staff to show them their rooms in the guest wing. Anwil could have been out there greeting them himself, but he chose the selfish option. He needed all the quiet he could get before spending the evening and most of the night with the rowdy kings and their men.

"Hiding?"

Anwil jumped and nearly threw the book across the room. "Ari!" He gasped, but it just made his sister laugh. She was dressed in a tunic and trousers, which bore wet patches from her sweat. She plopped down on the table and took the book from him. He could smell the stables on her clothes.

"The Iliad?" She handed it back to him. "Haven't you read that a thousand times?"

"This is new," he said, flipping through it. "With illustrations."

"Oh, that's lovely," said Ariadne, swinging her legs. "Anyway, are you going to be hiding up here all day?"

"I'm not hiding," he protested, but Ariadne gave him a look. "Fine, I'm hiding. And most likely, yes. Why?"

Ariadne shrugged. "Just wondering. Does Mother know you're here?"

"Ari, you want something," he said, putting the book down and folding his arms across his chest. If she had come straight from the stables, something was on her mind.

She stopped swinging her legs and looked down. "Well, yes," she said. "But I'm only . . . Well, I want your opinion."

Anwil leaned against the table and waited for her to continue.

She pushed stray hair, identical to Anwil's, from her face and let out a huff. "What do you think of Lyrion?"

Anwil blinked and let out a laugh that sounded more like a cough. "What? What do you mean, what do I think of him? He's one of my closest friends."

Ariadne buried her face in her hands. "No, I mean . . . what would you think if I married him?" Her voice was muffled behind her hands, and her skin turned red under all her freckles.

He blinked again, not sure if he'd heard her right. "Ari, what—did he ask you?"

Ariadne shook her head and slid her hands down her face. She looked distressed. "No. But I can't see any other option to stay in Camelot."

"Stay in Camelot?" Anwil repeated. Now he was even more confused. "What happened? Did Mother arrange a marriage? Are you going somewhere?"

"No, I just—" She blew out a breath. "With your wedding happening and men trying to court me . . . I just figured, if I marry Lyrion, I won't have to leave."

Anwil sat down next to her. "You shouldn't marry him just to avoid leaving. Lyrion is in love with you."

Ariadne whipped her head around and stared at him with wide eyes. "What?"

"Don't act like you didn't know." Anwil gave her shoulder a nudge. "He's been in love with you for ages."

Ariadne groaned and lay back on the table. "Well, I mean . . . obviously we fancy each other."

"You *do* like him, right?" Anwil asked, twisting around to see her. "You're not just leading him on?"

"If I didn't like him, I wouldn't risk sneaking out at night to—"

Anwil held up his hands. "I don't need to know the gritty details. But . . . you are being careful, aren't you?"

"Anwil!" Ariadne shoved at his shoulder. "Of course I am! I drink that tea every few months, just as Mirah instructed." She sighed and folded her arms across her chest. "I do fancy him, but I don't know about love. I think I'm just too focused on becoming a knight."

"Then keep focusing on that and don't worry about your marriage," said Anwil. "Besides, you can't marry anyone without my permission anyway, and if you want to stay in Camelot, then that's fine with me. More than fine. I'd rather have you here."

Ariadne sat up. "You'd let me stay here and not arrange for a foreign king?"

Anwil put a hand to her forehead. "Are you feeling well? You *know* I'd rather you stay here. All I want is for you to be happy, Ari. You're my sister and my best friend."

Ariadne threw her arms around his neck, and he stiffened. She was still wet with sweat and, quite frankly, stunk. He would have to bathe again. Ariadne also rarely touched anyone and hated hugging. She tolerated it from their mother, but the only other person besides him and their mother he'd ever seen Ariadne hug was Mirah.

"Guess I just needed to hear it again," she said and pulled away. "Thank you, Anwil."

"Welcome," he mumbled, brushing off his tunic. "Now leave me in peace. And take a bath."

She stuck her tongue out at him but hurried out of the library. Anwil sighed and ran a hand through his hair. At least one of them should marry for love and not political alignment. He liked Yvanne well enough and considered her a friend, but their marriage was to strengthen the High Throne. A Briton princess would produce Briton heirs. The petty kings had not been fond of the idea of a foreign princess, even if it opened a new trade network. And Yvanne was the only choice; the other Briton princesses were already married or too young. Anwil also had a secret inkling that his mother and King Constantine had been conniving to arrange their marriage anyway. They were rather close, Guinevere and Constantine. But Anwil didn't want to dwell on that either.

He peered out the window again. More guests were arriving. He really should at least make an appearance out there. Anwil replaced *The Iliad* on the shelf and made his way out of the library, bidding Master Umar goodbye as he passed his desk. Sometimes he hated his sense of duty.

The orange glow of sunset covered the courtyard, and Gawaine clapped Anwil on the back. "Go wash up real quick. You look tired."

Tired didn't come close to how he felt. Anwil had spent the last five hours greeting and small talking the guests that came through the gates. King Bors III of Gwent had sized him up, asking when he would compete in tournaments, and King Elyion of Northumbria made passive aggressive comments about his daughter marrying a duke in Gaul. His daughter was nearly ten years older than Anwil and had already been widowed twice. He had felt bad for her. She had kept tears back the entire time he met with her last year and barely said a word. King Caewlin of Mercia at least seemed genuinely happy when he congratulated Anwil.

"I'll be quick," Anwil mumbled and trailed behind some servants as he made his way up the stairs only to find Merlin waiting for him. "Master Merlin?"

"I was wondering if we could have a chat, Your Highness?" said the wizard, leaning with both hands on his staff.

"Of course," Anwil answered automatically. "Would you mind walking with me to my rooms? I want to wash up before the feast."

Merlin bowed, and they fell into step together, walking slower than Anwil was used to.

"I wished, of course, to offer my congratulations," said Merlin. "And to offer you my advice, if you shall ever need it."

"I thought you were trying to retire? Are you saying you'll stay on as an advisor?"

"It would seem I shall stay longer, yes," said Merlin. "I also wished to speak with you about these attacks. There's more to them, I think. I've been having strange dreams lately, unlike I've had before. It is hard to interpret them, but something is coming."

"What kind of something?" Anwil did not like the grave look on Merlin's face.

"I do not know. Perhaps a war, an invasion . . . a severe storm? Hard winter, perhaps? It could be anything, but I believe whoever is behind these raids on abbeys is linked to it."

Anwil's stomach twisted. If Merlin was worried enough to delay his retirement, then it must've been bad. If Anwil had thought he was nervous before, it was nothing compared to the sinking feeling he had now. Becoming king was terrifying enough, but to be a new king with a foreboding future for his kingdom . . . it would either make or break him. And Anwil feared the latter. He was not as strong as he made himself out to be. It was all a farce, a mask he put on whenever he left his room or the library. It was as if he were an actor in a play and his role was Anwil Pendragon, son of the Once and Future King Arthur, future High King of Briton. Sometimes he wished the songs were true, that his father would rise again in Briton's time of need and Anwil needn't wear the crown.

"What should we do?" Anwil asked quietly. He was woefully naïve on matters like this. Most of his mother's reign had been peaceful. There was a rebellion not long after he and Ariadne were born, but of course, he wouldn't remember that.

"At the moment," said Merlin, putting a hand on his shoulder as they stopped at the bottom of the winding stairs that led to the private quarters, "enjoy your wedding. I used to tell Arthur to never take the happy moments for granted, for you will need them to hold on to in dark times."

"Is this a dark time?" Anwil whispered.

Merlin didn't answer for a long time. He looked at the tapestry on the wall of Sir Galahad holding the Grail but his eyes were distant. "For the first time in my life," he said finally, "I do not know."

CHAPTER SEVEN

GUINEVERE

G uinevere waited in front of the heavy wooden doors that led into the great hall. They were closed and guarded, but she could hear the rumble of voices behind them. All the kings of Briton and noble guests were on the other side, waiting for her and her children—Anwil specifically. The day after tomorrow was his wedding, and Guinevere was equally excited and sad. Excited that her son was now a man ready to take on his future, but sad her baby boy was all grown up. She remembered bouncing him on her knee, playing with him in his rooms, caring for his scraped knees, and tucking him in at night. Those were the best years of her life, when her children were young. She had loved every minute, even the exhaustion of the newborn stage. She had insisted she care and feed them on her own, not wanting a wet nurse for either of them. They were *her* children that she had fought and sacrificed for.

Guinevere shook herself from her thoughts and turned to her ladies, Blanchefleur and Dindrane. They dressed to match in red and yellow dresses, though Blanchefleur opted not to wear a veil over her light hair and pulled half of it from her face, with delicate curls framing her eyes. Dindrane, while unmarried, always wore a wimple, as she hated styling her own hair. *"It's much easier and practical this way,"* she had always said. Blanchefleur also wore dangling gold and pearl earrings with a matching circlet and necklace. Her red overdress was plain to accent her jewelry, and the yellow underdress poked out of the long sleeves with red embroidery at the edges. Dindrane was dressed similarly, with less jewelry than her sister-in-law, but her earrings matched Blanchefleur's.

Guinevere had told them they needn't wear the Pendragon colors, but they'd insisted on showing unity. Guinevere wore a dress of blue and red to signify the joining of the Pendragon and Dumnonia houses. Her jewelry was all gold, as was her veil. Her hair was neatly braided into two to fall over her shoulders and studded with pearls. It was a simple style but comfortable, as it would be a long night.

"Your children are late," Dindrane said, putting her hands on her wide hips.

"Oh, stop fussing," said Blanchefleur. "It's Anwil's celebration. He can arrive precisely when he means to."

"It won't do to keep guests waiting," said Dindrane. "They're an impatient lot, especially the old kings."

"There they are!" Blanchefleur waved down the hall, where Anwil and Ariadne were rounding the corner.

Guinevere smiled, her heart swelling. Sometimes she forgot they were twins, with them being so different in personality, but when they walked together, she was reminded of how similar they were. They looked wonderful, Anwil in the new red damask tunic Guinevere had made for him and Ariadne in a sleeveless red gown belted at the waist with a square gold belt and a sleeveless gold-and-cream open surcoat overtop. Two thick gold bracelets looked more like armor than jewelry wound around her wrists, and her hair was pulled up in a twist. She did not wear a circlet, but a gold hair pin glinted in her curls.

Dindrane faced them. Her infamous disapproving stare made Ariadne and Anwil falter. When Guinevere had other duties, Dindrane had taken on the role of governess, caring for them when they were younger. Dindrane had been better at discipline, as Guinevere found it hard to be angry with them at all, especially when they were young. But Dindrane had known exactly how to keep the rambunctious toddlers in line.

"You're late," said Dindrane, her arms folding across her chest and her foot tapping.

"It's all right," said Guinevere, closing the distance between them. She kissed both her children and took their hands, leading them to the doors. "Are we ready?"

When they nodded, Guinevere squeezed their hands, and Anwil switched positions so he could escort her in properly. Guinevere wrapped her arm through his and let go of Ariadne's. Guinevere signaled to the guards, and they opened the doors. The immediate rush of noise hit her ears. The hall was bright, with a roaring fire in the main hearth and floating candles, courtesy of Merlin. As they stepped through the threshold, a trumpet sounded, and the hall quieted.

"Rise for Her Grace, Queen Guinevere of Camelot and Briton, and Their Highnesses, Prince Anwil and Princess Ariadne." Lord Roland's voice boomed around the hall, and the guests all rose to their feet.

Guinevere smiled and made her way to the High Table with Anwil and Ariadne. Anwil pulled the chairs out for her and Ariadne, and once they were at the center of the table, Guinevere held out her arms.

"Welcome, good gentles!" she called out. "I shan't bore you with a long speech. Instead, I will merely share our gratitude and appreciation for all of you here. Not only are the kings of Briton present, but guests from Gaul, Constantinople, Egypt, Byzantium, Persia, Ireland, and many other wonderful places with rich cultures. And we welcome each one of you to our humble kingdom of Briton." Guinevere picked up the goblet in front of her that was already filled with wine and raised it. "To all of you who join us here tonight and to my son, Anwil, may happiness and prosperity join you in this new chapter of life."

The crowd cheered and clapped, sipping on their drinks. Guinevere sat, and the hall followed. The musicians started a lively tune, and servants flooded in through the servant doors, pushing carts full of food and drink as discussion rumbled through the hall again.

"Caradoc is not here," Gawaine said from Anwil's other side, digging into his soup.

"No one is shocked," Ariadne mumbled into her goblet. Guinevere shot her a look. "What? We all knew he'd make a statement."

"I *had* hoped he would at least come for the wedding," said Guinevere. She was tired of the constant arguing with the king of Wessex. He had adamantly refused to vote for her as regent when Arthur died and had defied her in any way he could ever since. From refusing to show at festivities, withholding taxes, leaving messages unanswered, or voting down any new bills for the country, it was unending. Not that Guinevere could do anything about it. The kings had their rights, and he did the bare minimum of his duties to the High Throne by coming to the biannual Meeting of Kings. As long as he didn't invade or declare war against the High Throne or the other kingdoms, there was nothing significant Guinevere could do about his behavior.

"Why?" said Ariadne. "You hate him. We'll all have a much better time without him anyway."

Gawaine snorted into his mug, causing him to cough, and his wife, Lady Reya, patted his back.

"It's outright disrespectful to me," said Dindrane. "An insult. He should be punished."

"We cannot punish him for not accepting the invitation," said Guinevere, already feeling a headache. Her stomach rumbled, and all she wanted to do was eat. The rabbit stew smelled delicious, but if they all wished to talk, she'd never have time to properly eat it.

Dindrane rolled her eyes but thankfully did not reply.

"Well, I'm certainly glad he isn't here," said Ariadne as she scooped gravy with a slice of bread. "If Caradoc were here, then his foul son, Cerdic, would be here as well."

"Have care not to say such things too loudly, please," Guinevere said to her. "Lord knows we have enough gossip around here."

"Speaking of gossip," said Dindrane, nodding to the elderly woman slowly approaching the table. She leaned on her cane and on the young man escorting her. She was dressed in dark green velvet gown with a capelet of fox fur snug around her shoulders. Her white hair was pinned into a delicate twist at the nape of her neck. The young man bowed deeply as they approached, and the woman bowed her head. Guinevere stood and reached across the table to take the woman's gnarled hand.

"Lady Laudine," said Guinevere, putting a smile on her face. Lady Laudine was a force to be reckoned with and had been her entire life. She was wife to the late Sir Yvaine, one of Arthur's knights, and had inherited all his titles when he passed as they had no children. When she was younger, Yvaine killed her first husband, and Laudine persuaded the knight to marry her and protect the lands, especially the magical fountain her late husband had guarded. She was also brutal in her court games and infamously passive aggressive. She and Guinevere had had an odd relationship—not friends, but not enemies either.

"Guinevere." Laudine smiled. Her voice was raspy with age. "It is good to see you. You are as lovely as ever. And young Prince Anwil."

Anwil stood to his feet to shake her hand. "My lady," he said, bowing over their clasped hands. "Thank you for coming."

"Oh, I wouldn't dare miss a royal wedding. And aren't you handsome, even with that hair."

Anwil blinked, and his smile faltered. Ariadne giggled, and Guinevere nudged her leg with her foot.

"Guinevere." Lady Laudine turned back to her, and she braced herself for the back-handed compliment that was bound to come for her. "Can we do something about the roads, my dear? They are rather bumpy, and the carriage ride is simply atrocious. Is there not a way to smooth them out?"

"I am actually heading a project to improve the roads," said Anwil. "We've already begun gathering materials and workers."

"Ah," said Laudine. Her nearly extinct eyebrows shot up. "Well, marvelous. I shall let you get back to your supper. Come, Trevyn."

The young man bowed again and escorted Lady Laudine back to her seat. Guinevere sank into her chair and topped off her wine.

"I believe that was the most polite I've ever seen her," said Dindrane, her eyes wide.

"What's wrong with my hair?" Anwil mumbled, patting his curls.

"Nothing, darling," said Guinevere. "Percival." She leaned behind Ariadne to see her captain of the guard a few seats down. "Could you make sure no one else approaches the table? I'd like to eat tonight."

The rest of the feast went by much smoother. Guinevere shared in laughter and stories and ate more than she had in ages. The desserts of candied fruit, pies, and apple cinnamon scones were the best she had ever tasted. Her mood, though, soured when Sir Malcolm, Percival's second-in-command, informed her that Lord Cerdic of Wessex had indeed arrived and was currently at the stables. His father, King Caradoc, was not in attendance and was apparently ill.

"I'll go." Anwil stood, but Gawaine put a hand on his arm.

"No," he said. "This is your feast. You stay. I'll go. I know how to deal with him."

"Ari," said Guinevere. "You best go with him. One of us should be there."

Ariadne looked at her mother over her goblet. "Er, all right." She stood but was a bit wobbly on her feet. Guinevere pressed a hand to her forehead, already dreading the rest of the night.

"That man is not ill," said Dindrane, watching Ariadne leave with Gawaine.

"He is getting up there in age," said Blanchefleur. "He may likely be ill."

"The gods aren't that merciful." Dindrane snorted.

Guinevere filled her goblet with wine once more.

CHAPTER EIGHT

ARIADNE

Ariadne grumbled under her breath as she steadied herself on Gawaine's arm as they descended the courtyard stairs. She wasn't drunk, but she *was* feeling the two goblets of wine she'd had.

"Steady now," said Gawaine. The stairs were soaked from the rain, and she clung onto him until they were safely on the ground. She took in a deep breath and gave herself a shake as Gawaine waited with a raised eyebrow.

"All right," she said. "I'm good."

Gawaine nodded but didn't look too convinced. "Just, er, let me do the talking."

Ariadne did not argue with him. Not talking to Cerdic was perfect. The last time they'd spoken, he made an inappropriate comment about her chest in front of everyone on the training field. She'd quieted him by sending an arrow whizzing past his ear, but it hadn't lasted long. He was back to his usual uncomfortable *flirtations* the very next day.

Ariadne stumbled into a puddle and cursed. Her shoes and stockings were now soaked. She let out a frustrated growl and leaned on Gawaine again. She hiked her skirt to see the damage, and her brown leather shoes were nearly black with water.

"Come on," said Gawaine. "Let's get this over with quickly. You can change your shoes when we get back."

Ariadne protested, but Gawaine just nudged her on. Normally, they would shortcut through the grass field, but it was muddy and full of water, so they took the winding path along the outskirts of the courtyard. Not that it was much better. She tried hiking her skirt up, but the mud was relentless. Her hem was brown and soggy.

"Mother is going to kill me," she muttered. "This is a new dress."

Gawaine glanced over at the stables that were now in view. A large group of men huddled around, unpacking their horses. Ariadne did not see a stable hand in sight. They would never hear the end of that from Cerdic.

"Stop grumbling about your dress and sober up," said Gawaine sternly, but there was an amused spark in his eye. "Come on."

Ariadne glared at him but followed quietly. Her feet squeaked in her shoes, and she cringed with every step. They reached the stables, where about two dozen men were unloading their horses and leading them into open stalls. She could do this. She could be polite and welcoming and not give them a reason to sneer. Hopefully.

"Cerdic," Gawaine said to a tall thin man in a burgundy cloak. His pale hair was receding, and a few scars crinkled his face. His nose was crooked, as if broken a few times. He glanced over his shoulder at them but went back to fiddling with his horse's saddle. Ariadne pursed her lip at the dismissal but said nothing, just as Gawaine had asked.

"Gawaine," said Cerdic in a smooth voice. "Grand welcome party, I see. Her Royal Majesty couldn't even be bothered to say hello?"

"You missed the welcome party." Gawaine folded his hands across his broad chest. "And most of the feast. You're late. Where's your father?"

"Ill," Cerdic answered, not bothering to turn around. "Healers said it would be unwise for him to travel."

"Well, there's still plenty of food left," said Gawaine. "You're welcome to join in or head straight to your rooms in the guest wing."

"Guest wing?" Cerdic asked, finally turning around. His gaze caught Ariadne, and he wasn't subtle about his eyes roaming up and down her body. She folded her arms across her chest.

It didn't escape her notice that Gawaine shot her a warning glance.

"Aye," said Gawaine, turning back to Cerdic. "Just finished the renovations on it. The aqueducts even lead to it, so each room has running water. Now you won't have to complain about the bathhouses."

Cerdic blinked at them, and his face transformed into a scowl. "Aqueducts? Last I checked, we were Britons, not Romans." The last word he spat out like he'd eaten something disgusting. He and his father had been adamantly against Camelot incorporating Roman ideas into Briton, but Ariadne thought it genius. Use the enemy's ideas against them—although Rome wasn't much of an enemy anymore. Not after the fall of the Empire. Though the rising Catholics were growing in power and trying to needle their way into things.

Gawaine shrugged. "If you don't want to enjoy the water in your washroom, that's up to you. Now, if you don't mind, I'd rather like to get back to the strawberry pie."

Ariadne breathed a sigh of relief when she and Gawaine turned around to leave, but Cerdic apparently had other plans.

"Now hold on," he said. "You come all the way out here with the princess, who doesn't even bother to greet us?"

Ariadne held back a groan, and Gawaine gave her a warning look. She turned back around and put on her best polite smile.

"Welcome to Camelot, Lord Cerdic," she said in a fake sweet voice. "We hope you enjoy your stay."

Cerdic was still for a moment before letting out a laugh. "Straight to business, then," he said with a glance at his men. "Well, all right." He bent into a mock bow. "We are humbly grateful for your hospitality, Your Highness."

His men laughed, and anger bubbled in her stomach. Ariadne clenched her fists and bit down on her tongue. She had plenty she wanted to say to him but didn't want her mother or brother to have to deal with the repercussions. Still, their laughter hit a nerve with her not-quite-sober self.

"As you should be," Ariadne said. "Come, Gawaine. We have more important matters to attend to." She turned on her heel, her water-heavy skirt billowing out behind her, and stalked off. She could almost hear Gawaine's disapproval as he hurried to catch up to her.

"I thought you lot were all about chivalry and honor?" Cerdic called after them. The laughter from his men echoed, and Ariadne tried to turn back around, but Gawaine grabbed her arm.

"Ignore it," he grumbled into her ear. They were silent all the way back to the courtyard, which was illuminated by the moon's light. "Well, that could have gone worse," said Gawaine as they headed back to the stairs.

"He's vile," Ariadne hissed.

"I know. Are you heading back to the feast?"

"I'm going to change first."

"Take a guard!" Gawaine called after her as she hurried away down the corridor.

She hadn't made it far when she nearly ran into a pair of people in the dark corridors stepping out of the hallway that led to Merlin's study.

"Mirah!" Ariadne squealed and threw her arms around the woman. Her closest and oldest friend returned her embrace with the same enthusiasm. Lavender and sage filled Ariadne's nostrils, as well as the smooth scent of Mirah's hair oils. She and her father had been gone for over a month. They'd traveled back to his family estate after Mirah's maternal grandmother passed away. Mirah had taken the news hard, as she and her grandmother had grown much closer after Mirah's mother passed a few years before. Ariadne would have gone with her to keep her company, but neither her mother nor brother thought it was a good idea while abbeys were being targeted.

Mirah pulled back, and her face split into a grin. Her tight black curls were loose from her usual braids, framing her head and pulled back from her face with a gold headband. "I've missed you!" said Mirah as her father stepped into the moon-light streaming in from the corridor windows.

He was a tall powerful man with dark brown skin and kind eyes. It was odd to see him in a formal tunic and cloak and not his usual red knight's tabard. He was the son of Sir Palamedes, who had been one of Arthur's Knights of the Round Table, and Sir Jabir had followed his footsteps after Sir Palamedes's passing at the Battle of Camlann.

"Have you only just returned?" Ariadne asked them.

"Aye," said Sir Jabir, his deep voice echoing in the hallway. "Just came through a mirror to Merlin's study. He is hiding from the feast, I see."

"He always hides from feasts," said Mirah with a slight roll of her eyes. "You know that, Baba. How many times has he tried to schedule lessons during a feast just to have an excuse to get away?"

Both Mirah and Sir Jabir were mages—humans touched with magic. Mirah's mother had been an apprentice to Sir Jabir's mother, a healer Merlin had met on his journeys to North Africa. She had traveled back to Camelot with Merlin and fell immediately in love with Sir Palamedes. Ariadne had heard the tale for many years. The bards loved to sing of their love story. And now Mirah was Merlin's apprentice, having inherited magic from both her parents.

"Well, I, for one, am starving." Sir Jabir kissed his daughter's head. "Do not get into too much trouble now." He gave a look to Ariadne before heading into the hall.

"Do you wish to attend the feast?" Ariadne asked as soon as Sir Jabir was out of earshot. "Or do you want to sneak down into the city and see Captain Stout play at the Crown and Dragon?"

"Doesn't the feast have entertainment?" said Mirah.

"Yes." Ariadne slid her arm through Mirah's. "But the Crown and Dragon doesn't have kings and nobles we have to impress."

"You know your mother would have your head if you left the feast," Mirah said, tugging her toward the great hall doors.

Ariadne groaned but let Mirah lead her back into the hall. Mirah was the rational one out of the two of them and usually kept Ariadne out of trouble, but every once in a while, Mirah let her wild side show. They made room for Mirah at the table in the hall, and Guinevere greeted her with a tight hug and kiss to her cheeks.

As Mirah ate, Ariadne let her be and watched the acrobats in boredom. They were fantastic, climbing silk ropes that hung from the ceiling and swinging on hoops, but she wanted to dance, to be surrounded by people she could relax around. It wasn't often she could venture into the city without duties to attend to. Especially now with the attacks on the abbeys. She hadn't been to the city in weeks and missed the revelry, the people, and being somewhere she didn't have to constantly think about what she said or how she said it. She didn't have to play political games with the people in the city.

Her eyes roamed over the guests in the hall and landed on the table full of the younger Knights of the Round Table. Lohengrin, her cousin Gingalain, Lyrion—although he was not yet a knight, he usually sat with his brother—Malcolm, Xiang, and Brionna. One day, Ariadne would sit with them, knighted and their equal, not above them. When this wedding was over, she would throw herself back into training and be worthy of the Trials and finally become a knight. Then she could live a life that truly mattered.

CHAPTER NINE

ANWIL

He was getting married today. The realization hit him hard the moment he woke up and saw one of his grooms, Leofwine, setting out the clothing he was to wear. For a while, it had seemed too surreal to be happening, but now that the morning was actually here, Anwil was terrified. Would he be a good husband? Would Yvanne be a good wife? And what did all that mean, exactly? Of course, treating each other with respect was a given, but exactly what did one do day to day as a husband? He knew what his duties were as a prince and eventually a king, but how should he go about doing them as a husband as well? How could he have not thought to ask anyone?

"Are you well, Your Highness?" Leofwine broke him from his thoughts, looking at him worriedly. "Shall I call for Master Cassius?"

"No," said Anwil. "No. I'm fine. Er, have you brought—ah, water. Thank you." A plate of fruit and a pitcher of water and a pot of tea sat on his bedside table.

"I've also drawn you a bath, sire. Do you need anything else?"

Anwil shook his head and dismissed Leofwine. Anwil let out a deep breath as the door closed with a soft click. His stomach twisted in knots, and he needed to get out of bed, but his body wouldn't move. He squeezed his eyes shut and pressed his hands to his face. He could do this. He *had* to do this. Anwil pushed himself out of bed and made his way to the attached washroom, where the large stone tub was full of steaming water. It was a plain room, with nothing but the tub, spigot, and a smaller table with a basin and plenty of soaps, oils, and drying cloths. Anwil went over to the basin and splashed the cool water on his face. Every movement was hard, as if he were forcing every muscle in his body. His chest was tight, but he got into the bath, and the hot water eased a bit of the tension in his muscles. The water was sprinkled with lavender, and he inhaled, silently urging the herb to work magic on his nerves.

The water was almost cold when a knock echoed on his door. Anwil jumped from the bath and dried off, throwing on a dressing gown before calling the knocker to enter. Gawaine stepped inside and took in Anwil's appearance.

"A bit of a late start?"

Anwil nodded, rubbing a drying cloth over his hair. Gawaine let out a hum of disapproval but didn't comment as he closed the door. He wore the uniformed red tabard with a yellow dragon of the Knights of the Round Table over shining mail with a red velvet cloak clasped with his chain of office. He wore a ceremonial sword at his hip, but Anwil knew it to be just as sharp as any of the swords he fought with.

"Let's get you dressed."

Anwil's outfit comprised a lot more layers than he normally wore. A red brocade short-sleeved tunic was worn over a long-sleeved cream shirt with matching trousers. Golden bracers were strapped to his wrists, and a belt with a gold ring was tied around his waist. His father's old ceremonial sword was tied to his hip, and three rings were worn on his fingers: the seal of the Pendragon, the gold ring of the High King, and the ruby ring his father had left for him before he died.

When Anwil finished, he regarded himself in the mirror as Gawaine clasped the heavy cream-and-gold cloak about his shoulders. "I look ridiculous," he mumbled.

Gawaine huffed out a laugh. "I've never liked ceremonial dress myself. Too restrictive."

"I'm going to be a sweating mess." Anwil moved his arms about. Gawaine was right about the restrictions. He could barely lift his arms above his head.

"That's what all the flowers are for." Gawaine leaned on the arm of the chair by the hearth. "Have you eaten yet?"

Anwil shook his head. "I don't think I can."

"You must." Gawaine crossed the room and regarded the tray of fruit. He tossed Anwil an apple and poured him some tea. "Can't pass out from an empty stomach halfway through. You won't have time to eat until tonight otherwise. They should have brought you a better meal. Eggs, sausage—I'll have some brought to you. You should have just enough time."

"Gawaine, I'm not . . . I'm not sure I can eat." Anwil fiddled with the apple in his hands.

"Are you all right, lad?" Gawaine's voice softened.

"Just nervous," Anwil whispered. How could he explain to Gawaine that he'd rather be doing anything else in the world than getting married today? That he didn't know what he was doing or supposed to do. Yvanne had been brought up to one day be queen, a king's wife, but he had never been taught how to be a queen's husband. Was he supposed to treat her as he had during their friendship? He saw how Lohengrin was around Ellyn, and the other knights around their wives while at court, but what about behind closed doors? What were they supposed to do with each other?

"You'll be all right." Gawaine squeezed his shoulder. "I was nervous before my own wedding as well. Now, about tonight. Do you, er, have any questions?"

It took Anwil a moment to register what Gawaine meant. "What? No! No, I-I'm good." He knew *that* part. He wasn't a prude, and he had slept with a girl before. They had been barely sixteen and kept breaking out in fits of giggles, scared to be caught in the act.

"All right, then," said Gawaine. "Let's get going. But we'll stop by the kitchens to break your fast. You need the food."

If Anwil's stomach had been heavy before, that was nothing after Gawaine had forced him to eat two eggs, four pieces of sausage, some bread, and a jug of water. The sun, which was bright in the unusually clear sky, did not help matters. He was already sweating under his cloak, and Gawaine had to hand him a handkerchief to wipe the sweat from his forehead as he mingled and made small talk with the guests that had packed themselves into the courtyard. He was surrounded by guards but guided by Gawaine to greet as many guests as he could before Yvanne arrived. The crowd was a mix of nobility and commoners, and Anwil greeted the commoners the same as the nobles. He knew many of the people from the city, as they were shopkeepers or acquaintances he'd made during his visits to the market. After what felt like an eternity with the people, trumpets sounded.

He and Gawaine pushed their way back to the courtyard steps where guards and knights lined the sides. At the very top were his mother and sister, along with Merlin in formal blue robes.

Guinevere reached her arms out to him, and he took her hands, kissing her on both cheeks. "You look so handsome, my darling," she whispered, tears glistening in her eyes.

"Thank you, Mother," he mumbled.

Ariadne gave him a playful punch in the arm and a warm smile.

"Lady Vivienne arrives," Merlin said, looking out over the crowd below.

Anwil turned just in time to see a company of five riders enter through the gates. The horses were so white, it seemed as if they glowed with light. As they walked closer, Anwil realized they were not horses at all, but unicorns. Each carried a rider in billowing blue robes of silk that shimmered in the sunlight like sun on water. Their hoods covered their faces, but the crowd parted for them in a stunned silence.

They halted their unicorns at the bottom of the stairs. Anwil descended with Merlin and Gawaine, and as they approached, the lead rider pulled her hood down. Anwil's breath hitched in his throat. She was the most beautiful woman he had ever seen. She was neither old nor young. Her waist-length black hair tumbled out of her hood like waves down her back, and her eyes were the most brilliant shade of purple. Her skin was slightly silver, like moonlight, and she beamed at him as his arm reached for her.

She took his hand, and her skin was so smooth it felt like velvet. She slid off the unicorn with ease, and her pointed ears poked out from her hair. Anwil was vaguely aware that Merlin and Gawaine helped the others, but he couldn't take his eyes off this woman.

"Anwil Pendragon," she said. Her voice bounced around him like echoes in a cave. "We finally meet."

Anwil tried to say something, anything, but he could not find his voice. His heart raced against his chest. Merlin thankfully saved him from embarrassment by putting a hand on his shoulder.

"Anwil," he said. "This is Lady Vivienne, or as you know her, the Lady of the Lake."

Anwil bowed and cleared his throat. "Welcome, my lady." His voice cracked, and he cringed. "It is an honor to have you here to officiate the ceremony."

She squeezed his hand, and he felt the tension leave his body. His shoulders relaxed, and his heart didn't pound so hard against his chest. He wasn't even hot under his cloak anymore. Before anyone else had the chance to speak, trumpets sounded again. Anwil jumped, startled by the noise. He led the Lady of the Lake up the stairs with the others trailing behind, and they took their places at the top as a carriage pulled through the gate. Men on horses in bright blue and yellow followed it.

"Places!" Guinevere ordered.

Anwil stayed where he was as Lady Vivienne and Merlin stood on the threshold, along with Father Ifan from Glastonbury Abbey. The priestesses that had come with Lady Vivienne gathered just off to the side.

"Remember," came his sister's voice in his ear, "if you need to empty your stomach, aim for Lord—"

"Ari!" Guinevere snapped, and Ariadne hurried to her place next to her.

Anwil's heart pounded again, and he straightened, attempting to stand tall. The carriage stopped at the bottom of the stairs, and the driver opened the door. First to step out was a man with pale hair in a blue velvet cloak and a gold crown. King Constantine of Dumnonia held out his hand, and Princess Yvanne stepped out. A veil covered her face, and her gown was the same cream and gold as Anwil's undertunic. She held a bouquet of blue, red, and yellow in her hands. Anwil's stomach fluttered, and sweat dripped down his face. The calmness he'd felt when holding the Lady's hands was gone, replaced by his godforsaken nerves. He breathed slowly in through his nose and out through his mouth, hoping to calm his stomach. King Constantine escorted his daughter up the stairs, and two ladies followed behind, carrying her train.

Anwil and King Constantine bowed to each other, and Constantine handed Anwil Yvanne's hand. Anwil kissed her hand, and Constantine stepped aside to stand by Guinevere. Yvanne smiled at him through her veil.

"Hello," she whispered.

"Hello," he whispered back.

"You're supposed to take my veil off now," she said just as quietly, amusement in her voice.

"Oh, right!" Anwil carefully lifted the sheer fabric, and her smile widened into a grin. He couldn't help his own smile tugging at his lips. She looked beautiful. Her golden hair was down except for a few twists held back by sparkling diamond pins. Her round cheeks were dusted with the same color rouge as her lips. "You look beautiful."

Yvanne's cheeks flushed red under her rouge, and she laughed. "Thank you. So do you."

Anwil laughed, and his voice cracked again. Yvanne gave his hand a squeeze, and they faced the Lady, who had stepped forward with the priest.

The Lady called over the crowd in welcome, her voice magnified. Anwil tried to concentrate on her words, but he was too busy trying to keep steady. Yvanne must have noticed his shaking, because she squeezed his hand again. Both the Lady and Father Ifan assisted in the handfasting, tying the ribbons around their hands and wrists. Father Ifan said a Christian prayer, and the Lady gave a blessing of her own. Anwil and Yvanne exchanged vows and were each given a crown of flowers on their heads.

When the Lady called to seal the vows with a kiss, Anwil froze. But Yvanne leaned forward and pressed her lips gently against his. He pushed his hand to slide around her waist, but it was over as quickly as it had begun. When she pulled away, the roar of the crowd filled his ears. Merlin raised his staff high. The crystal emitted a yellow light, and fireworks burst above the crowd. Yvanne jumped and grabbed Anwil's arm. He pulled her to him, and she laughed into his shoulder.

"To the joust field," Guinevere whispered into Anwil's ear.

Anwil led Yvanne down the stairs, and the crowd parted for them. Flower petals were thrown, hands reached out, and other gifts were shoved in front of them, but the guards kept everyone back, giving them room to move. The joust field had been decorated with flowers and banners in both the Pendragon and Dumnonia colors and sigils. Anwil took Yvanne to the dais as their families followed. The guards bowed to them as they stepped up and took the tallest seats directly in the center of the dais. Yvanne set her bouquet down and leaned over the railing, watching as the stands across the sandy field filled with people. Anwil stood, hands behind his back, and watched her laugh and wave.

"It's been so long since I've been to a joust," she said, returning to Anwil's side. She slid her arms around his waist and kissed his cheek. "That was a wonderful ceremony, wasn't it?"

Anwil nodded. He had almost forgotten her energy. He had known Yvanne since they were children, and her innocent glee at the world had always been one thing Anwil liked most about her.

"Oh, Anwil, this is so exciting," she said as their parents took their seats in the smaller chairs next to them. "I was so nervous, especially when I saw all the people. I'm glad it was you by my side up there."

A flutter twisted his stomach, but it was different. He didn't want to throw up. He wanted to pull her to him and—

"Drink." A goblet full of water was shoved into his face. Gawaine. Anwil took it with a mumbled thanks. Yvanne was given her own goblet of water, and they sat in the throne chairs. Yvanne squealed when Ariadne and Mirah took their seats on Yvanne's other side.

"Ari! Mirah!" She jumped up to hug them both.

Anwil watched them talk excitedly until more trumpets sounded and Lord Roland rode onto the field. His horse was dressed in a caparison matching his own house colors of red and black. Roland wore light armor, shining mail under his red-and-black tunic, and steel bracers at his wrists. He raised a hand, and the rumbling of spectators quieted. The stands were filled, and many people stood on either side, huddling as close as they could to get a view of the field.

"Good day and well met, good gentles!" Roland called. "Who among you has come to see a joust?"

The crowd roared with pleasure. Sir Roland dripped with charisma and commanded the field well. He was Anwil's favorite part of the joust. Roland settled the crowd with an emphatic gesture of his right hand, the horse's reins loose in his left.

"Well. I'd say a good many of you! Very well. Let us not gild the lily any longer than we must. As you well know, today is a most auspicious day! For on this very morning, your very own most beloved Prince Anwil Pendragon was wed to the fairest princess, Yvanne of Dumnonia!" The crowd roared and settled. "Now, good people, please rise to your feet for Their Royal Highnesses, Prince Anwil and Princess Yvanne. Hip, hip!"

The crowd let out a booming "Huzzah!" as Anwil and Yvanne stood at the railings and waved. The crowd followed Roland's cheer twice more before Anwil motioned for them to sit and he escorted Yvanne back to their seats.

"And now!" called Roland, his hand reaching out to the side of the field. "Let us call forth the noble knights who will compete for you this day! Hip, hip!"

The ground rumbled with the echoes of horses' hooves as brightly colored knights rode onto the field carrying flags bearing their own house colors. The stands erupted with cheers and clapping and even pounding on the rails and steps. The joust was the most popular sport in Camelot, and even Anwil enjoyed watching. He could finally take a small breath of relief while the knights flirted with the crowd, taking the attention away from him for the moment.

Roland rode over to the north section of the field, next to where a corner of the stands was decorated in red and blue. Lord Roland held up a hand, and the crowd quieted.

"For those of you in the noble colors of blue and red, I bring to you a knight who needs no introduction. A knight known well upon this field for his prowess and honor, and not necessarily for his language skills. I call forth to this field Sir Ulrich!"

Sir Ulrich took the field, his gigantic frame belying his skills on horseback—by far the best horseman in Camelot, and he knew it. His ride onto the field was brief. He effortlessly slowed his horse to a trot and approached the dais, stopping before newlyweds and cuing the horse to bow before them as he did the same. The crowd *ooohed* and *ahhhed* as he turned and raised his fist, eliciting a great roaring cheer from the crowd.

"Wonderful display, Sir Ulrich!" said Sir Roland. "And now, good gentles, I call forth for those of you in purple and gold a young knight worthy of your love and cheers, eager to prove himself on today's special field. I give you Sir Lohengrin!"

Sir Lohengrin took the field, though not as gracefully as Sir Ulrich but with more determination and just as much good cheer. He made a full lap around the list as he called good-naturedly to Sir Ulrich, "Show-off!"

Ulrich roared with laughter, as did the crowd. Although the knights often jested this way, today, the joy was palpable and infectious. Anwil found himself grinning, his nerves forgotten for the moment.

"And now, my good people, rise you up a cheer for another knight well known in this kingdom, whose prowess is known not only on the field, but in many bedchambers across Christendom. Ladies, you know him as 'my love,' gentleman as 'that knight.' Good people, I give you Sir Gingalain the Maiden Bane!"

Cheers rang forth, and Anwil noted with a laugh how the pitch in the crowd rose and women stood and waved. Sir Gingalain, the only son of Gawaine, rode forth in his family colors of green and gold, lapping the list and approaching the dais with a respectful bow and a sly smile. Anwil watched as Gingalain turned to the crowd, and began throwing roses to them.

Ulrich laughed. "Where did he get those from?" His voice was loud enough to carry across the field.

"He definitely wasn't holding them when he rode out." Sir Lohengrin called. "Else he would have fallen off."

Sir Gingalain made a rude but good-hearted gesture at them as Roland rounded the list and came to a stop in the middle.

"Finally, last but certainly not least," Roland called out, "hailing all the way from the Frankish Empire, I give to you in burgundy and white, Sir Benoit of the Tumble!"

The knight sprung forward, his horse pulling hard at the reins. The knights' laughter rang out as the horse ran, completing the lap around the list and running past the dais. The crowd laughed once more as the second lap came to a close with an abrupt turn that tossed the knight from the saddle. They gasped as he hit the ground and rolled gracefully in the sand, then sprung back to his feet. The crowd chuckled uncomfortably while Lord Roland stepped his horse forward.

"Sir Benoit." Anwil could see Roland struggling to hold back a laugh. "Are you well?"

"All is well but my pride!" He laughed, and the crowd chuckled with relief. "Apologies, Your Majesties," he said, bowing. "This horse is very . . . spirited."

Giggles caught Anwil's attention, and he glanced over to see Ariadne and Mirah, both barely holding their composure, chests convulsing with laughter.

"It is well, Sir Benoit. That horse is named Slater. I know him well. Good luck," Lord Roland said good-naturedly to the knight.

Ariadne stood up to call, "He'll settle in. Just give him a pass or two."

Lohengrin turned on his horse and caught her eye, sending her a wink.

"Oy, now!" Gingalain called, pushing his wavy black hair from his face. "What have you two conspired?"

"Me?" Ariadne put a hand to her chest and feigned surprise. "Why, I would never! I am perfectly innocent!"

Anwil sniggered. He realized exactly what Lohengrin and Ariadne had done. Slater was unpredictable. They were testing Sir Benoit. Anwil hoped the knight took it well. He didn't wish to have an angry foreign noble on their hands.

Gingalain snorted. "Innocent, right. I've known you since you were a babe, cousin. You've always had a trick up your sleeve! You were never innocent."

The crowd let out an "Ooohhh!" and Roland waved his hands for them to settle down. "Now, now," he said. "Sir Benoit is our invited guest!"

"Aye, that he is!" Anwil rose and came to the ledge. Courage sprouted in him to take part in the teasing, and to keep it light-hearted. He couldn't have Lohengrin and Ariadne having all the fun on his wedding day. "And he shall be treated as such!"

Anwil turned to Ariadne, a teasing smirk on his face. "Sister, did you not wish to favor our guest?"

Ariadne shot him a look as the excited whispers and whistles echoed through the crowd. Ariadne quickly put a smile on her face, but her eyes were shooting daggers at Anwil. She yanked her handkerchief from her belt and held it out to Sir Benoit. He hurried over and reached up to take the piece of silk.

"Thank you, Princess." He flashed her a charming smile. "I will carry this with honor." He bowed deeply and ran back to his horse and cheers.

Ariadne gave Anwil a look that told him she would have her revenge on him, but he merely chuckled and returned to his seat. Yvanne took his hand and laughed with him, biting at her lip.

"If there be any other noble ladies who wish to favor these knights, step you forward!" Roland turned his horse around to face the dais.

Lady Ellyn dashed to the ledge, holding out her scarf. Lohengrin trotted his horse over and reached up to kiss his fiancée to whistles and cheers from the crowd.

"I'll get you back for this," Ariadne whispered in Anwil's ear as Gingalain collected many, many handkerchiefs.

"You'll try, sister," he said, although he would be checking under his pillows for weeks. Yvanne squeezed his hand as the knights once again, took time to flirt with the crowd.

"This is so much fun!" she whispered. "Who do you think shall win?"

Before Anwil could answer, Roland held up a hand.

"Knights!" Roland bellowed. "To your ends and prepare! Let the games begin!"

The crowd screamed, and squires ran onto the field to set up targets, rings, and quintains for the obstacle games. One squire, though, ran up to Roland and handed him a scroll. Roland read it, and his eyes went wide. He glanced at the dais and held up both of his hands.

"Hold!" he called.

Squires echoed his command, and everything came to a halt, even the noise from the crowd. Anwil glanced at his mother, who looked just as confused as he was. Roland rode up to the dais and held out the scroll. Anwil got to his feet and took it from him.

It was a coat of arms he did not recognize and a request to enter the tournament. Anwil looked for a name, but it only said *Knight of Briton* along with the royal seal. He did not remember this. He knew all the knights competing, all the papers he'd signed, and this was not one of them.

"What is this?" Anwil looked up just as whispers erupted in the crowd. A rider entered the field. His armor was a mix of leather and plate, and it was all black. Even his horse bore black armor and trappings. The knights on the field rode out and lined up, stopping him from going too far. There had only ever been one Black Knight in Camelot: Lancelot. But he had been presumed dead long ago, after he was banished from Camelot. And even if he were alive, he'd be well into his eighties.

"Who are you?" Anwil called to him. Guinevere was suddenly at Anwil's side, and he could hear her ragged breathing. Her face flushed with anger.

"How *dare* you show up in those colors and make a mockery of this tournament!" she called out. "Show yourself!"

The knight did not answer or move to remove his helm. The squire who'd handed Roland the scroll stepped in front of the knight's horse. He wrung his hands together and bowed.

"My lord would beg permission to compete, Your Grace," he said, keeping his eyes on the ground in front of him. The poor boy was terrified. Anwil's heart reached out to him.

"What is your name, lad?" Anwil asked him gently.

"M-Marcus, sire." The boy bowed again.

"Marcus, are you this knight's squire?"

The boy glanced back at the knight. "Er, for today, sire."

"What is his name?" Anwil pressed for more information.

"I do not know, sire." The poor boy was on the verge of crying. Yvanne came to his side, clutching a hand over her chest.

"Well, how did he come upon you?"

"I live in the city, Your Grace. H-He saw me and said I would get ten gold coins if I squired for him at the tournament."

Anwil's eyes widened. That was a good amount of money. Whoever this knight was, he was powerful if he had that much to give away. But Anwil knew all the names of the noble houses of Briton, and none of them needed to hide or disguise their names. He looked at his mother, but she was glaring at the knight in black.

"Enough with the questions! Let the man compete!" Lord Cerdic called from his seat below the dais. "Let's see how he does. It's high time we had some real entertainment." He sniggered at the laughs he pulled, but Anwil clenched his jaw.

"Are we *not* real entertainment, my lord?" Gingalain called out to him. "Have we been boring you? My most sincere apologies!" Gingalain gave a mocking bow on his horse. Some of the crowd laughed, but it did not break the tension.

"He cannot compete," Anwil said. "I did not sign this declaration, nor do we know his name. The rules are clear—"

"It's just a wedding tournament," said King Bors. "Who cares? It's all for fun anyway. I say we give the people something to talk about!" He raised the goblet in his hand, and the crowd cheered.

"King Bors, I must protest—" But jeers and boos drowned Anwil out. He glanced again at his mother, whose face was now red. He sighed and turned back to the list. Lohengrin caught his eye and shrugged.

"Have no fear, Your Majesties!" Sir Benoit called out. "I shall defeat him forthwith! I'll take him in the first pass."

To Anwil's annoyance, the crowd clapped. Anwil held his hands up, calling for silence. He knew when he was defeated. When the crowd finally quieted enough for him to speak, he said, "Very well! If the people wish to see him compete, he will compete. However"—Anwil looked back to the Black Knight, directly into the slit in his visor—"my guards and knights *will* be watching you. You will follow all rules and conduct yourself with dignity and honor. One wrong move, *sir*, and it will be your last."

Out of the corner of his eye, Anwil could see the subtle shift in the guards. The guards stationed around the field moved almost imperceptibly; some shifted their hands from the pommels of their swords to tightly grip the handles, and others knocked arrows in their bows. The knight in black bowed his head and motioned for his squire to follow him to the end of the list. Anwil slowly sank back into his seat. Yvanne took his hand and gave it a squeeze.

CHAPTER TEN

GUINEVERE

There were not enough words in the Briton language to describe how furious Guinevere was. She whirled on her feet and turned for Gawaine and Percival, who had been at the back of the dais to guard the stairs. Gawaine's face was nearly purple with anger, and although Percival could be perceived as calm, his jaw was clenched, and his hand gripped the pommel of the sword at his hip.

"Go find Merlin," Guinevere hissed at them. "And find out who that man is. I want to know how he got past our guards."

They nodded and raced off, a trail of guards hot on their heels. Guinevere sank into her chair, gripping the armrests with white knuckles. Constantine put a hand over hers, but she ignored it. They had been breached somehow, or someone had decided to perform a nasty and offensive prank, knowing what the Black Knight meant to Camelot. To her.

Her mind raced. She wanted to leave, to find out what was happening, but she couldn't leave the dais. There would be enough gossip already, especially about how she'd lost her temper. As a woman and queen, she had to keep her emotions in check. Anything too rash, and she was considered too emotional and unfit to rule. And perhaps she was being rash. The man had technically done nothing wrong, but to show up unannounced for a royal tournament dressed in black armor—the colors Lancelot used to wear? Someone meant to offend Guinevere and send a message. And she would find out who and snuff them out before they could do anything further.

Guinevere kept her eyes on the knight in black as the games began. He racked up points in the obstacle games, never missing a target. His ease and demeanor were just as Lancelot's had been. But Lancelot was dead, or at least she had assumed. He had been older than Arthur and banished nearly twenty-five years ago. If he wasn't dead, he was close to it.

"He shouldn't be competing," Constantine growled under his breath as the knight in black was declared winner of the games, to the anger and frustration of the other knights competing. Lohengrin mumbled something to his brother, Lyrion, and Sir Ulrich stared hard at the knight, who still had yet to take off his helm.

"No, he should not," said Guinevere with a glance to Anwil. He was watching the field, his face a mask, just as she'd taught him, but Guinevere could see the creases at his eyes and the fidgeting of his fingers. "We were unfairly put on the spot." They should have stuck to the rules, no matter the unpopular choice it would have been. The people lived for excitement and drama like this, but their safety was most likely in danger. If they had been breached somehow, everything she and Arthur had worked so hard for would crumble.

"Not just that," said Constantine, glaring, "but to wear the black armor? It's an insult to you and Anwil. And now my daughter. To taint her wedding day."

Constantine shook his head and leaned back in his seat. It was an insult. Constantine was right. It was a humiliating insult that would put a dent in her reputation, and Anwil would suffer for it. The rumors that Lancelot had fathered her children instead of Arthur, no matter how illogical, as he had been banished years prior, had nearly cost her the throne and her children's lives. Thankfully, those rumors had been put to rest when they came out looking nearly identical to Arthur.

Guinevere was pulled from her fury as Merlin arrived, along with the Lady of the Lake. Merlin, always calm, regarded the knight with more curiosity than anything, but the Lady of the Lake—Guinevere could have sworn she saw white-hot flames dancing in her pupils. Merlin leaned on the rail, watching closely as the jousting began and the knight in black struck Ulrich's shield hard enough for his lance to split. Lady Vivienne hovered behind Guinevere's chair, and Guinevere felt a radiating vibration in the wood beneath her feet. It was unnerving to be so close to her. Magic emanated from her, and it made Guinevere dizzy. Even the smell. Vivienne smelled of clear water and an early spring morning—a pleasant smell on its own, but coming from Vivienne, it was too much for Guinevere.

"There is magic surrounding him," Lady Vivienne whispered, and Guinevere tensed. "But *he* is not magic."

"Who is he?" Guinevere demanded, turning around in her chair. The entire dais was looking at Lady Vivienne now, but the priestess shook her head.

"He is but a simple human male," she said with a half shrug of her shoulders. "I do not know him."

"But what about the magic?"

"Someone else is protecting him." Merlin pointed toward the knight. "See there. Look at his shield. Lohengrin's lance hit dead center, but there are no markings. No scratches, no dents."

Guinevere moved to stand from her chair, but she thought better of it and grabbed Anwil's hand, who had been listening intently. He needed to take control and lead. "He is cheating. Call him on it and disqualify him."

Anwil's eyes widened, but he nodded and stood at the railing. Yvanne hurriedly joined him and called out for Roland. Roland paused the joust to the confused murmurs of the crowd. Guinevere was again reminded of why she had picked Yvanne for Anwil. The young woman was built to rule, and she would be a steady shoulder for Anwil to lean on.

"Your Highnesses." Roland bowed his head as he turned his horse toward them.

"The Black Knight cheats!" Yvanne called. "He is using magic!"

A gasp echoed throughout the crowd, and Anwil held up his hands.

"Sir Black Knight," Anwil called. "Come you forward and remove your helm. You stand accused of cheating."

The crowd hushed as the knight dismounted from his horse and walked over to stand in front of the dais. Instead of removing his helm, he removed the gauntlet from his right hand and tossed it on the ground in front of Anwil. There was a near immediate uproar from the crowd, and the other knights quickly moved on him, swords drawn. Guinevere leapt from her chair, but Constantine grabbed hold of her. Merlin raised his staff and slammed it on the ground. A booming bang erupted, and the crowd quieted.

Anwil, breathing hard, gripped the railing with white knuckles. "You dare challenge me? On my wedding day?"

Guinevere's breath hitched in her throat, and the crowd angrily shouted at the Black Knight. Anwil could not fight him. A challenge was to the death. But why? Anwil had done nothing to prompt anyone to challenge him.

Guinevere looked at Merlin. "Do something," she hissed, but Merlin either did not hear her or ignored her. His eyes narrowed at the knight. Lady Vivienne joined him at the dais as Yvanne spoke.

"Why do you wish to challenge my new husband, Sir Knight?" Yvanne's cheeks flushed with anger.

"To see if he is worthy," came a gruff but muffled voice from inside his helm.

"Worthy?" Anwil repeated. "Worthy of what?"

"King."

Fury filled Guinevere's veins, and Constantine must have noticed, because he clasped her waist. Guinevere had never been one to back down from a fight. She had never hesitated to protect her children either. If she needed to become a mother bear, then so be it.

"A fight will not determine that," Anwil replied. "And I am afraid I shall only disappoint you. I am not the master swordsman my father was, if that is what you seek. I shall follow in my father's other footsteps, however. As a seeker of justice and compassion. A king who loves his people equally, no matter their status."

Guinevere's heart swelled with pride. The cheers and whistles from the crowd threatened to pull tears from her eyes. Guinevere had worried for Anwil, knowing how his nerves had been a battle for him his whole life. They would see his compassion and empathy as weak, especially the kings and warlords, but Guinevere knew it to be his greatest strength. It had been Arthur's greatest strength too.

King Elyion of Northumbria stood to his feet on the smaller dais below. "Sir Knight," he called, his mustache moving with his breath. "I find it quite offensive that you wish to spoil this celebratory day with your foolish and uncalled for challenge. I call for this man to be taken off the field and the tournament to continue properly forthwith!"

Argument broke out amongst the nobles. Lord Cerdic jumped to his feet, whirling on King Elyion, but King Bors got in between them. Their shouts were muffled by the crowd.

"This is preposterous," Constantine growled, finally letting go of Guinevere.

"The rules of a challenge are clear!" Cerdic's voice broke through the shouts. Of course he would jump at this opportunity. Anything to humiliate the Pendragon's.

"The challenge is ridiculous!"

"Denying a challenge is unworthy!"

Guinevere's mind was racing. She needed to handle this carefully.

"Mother, what do I do?" Anwil whispered, breaking her from her thoughts. Guinevere's heart sank as she turned towards him. He looked so out of depth. But before she could say anything, Ariadne shoved her way to the railing.

"I'll take your challenge!" she yelled. "I'll champion for my brother."

CHAPTER ELEVEN

ARIADNE

Ariadne ignored the protests of her family and stared down the mysterious knight. If he had the audacity to think he could control this situation, he thought wrong. No one would challenge her brother on what should be a happy day and not be punished for it. He was making a mockery of them, and Ariadne would not put up with it. His helm moved barely an inch to look at her. He wasn't too tall—perhaps an inch or two taller than her. It was hard to tell his physique under his armor, but if magic was involved, his looks could very well be deceiving.

"Ari," Mirah whispered behind her, but she ignored her too. She did not need Mirah's voice of reason at the moment. She had to do this.

"However!" Ariadne called out to the knight once the protests had died down a bit. "The challenge shall not be to the death. If you wish to engage in this stupid fight, then you shall play by *my* rules. No magic, no cheating, no killing. It is bad luck to spill blood on a wedding day, after all."

Anwil grabbed her arm, but she shook him off, determined to keep her eyes on the knight. She couldn't see underneath his helm, but she knew she held his gaze. She stared him down, silently daring him to dismiss her offer. If he wanted to play games, then so would she. The knight finally bowed and walked off the field, leaving his gauntlet in the sand. Guinevere spun Ariadne around. Her face twisted with such fury that Ariadne took a step back.

"What the devil do you think you're doing?" Guinevere spat. Ariadne had never seen her mother so angry. "Ariadne, you rescind the challenge right now!"

"There is no way out of this!" Ariadne shot back. She straightened to her full height. "Honor demands it. Anwil's dignity—"

"My *dignity* does not need saving!" Anwil took her by the shoulders. "You cannot do this! I forb—"

"Don't!" Ariadne threw his hands off her. "You promised you'd never say that word to me!" She saw the hurt and regret that flashed across her brother's brown eyes, but he shook his head.

"I will not watch you die!"

115

"It's not to the death!" The longer they stood there arguing, the more time they wasted and the more fuel was given to the fires of gossip.

Guinevere scoffed. "Ariadne, I did not raise you to be that naïve. That man cheated his way into this tournament! What makes you think he will honor your request now?"

The words stung, but Ariadne would not back down. They needed to show the people and the kings especially that they were fit to rule. The warlords of Briton cared more for brute strength than wisdom and compassion. At least most of them shared the same line of thought about the challenge she and Anwil did, but they also needed to be seen taking care of issues themselves rather than having the guards or knights fight their battles for them. In all honesty, she had been impulsive to take the challenge. She had jumped from her seat before she could stop herself or think twice about it, but to back out now would be even worse.

"It's done," she said, her voice shaking. "I *will* do this."

Guinevere hesitated, and Ariadne used that to storm from the dais. She headed towards the knights' tents set up on the far edge of the field. She told one of the guards to find a maidservant to bring her clothes and armor. Her mother and brother trailed after her, but Brionna quickly caught up with her and pulled her close. The crowd mostly parted for them, and Ariadne heard the whispers that had made her blood boil for years.

"Why would she fight?"

"This is insanity!"

"Women can't fight!"

Ariadne would show all of them that they were wrong. And what did they think Brionna was? She was the best fighter in Camelot, but even she was not safe from the jeers. Ariadne *had* to prove them wrong.

"What do you think you are doing?" Brionna hissed in her ear as they approached the knights' tents. "This is a terrible idea. You are not yet ready—"

"I've been training for months," said Ariadne, offended by her friend's words. "Under *you*."

"This is different!" Brionna snapped and stopped Ariadne in her tracks. She had never known Brionna to show such frustration before. "He will not fight with honor. I have not yet prepared you for that, and I am afraid we may not be fast enough to defend you. He is using magic, Ari."

"Merlin and Lady Vivienne are here," Ariadne pointed out.

"Yes, but they are not all-powerful. Everyone has their limits, and if they do not know whose or what magic he is using, it will be hard to defend against it. You should not have volunteered yourself."

Tears of anger threatened to fall from Ariadne's eyes, but she bit back a reply and instead blew through the flaps of the knights' tent. Chairs, small tables, weapons, and armor racks lined the cloth walls. The stench of sweat, dirt, and horse filled her nostrils. Lohengrin and Lyrion entered nearly at the same time from the other side, and they both rounded on her, wearing identical dumbfounded and angry looks.

"Are you mad?" said Lohengrin, his eyes ablaze, and it took her aback. "Why would you—"

"Ari, tell me you are not going through with this," Lyrion pleaded, taking her hand. "This has to be a jest. Surely you cannot fight him."

"Enough!" Ariadne yelled, holding out her arms and backing up a step. "It's done. I can't take it back now." She looked away from Lyrion, who was giving her a look she could not quite place.

"You absolutely can," said Guinevere, entering the tent with Anwil, Yvanne, and Brionna. "Lohengrin, get your father—"

"No!" said Ariadne, and she turned to her. She had had enough. "Mother, don't. As of right now, we cannot arrest this man. He's committed no crime. He can be banished from tournaments for cheating, but nothing else. If he attempts to take my life, he *can* be arrested, and we can easily keep him under custody and find out exactly who he is and why he has entered the tournament. I think he intended to challenge Anwil from the beginning." The words spilled from her mouth, surprising herself a bit.

Guinevere's mouth opened and closed a few times. She stared long and hard at Ariadne before letting out an exasperated sigh. "Men, out!"

There was no hesitation from Lohengrin, although he did give Ariadne a hard look on his way out. Lyrion tried to talk to Ariadne, but she turned her back on him and he left with Anwil.

"This is madness." Guinevere paced the tent as Brionna helped Ariadne into her armor. It had taken a bit for the maidservant to reach them through the crowds with Ariadne's armor. Ariadne could hear the restless crowd through the thick tent and tried to ignore them. Her nerves had set in.

"There," Brionna mumbled, tightening the last of the straps on her shoulders. Ariadne raised her arms and shifted her shoulders. The plate cuirass was much heavier than her leather one, but she could breathe. Brionna knelt and held a steel cuisse to Ariadne's thigh and reached to buckle it around her leg, but Ariadne shook her head. "They'll only slow me down," she said. "I need to move fast."

Brionna sighed. "If he cuts into your thigh and hits your femoral artery, you will bleed to death." Brionna shook the armor, and Ariadne helped to put them on. At least they were only half legs, covering the front. Brionna did not argue with her about the greaves, thankfully. Ariadne hated those, They dug into her ankles and hindered her footing too much. Ariadne took a few steps, getting used to the weight, letting the armor settle into place on her legs. She rolled and shrugged her

119

shoulders, adjusting the cuirass as Anwil ducked into the tent with Lohengrin, his lips a thin line. He folded his arms across his chest but didn't say anything.

"I've never seen a woman fight in a tournament before," Yvanne said, touching Ariadne's pauldron. She had been watching quietly from the corner of the tent.

"She shouldn't be fighting at all," Anwil grumbled. "I should have accepted the challenge."

Lohengrin snorted, plopping down on a stool. "Absolutely not. Not on your wedding day. If Ari hadn't volunteered first, I would have. I'd like to give that cu—"

Anwil knocked him on the arm. "Watch your language!"

Guinevere stepped in front of Ariadne. "Darling," she said, putting her hands on Ariadne's shoulders. "You do not have to go through with this. I can have him arrested, and we can carry on with the tournament."

Before Ariadne had the chance to reply, Lord Roland stepped inside, holding a red shield with the gold Pendragon dragon and sword. He cleared his throat. "Your weapons, my lady."

Ariadne took them from him. She adjusted the shield on her left arm with Roland's help and rolled the sword with her wrist in the other. Roland watched her, being a weapons master, and nodded, mumbling to himself.

"Whose shield is this?" Ariadne asked him.

"Yours," he said, putting his hands behind his back. "I had it made for you and was waiting to give it to you when you were knighted, but I think you need it today."

Ariadne's breath hitched in her throat, but she didn't get a chance to thank him because Gawaine entered and told them the crowd was growing restless. Ariadne took in a deep breath, and looked around at everyone. "Well, here it goes." She tried to give them a smile, but it came out as more of a wince. She rolled her shoulders again, trying to shake away the nerves that had started to set in.

"Wait!" Yvanne pulled a handkerchief from her sleeve and tucked it under Ariadne's vambrace. "For luck."

"Thank you," said Ariadne, and Roland, Brionna, and Gawaine escorted her out of the tent. She held her head high and didn't make eye contact as the crowd parted to let them pass. Some of the nobles were still grumbling to each other, but she ignored them. As they came upon the field, the cheers were so loud, they nearly knocked her off her feet. Brionna held out her helm, but Ariadne shook her head. She hated that thing and couldn't see out of it. Brionna did not back down.

"You will wear it," she said, still holding it out. "I had the visor pulled. The cage will offer a great deal less protection, but more visibility. You must be cautious—a well-placed thrust could be the end—but you will have the protection."

Grudgingly, Ariadne lowered the helm onto her head and was relieved to find that she could see much better between the thick bars. She and Roland approached the knight, who stood unmoving in the middle of the field, and Roland stopped in between them. Roland lifted his hands high, and the cheers quieted down.

"A challenge has been made, and honor demands satisfaction." Roland turned to Ariadne. "My lady. Do you accept?"

"Aye!" Ariadne called, her voice muffled by her helm.

Roland turned to the Black Knight. "My lord?"

The Black Knight nodded once.

"Very well. How'ere, with this being a wedding celebration, there will be no bloodshed. First to disarm shall be declared the victor!" Roland called. "No cheating, no magic! If you break the rules, you will face dire consequences. Lord Merlin?"

Merlin walked onto the field and stood directly in front of the knight. Merlin held out his hand, and after a moment, the knight held out his. Merlin took hold of him, and a sound of wind being sucked into a hole echoed, and the knight trembled. And just as fast as it had happened, it was over, and Merlin stalked off the field.

"Very good. Thank you, Lord Merlin," said Roland. "Princess, Sir Knight, you will both conduct yourselves with dignity according to the Code of Chivalry our late King Arthur laid down. Do you both agree? Aye? Huzzah!" Roland crossed the field to give them room. "Knights! Salute!"

Ariadne lifted the sword to her face, cross guard just below eye level, and bowed, but the Black Knight didn't move and was jeered by the crowd. Ariadne stepped back into position as she raised her shield and rolled her sword into position: high guard over the shield, the dulled tourney sword's point on her opponent as she'd been trained. *It's just training with Brionna*, she told herself. *Just pretend it's training.* She could hear her breath in her ears, and time seemed to slow as her vision narrowed, blocking out everything but the Black Knight, who stood out in sharp clarity against the blurred field around him.

"Knights!" Roland called. "Lay on!"

The Black Knight didn't hesitate, shifting forward and bringing his sword around in a hard arc at Ariadne's head. She managed to raise her shield and block the blow, but just barely. The top of her shield tilted and struck the outside of her helm, blurring her vision and ringing her ears. He came for her, and his blows were hard and swift. He drove her back, blow after blow. Her arm screamed in pain from the concussive force, and the weight of the shield was becoming unbearable. Ariadne could hear Brionna's voice but could not make out the words. She could barely think herself. The knight was coming too fast for her to comprehend anything else.

He came at her again, this time bringing the sword down on her from above with both hands, like an executioner at the block. All she could do was lift her shield above her head and deflect without bringing the full force onto her head. She cried out as the blade scraped the heavy steel of the shield, taking shavings of fresh enamel. Her breath came in gasps that echoed in her ears. But she pushed off her back foot and drove forward. She dropped her shield to the front, hoping to catch her opponent off guard and break his balance with her own body weight. The knight sidestepped her easily, however, and she stumbled forward, turning just in time to catch another strike with the shield, and the volley began anew. With every blow, her shield arm shook. She had to get rid of it. Its weight was too much. She needed to use her speed.

Ariadne planted her feet and braced the shield with the gauntlet of her sword hand. She yelled out as the knight's sword came again. She stopped the blow cold and pushed the sword away, releasing the shield's handle with numb fingers. It flew off her arm, whirling toward the audience. Screams sounded, but it bounced in the sand in front of the fence.

Ariadne barely had time to register the crowd and rolled clumsily under a blow from the knight. Ariadne scrambled to her feet, dodging a low cut at her stomach. As the knight's sword swung fast and clear, the sun flashed on his unguarded breastplate. Ariadne took the opportunity to flip her grip and smash the pommel of her sword into his stomach. He faltered, and Ariadne swung again. She barely scratched his armor, and Ariadne registered too late that he had let go of the sword with one hand. His fist came rushing at her face. His steel gauntlet slammed into the barred visor and rocked it back into the soft bone of her nose. The crunch of bone echoed inside her helm, and her eyes immediately filled with tears. Blood gushed down her mouth, and she stumbled, then fell to all fours. She crawled and gripped her sword with all of her remaining strength. Her vision swam, and she spat blood into her visor. Bloodshed. He broke the rules.

Someone shouted, "Get up!" from the crowd, but the sound felt far away. Ariadne gripped her sword with shaking fingers. The only thought she tried to hang on to was to not drop it. *Don't drop the sword.*

Before she should get to her feet, something hard slammed into her stomach, rolling her over to her back, splayed out and gasping. Every breath was a fight, even under the breastplate. A shadow crossed her vision, and she screamed when a foot ground her wrist into the sand, trying to make her let go of the sword, but she refused. Lifting her head a little and blinking sand from her eyes, she spotted her shield. She reached out as the foot dug into her wrist, screaming once again as she felt the break. Hot tears stung at her eyes, but she managed to grip the shield's handle and swung it hard, connecting the dull heavy edge with the knight's knee. He fell forward, releasing her wrist, and she scrambled to her feet, grabbing the sword with her left hand. She was now very grateful Brionna had insisted she learned to use both hands. The knight got to his feet, but Ariadne swung first, then again and again. Anger forced itself from her mouth in gasping screams with every swing. This was no longer a fair fight. He wasn't planning to disarm her and win a challenge. He was planning to kill her.

Her burst of adrenaline kept the knight at bay. He jabbed pitifully at her side, but she blocked it and aimed a kick at his chest. It was just enough that he tipped over and fell flat on his back. Ariadne quickly kicked the sword from his grip, scrambled backward, and finally fell to her knees, exhausted. She cradled her broken wrist to her chest, her arm shaking.

Guards swarmed the list, and Ariadne slumped to the ground. Hands gripped at her and pulled her up. Her limbs shook, every movement sending sharp pains through her wrist like knives. Her vision swam, and she hissed as someone took the helm from her head. Cool air rushed her face, but it also brought more pain to her nose. Colorful blurry figures danced in her vision. Someone was yelling, but she couldn't fully make out the words. She was so tired. She just wanted to sleep. Her eyes slid closed, but a hand forced her head up, and she cried out.

"Ari!" Her mother's voice was sharp. "Ari, stay with me!"

"Don't fall asleep," someone said in her ear—Mirah. "Stay awake." Something soft and wet pressed to her nose, and she cried out in pain. It made the throbbing worse and stung. Mirah wiped at Ariadne's face, and she bit out a sob. "I know. I'm sorry."

"Ari, stand up," Guinevere ordered, standing over her. "Come on. Stand up."

But she couldn't, not on her own. Why couldn't she fall asleep? That's all she wanted to do—just lie back and sleep.

Someone took hold of her and hoisted her to her feet. Anwil. Ariadne swayed again, and Anwil caught her, blood smearing on his cloak.

"I've got you," he said, holding her up. "Lean on me, but you have to walk."

She groaned. "Why?"

"Don't let them see you weak," he said in her ear.

She pushed herself to walk, Anwil giving her support. Although she moved her feet, it was mostly Anwil that half carried her to the infirmary tent where Lady Vivienne was waiting.

Lady Vivienne ordered everyone out, while she and Mirah stripped Ariadne of her armor and gambeson. Guinevere held on to Ariadne, dabbing at her face and wiping away the sticky blood. Ariadne grumbled an "Ow" every time her mother got too close to her nose. The pain had set in and tears streamed down her face. Her head and sides hurt. She had taken beatings before, during her lessons, but nothing compared to this.

Once her armor was off, Lady Vivienne stepped directly in front of her, bracing her hands on Ariadne's shoulders. "I'm going to set your nose," she explained. "Are you ready?"

Ariadne took her mother's hand and nodded. Lady Vivienne pressed a finger to Ariadne's nose, and Ariadne screamed as white-hot pain shot through her nose. It lasted only a second but left her breathless.

"Breathe," Lady Vivienne instructed as Mirah came over with a fresh washcloth. "Through your nose."

It took Ariadne a second to muster the strength, expecting it to hurt, but the pain never came. She breathed normally, although winced at the pain still in her side.

Lady Vivienne smiled. "Good, now let's fix the wrist and ribs."

Ariadne nearly passed out when Lady Vivienne healed her wrist, but once her bones were no longer broken, she was given a reprieve. She laid her head on her mother's shoulder and just breathed, closing her eyes. Guinevere held her tight, stroking her hair. The Black Knight had been strong, too strong for an ordinary human even though Merlin had taken the magic that he used in the tournament. It was pure luck that she beat him at all. Something sold pressed itself onto Ariadne's side and she jumped. Mirah mumbled an apology and rubbed a salve onto the bruise that was already forming.

"Drink this." Lady Vivienne held up a small vial of brown liquid in front of Ariadne's face. "It'll help."

Ariadne did as instructed and gagged. "Oh, it's awful." She coughed.

"Yes, the taste is terrible, but you should start feeling the effects right about . . . now." Lady Vivienne gave her a small smile.

Ariadne blinked up at her. And then shivered. Not from cold, but a tingling sensation that rolled its way down her limbs. The fatigue and pain left her body. She took in a deep breath, and the fog in her brain cleared as well. "Wow," she mumbled. "I feel...fine?"

Guinevere sighed in relief.

"Good. Now, do not overindulge tonight," said Lady Vivienne, giving Ariadne a stern stare. "That tonic will not last forever, and you need to let your body heal on its own. You'll feel sore tomorrow, so I'll leave something to help with that."

Ariadne nodded and pushed herself off her mother. She stretched, her back cracking, and rolled her wrist, eyes wide. "I don't feel any pain."

Lady Vivienne smiled. "You fought well. You are very brave, Ariadne Pendragon."

Ariadne blushed under Lady Vivienne's intense gaze. Now that she could think properly, it sunk into her that the Lady of the Lake had healed her herself. The Lady's shining black hair was tied back in a single braid and she had an apron on over her glittering dress. Ariadne had never met her before, had only known her through the tales and legends sung by bards, or by the rare occasion that Merlin spoke of her. The Lady of the Lake was said to be a child of the gods, magic incarnate, and yet here she was, the hem of her dress dirty and blood smeared on her apron like any normal healer. Ariadne almost felt a bit embarrassed.

Guinevere stood and kissed Ariadne's forehead. "Go wash up and meet us in the hall. Take your time, darling."

Ariadne hugged her mother and thanked the Lady of the Lake before leaving with Mirah. She stepped out of the tent in her sweaty bloody tunic and trousers, only to find a small crowd waiting for her. Lohengrin, Lyrion, and a few other nobles and commoners all turned to her. At the forefront were Anwil, Yvanne, Brionna, and King Constantine. Anwil launched for her, throwing his arms around her. Ariadne stiffened, expecting pain, but none came. Lady Vivienne's magic at work.

"Ari," Anwil whispered, hugging her tighter.

"Ow, Anwil, you're squeezing," she rasped, and he jumped back, eyes wide. "I'm fine. I'm fine. Lady Vivienne healed me."

Anwil looked over her face and clothes. "Ari, I am so sorry. I—"

Ariadne shook her head. "I'm fine. I would really like a bath right now, though." She also wanted to get away from the crowd as soon as possible. She could see a few of them itching to talk to her.

Anwil nodded and hugged her again. He sniffed, and Ariadne tightened her hold. She did this for him and would do it again in a heartbeat. He never would have survived the fight. Anwil could defend himself if need be, but he was not a fighter and would not have lasted in a fight against the Black Knight. And if the Black Knight had truly been out to kill him... "Go enjoy your wedding," she whispered, pulling away and shaking those dark thoughts from her mind. "I'll see you at the feast."

Anwil nodded and turned to Mirah. "*Is* she fine?"

"Yes," Mirah assured. "She'll be fine. I'll keep an eye on her."

Anwil stepped back for Brionna to join Mirah and Ariadne. As they made their way through the crowd, onlookers offered her congratulations and a few words of encouragement. She smiled and thanked them, but didn't stop to talk. She quickened her pace, but a familiar voice called her name.

"Oy." Lohengrin broke through the crowd and took her by the arm. "Don't do that again, though, yeah? I swear I felt my heart stop."

Ariadne snorted and gave him a playful push. Lohengrin had adopted a protective older brother mentality with her years ago. She didn't reply though as Lyrion caught her eye. He, too, was dirty from the tournament. He took her hand and entwined their fingers. Ariadne's heart fluttered at the contact, but there was an odd expression on his face.

"Save me a dance," he said, his voice strained.

She wanted to ask him what was wrong, but his hand slipped from hers, and then he was making his way back to the infirmary tent.

"Come on," said Mirah, sliding her arm through Ariadne's. "Let's get you a bath."

CHAPTER TWELVE

GUINEVERE

G uinevere held up Ariadne's gambeson, wet with sweat and covered in the sand and dirt from the field. She remembered the countless of times when she helped clean Arthur's wounds and gathered his torn and bloody clothes to wash and repair. She would now do the same for their daughter. Arthur would have been proud of her, of both of their children. They handled the situation well. Much better than she had. Her anger had taken control of her, a rare instance, as she had learned long ago to keep her emotions in check.

"That man was shouting as the knights took him away." Lady Vivienne's voice cut through Guinevere's thoughts. The Lady was cleaning her hands in a water bowl. "That you killed his wife."

Guinevere froze. "I beg your pardon?"

Lady Vivienne raised a black eyebrow and dried her hands on a cloth. "To others, his shouts may have seemed nonsensical. But to me . . . Well, he said—and I quote—'You killed my wife with a curse so your bastards could live.' Guinevere, I can sense the magic in their blood. I thought it may have been from Arthur, left over from when Merlin helped Uther conceive him, but I've always thought it strange how powerful it is."

Guinevere's entire body went tight, and her breath hitched in her throat. It couldn't be. No one had known. No one save for Guinevere and *her*. And she hadn't been seen in so long she was presumed dead. Guinevere had never told a soul, not even a diary. She'd kept herself from even thinking of it. The guilt had eaten at her during her pregnancy, but once her children were born, it had been easier to ignore it. But magic in their blood? Neither Anwil or Ariadne had ever shown signs of magic.

The Lady stared her down, but Guinevere stood her ground.

"I do not know what he means," she lied.

She knew the Lady did not believe her, could see through her, but Guinevere was saved by Merlin ducking in.

"The Black Knight—or Hywel, as we have found—is in the dungeon," he said, leaning on his staff. "Percival and Gawaine are interrogating him now and—" Merlin stopped, catching the look between the two women. "What have I missed?"

"Nothing," said Guinevere, laying Ariadne's gambeson down. "Thank you, Merlin. And thank you, Lady Vivienne, for healing my daughter."

Guinevere hurried out of the tent before either of the two could say anything. They would surely discuss what Vivienne heard and interrogate her about it later, but Guinevere was not ready for that now. Dindrane and Blanchefleur were waiting for her just outside with guards and Lord Roland. The tournament field had cleared, only a few lingering about.

"The guests have moved to the hall, Your Grace," Roland said gently.

"Thank you." Guinevere ran a hand over her forehead. "I, er, will need to freshen up." She looked down at her dress, which bore stains from Ariadne's blood and sweat. She also needed to compose herself before confronting anyone else.

"Of course." Roland gave a curt bow. "I'll take care of the guests."

Guinevere took his hand in both of hers. "Thank you, Roland."

"Of course, Guin." Roland bent to kiss her hand and left for the castle.

Guinevere took in a deep, shaking breath and smoothed her hands on her skirt. Her mind was spinning. How could that man have known? She hadn't told anyone, not even Merlin, and yet this man knew. Or was he bluffing, trying to get a rise out of them and cause discourse? The people, and Christian leaders especially, were already angry enough they they had not yet managed to catch whoever was ransacking and burning abbeys. She was angry too, of course. it had never been this hard to catch a foe before. Perhaps this was a larger problem then they all realized.

"Are you all right?" Dindrane asked, handing her a handkerchief and snapping Guinevere out of her thoughts.

"I'm fine," said Guinevere, dabbing at her face. "I should make a quick trip to the dungeons before I wash up." She needed to know more about this man and what more he knew.

"Would you like company?" said Blanchefleur.

"No." Guinevere shook her head. "I need you in the great hall, please. I'm sure the people are already alight with gossip."

"I'll handle the rumors," said Dindrane. "You go on. Do what you need to do."

Guinevere nodded, and just as she turned, Merlin ducked out of the med tent. He looked at her as if he were seeing into her soul, and she knew he now knew. His storm-gray eyes were cold, and he frowned. He must have always known. Her stomach sank . She should have known she could never hide anything from him. He had said nothing, or perhaps she'd been too distracted by the joy of finally being with child to see it. They stared at each other long and hard, and she braced herself for the tongue-lashing he was sure to give her.

"The ramblings of a madman, it would seem," he said loudly and to no one in particular. But his eyes never left Guinevere.

"Poor fellow has gone out of his mind. Dabbling in magic when one should not can strain the mind and cause madness. He is safer in the dungeons, where he cannot hurt anyone else."

The crowd that had lingered nodded their heads and agreed. Guinevere raised her eyebrows at Merlin, but he just turned away from her and headed back to the castle.

"Merlin's right," said Dindrane as she led Blanchefleur away. "Mental. Completely mental."

Guinevere slowly made her way with the crowd back to the castle, grateful for Merlin's influence. A trail of guards followed her, but they kept to a distance, giving her some room to breathe. She had not visited the dungeons in years. Not since her sister had been locked up for impersonating her and trying to frame her for treason by sleeping with Lancelot. And that had been nearly twenty-five years ago, the last time she had seen her sister as well. Gwenyth had lived out the rest of her life at a convent under house arrest. Guinevere did not have the heart to order her sister's execution—a choice she came to regret when it sparked a rift between Arthur and his nephew (and heir at the time) Mordred, leading to Mordred's rebellion and Arthur's death. Mordred's rebellion had also sparked something in her: a desperation for a son, a true heir for Arthur. Guinevere had not thought about what she had done for a long while. She'd pushed it into the back of her mind so far that it almost wasn't real anymore. As if it had been just a bad dream. But now, this man, this disgrace who donned the black armor and threatened her and her children, had brought it back to the forefront.

The castle halls were empty, but Guinevere could hear the roar from the great hall as she wound her way through the corridors and down a small set of steps to the dungeon's entrance. Two armored guards stood on either side of the hidden door, tucked away under a stair case. Guinevere slowed her steps, gripping at her skirts. Her heart raced in her chest.

"Is everything all right, Your Grace?" The young guard on the left was looking at her with concern.

"Just a little rattled," she said. "Thank you." But Guinevere hesitated. She needed to see him. Needed to find out his game before he could make any more accusations, but could she?

"Open the door," she ordered, before she could second guess herself even more.

The smell hit her first. The long winding dark stairs were damp and humid, and the air stunk of human waste and rot. Guinevere held a handkerchief to her nose, but it helped little. The guards trailed behind her, and her foot splashed in a small puddle at the bottom of the steps. It had been a good idea to stop here first before she bathed. Sconces lit the hallway, though they brought little light. Her eyes strained to see, and she kept close to the center of the walkway as prisoners sneered and called out at her as she passed the cells. She ignored them all, keeping her gaze straight ahead where she could see two men holding torches at the end of the hall.

Gawaine and Percival were huddled around a cell at the far end of the corridor. They looked up as her footsteps echoed on the wet stone. Gawaine looked surprised to see her, but he said nothing as she approached. The Black Knight impersonator had been stripped of his armor and wore only a simple brown tunic and trousers. Leather slippers were on his feet, and he sat back against the wall, his head hanging between his knees. His hands and ankles were chained and his dark hair was wet and plastered to his face. Guinevere did not recognize him.

"What have you gotten from him?" She asked Percival and Gawaine.

The two men squirmed, sharing a look. "Well," said Gawaine. "He talked a lot, actually. Accused you of murder."

Before Guinevere could reply, the man shot to his feet, lunging at her. Guinevere screamed and jumped back, but the chains were bound to the wall, and his fingertips barely brushed the iron bars of his cell. His eyes were wild and he snarled at her like a wild animal. He truly was mad.

"You murdering bitch!" he screamed, spit flying from his mouth. "You killed my wife! You killed my wife and *our baby*!"

Gawaine banged on the bars. "Oy! Shut your mouth!"

The man answered by spitting at Gawaine. Percival handed Gawaine a cloth.

"His name is Hywell," said Percival. "He claims you had his pregnant wife killed."

"Who?" Guinevere tried to keep her voice as even as possible, but her entire body was shaking.

"Her name was Enith!" The woman's name came out as a sob, and the prisoner fell to his knees. "Enith! And you killed her so your demons could live!"

Guinevere stepped back, doing her best not to react, but the memory tore through her mind as if it had just happened yesterday.

"Where did you hear that from?" Guinevere asked, keeping her voice even. "Who told you?"

"You're a murderer," the man growled. "Your children shouldn't be here. They shouldn't have been born! They don't deserve life!"

That was enough for Guinevere to snap. "Enough!" she boomed. "How dare you come here with these false accusations! How dare you make a mockery of this kingdom! You enter a tournament under false papers, you attempt to kill your future king and his sister, and now you say I am a murderer? You have earned yourself charges of treason. You'll stay here until your trial."

And with that, Guinevere spun on her heel and stormed out of the dungeons. Gawaine and Percival were right behind her, but neither of them said anything until they were out of the dungeon and the guards had closed and locked the door. Guinevere dismissed them and motioned for Percival and Gawaine to follow her to Arthur's old study. The room wasn't used much anymore. It was small and stuffy, but it was private.

As soon as Percival locked the door behind them, Guinevere whirled on them.

"This shall never *ever* leave this room. Do you hear me?"

Gawaine and Percival were taken aback. "Guin, what is it?" Gawaine took her gently by the shoulders. She was shaking, Out of anger, frustration, or shame, she did not know.

"He wasn't lying," said Guinevere, unable to meet his eyes. "I . . . I went to Morgana."

Gawaine's hands slid off her arms. "What?" he whispered.

"We tried for years, Gawaine," said Guinevere, wringing her hands. "You know that. Not once, not even a false hope or a miscarriage. Nothing. So I was desperate. I went to Morgana. But she told me that *Arthur* was infertile." Guinevere stopped pacing and swallowed. "She told me that Igraine had cursed Uther, that his line would end with Arthur, and that because Arthur was born of magic...But we needed an heir. Arthur told me how his first wife . . . how she . . . but I couldn't. I couldn't sleep with someone else." Guinevere wiped at her tears. "So I went to Morgana. And . . . it was a life for a life. I didn't know she was with child."

"Guin," Gawaine said again, his face draining of all color.

"She was sick, Gawaine! Sick! Already dying! I thought—I thought I was being merciful, that at least she wouldn't suffer. I just wanted . . . I just wanted to do my duty, to have a child, an heir." The sobs that she'd tried too hard to keep at bay erupted, and Gawaine was instantly on his feet, catching her, and Guinevere cried into his shoulder.

CHAPTER THIRTEEN

ANWIL

The great hall was hot and crowded. Anwil's heart raced against his chest, but he did his best to put on a smile and mingle with the guests. What he really wanted to do was check on his sister and mother, and talk to Gawaine to find out who that false knight was and why he'd called his mother a murderer. The audacity of the crazed man was appalling. Sure, Guinevere had seen to executions in her time as queen—all rulers had—but that did not make her a murderer. His mother had never killed anyone. Some guests had asked about it, but Anwil shrugged the questions off.

"The man was mental," he told the ambassador to Byzantium. "He called us demons and bastards. He must be left over from Mordred's rebellion. We have them pop up from time

OF CROWNS AND LEGENDS

to time." It was true. Every few years, a small rebellion would try to pop up, or a lone religious zealot, but they were always handled immediately before they became a problem.

"Mordred's rebellion?" the ambassador asked, raising an eyebrow.

"My father's nephew," Anwil explained. "He rebelled against my father, wanting the throne for himself. He was no longer heir, as my mother had become pregnant with me and my sister."

"There were other disagreements," said King Constantine, who came up behind Yvanne. Yvanne had stuck close to Anwil's side, almost like an anchor. "Mordred was—well, to put it plainly, a right mean bastard. He held a lot of hate in his heart for Arthur."

"But why make such accusations against the queen?"

Anwil narrowed his eyes. The ambassador was prying, and he did not like it. He understood that Lord Leontius was just doing his job, but this was not a matter he needed to pry his nose into. His reply was cut off by Constantine snorting.

"All sons of kings are accused of being bastards," he said. "It's the easiest way to claim the throne for your own. Pay it no mind, my lord. As a politician yourself, I'm sure you're used to such rumors. Now come, I wish to show you the water fountain."

Anwil was grateful for Constantine pulling the ambassador away and breathed a sigh of relief.

"I don't like that man," Yvanne mumbled, watching her father lead the ambassador away. "I don't trust him."

"I don't either," said Anwil. "I need a drink."

"Oh, good. Me too."

A roar of laughter filled the hall as Anwil and Yvanne wove their way through guests. A court jester had taken to the center of the hall, which had been cleared for the dance floor, to perform an insult act. Why anyone thought it was funny to be berated in public, Anwil would never know, but at least the jester was drawing the crowd's attention for a while. They made it to the wall where servants were pouring drinks, and Anwil made sure to grab a large goblet of red wine for both him and Yvanne. The wine was cool, kept cold by Merlin's magic and Anwil had to be careful not to just chug the entire goblet.

"Don't look now." Lohengrin's voice in Anwil's ear made him jump. "But Lady Ilsa is here and has been staring daggers at you all night."

"Lady Isla?" Yvanne giggled behind her hand. "Isn't she the one who fancied you when we were younger?"

"And chased him into a river?" Lohengrin grinned, putting an arm around Anwil's shoulders. "Aye, that's her. Still hung up on him too. Threw a fit when Anwil announced his engagement to you."

Anwil's cheeks burned as Yvanne and Lohengrin giggled. He had almost forgotten how well the two got along. "All right, that's enough."

"Someone's a bit touchy." Lohengrin dropped his arm and drained his goblet.

"Has someone forgotten what just happened?" Anwil hissed.

"No," said Lohengrin, his face turning serious. "But I'm not *not* going to enjoy this evening. You should be enjoying it as well. It is your wedding feast after all."

"I think once the feast actually gets started, it'll be easier," said Yvanne. "I'm starved."

"We'll start once my mother returns," said Anwil, craning his neck and gazing along the crowd to see if she had arrived yet or not. They wouldn't be able to stall the guests for much longer. It had already been a very long day.

"What about your sister?" said Yvanne. "Surely we should wait for her as well?"

Anwil shook his head. "She'll be in that bath for a long time. She wont' mind if we start without her."

"I think Lyrion snuck up to see how she's doing," said Lohengrin, wigging his eyebrows. Anwil glared at him.

Yvanne squealed in excitement. Her face lit up with her smile. "Oh, will there be another royal wedding soon?"

"Lyrion should not be in her chambers. That is not proper," Anwil snapped before he could contain himself.

Lohengrin barked out a laugh. "Proper? Oh please, coming from the man who snuck—"

"No, no," said Anwil. "That's enough." He glanced at Yvanne, but she was still giggling.

"Oh, it's all right." She slid her arm through his. "We've been friends for years, remember? I know what you were like."

"A bore?"

"Lohengrin!" Yvanne playfully slapped his arm. "Mayhaps you should find *your* betrothed and go bother her."

"I should." Lohengrin grabbed another full goblet. "And maybe we'll sneak out early too." He sent a wink to them before hurrying off, leaving Anwil wondering why he had ever become friends with him. Yvanne slid her hand into his and gave it a squeeze. She pulled him away from the drinks, but they did not make it far.

"You did well today, Your Highness." King Elyion said in his gruff voice, blocking their path. He was an older king, with a fluffy gray beard and shoulder-length hair. A simple gold crown circled his forehead.

"Thank you, my lord," Anwil said, extending his hand. Elyion grasped his wrist, and they shook. "And thank you for speaking out earlier. I'll admit, I wasn't quite sure how to handle the situation."

"It was unique, that's for sure. And uncalled for," said Elyion, his eyes darkening. "But you'll get used to it. You handled it well."

"Thank you," Anwil said again.

King Elyion clasped him on the shoulder and smiled under his beard. "Do not fret over it anymore tonight. This is a celebration! Now, enough talk of treasonous bastards. How are you faring, Lady Yvanne—or rather, Your Highness?"

Yvanne grinned. "I've been having a wondrous time, despite the hiccup," she said. "I do hope Princess Ariadne will join us soon. She was so brave!"

"Aye," said Elyion, stroking his beard. "She took quite the beating. I must admit, I did not think she would hold her own. It is...uncommon for women to fight so."

"Hopefully not for long," Anwil said. "Dame Brionna has been a Knight of the Round Table for over a decade, and Ariadne is on her way. I'm sure more women will follow."

King Elyion hummed and stroked his beard again. "Yes, well, we shall see. But in any case, I am glad she won against that crazed lunatic." King Elyion bowed and bid them farewell as Guinevere's entered the hall. She had changed into a bright red and gold gown. Although she was smiling, Anwil could see the tension in her face.

The crowd parted for her as she made her way into the hall with Gawaine and Percival trailing behind her. Anwil wished he could have an ounce of that commanding presence.

"Welcome, good gentles," Guinevere called when the crowd hushed. "I apologize for being late, but as most of you know, the duties of ruling never stop. Now, I believe it is high time for the festivities to begin! And to start-a feast!"

147

The crowd cheered, and Guinevere motioned for them to sit before the servants rolled out tray after tray full of food and drink. Anwil and Yvanne along to the High Table, where they sat at the center with his mother off to the side. It was odd, sitting higher than her, but she smiled up at him and winked. Yvanne had already started digging into her food and blushed when she caught Anwil's eye.

"Sorry," she whispered. "I'm just so hungry!"

Anwil couldn't help his grin, and he, too, dug into his food. He had taken a few bites of the rabbit stew when Ariadne finally entered with Mirah. Mirah caught his eye first in her yellow silk dress and wide-legged red pants. She caught his eye, and he glanced away, focusing on his sister. His jaw dropped in shock.

"That is a bold choice in clothing, my darling," Guinevere said as Ariadne kissed her cheek before she and Mirah took their seats. Ariadne had put on a navy blue dress, with a neck-line that wrapped around her neck, but left her shoulders bare. The sleeves were tight around her arms, ending in a point over the back of her hands almost like gloves. Her hair was still wet, and she had casually twisted it into a single braid over her shoulder, topped off with a silver circlet that matched the embroidery in her dress. It wasn't just bold, it was borderline scandalous! And on his sister!

"I didn't have another red dress clean at the moment," Ariadne scooped food onto her plate. "And I haven't a chance to wear this one yet."

"Where did you get that?" Anwil said to her and Ariadne raised an eyebrow at his tone.

"In the market," she answered.

"Why-"

Yvanne put a hand over his. "You look bloody brilliant," she said to Ariadne. "We must hit the market soon. I need a dress like that for myself."

Anwil struggled to hold back his reply as Ariadne beamed at Yvanne and they chattered about shopping.

"How are you feeling?" Anwil interjected, once he had breathed.

"I'm all right." Ariadne ladled thick gravy over her beef. "Lady Vivienne repaired all my breaks, but I'm sore."

"Breaks? Plural? How many?" But Ariadne just shrugged.

"I'm also keeping a close eye on her for any ill effects," Mirah said as Ariadne handed her the ladle. "Healing tonics affect everyone differently."

"I'm fine, I promise." Ariadne stuffed a forkful of beef in her mouth, and Guinevere playfully swatted at her shoulder.

"It's my wedding, sister, can you at least pretend to have manners?" Anwil teased.

Ariadne held up her fork with a dripping piece of meat. "Don't think I won't throw this at you. Even at your wedding."

Anwil snorted. "You wouldn't dare."

Ariadne picked up a large chicken leg and pulled her arm back, but Gawaine appeared behind her and snatched it from her hand. Mirah and Yvanne exploded in a fit of giggles and even Guinevere hid a smile behind her goblet.

"Don't mind if I do," Gawaine said and bit into it.

Anwil shook his head and let his shoulders relax. He surveyed the room and took in the laughter, the lively music, and decorations. Yes, he could enjoy the night.

CHAPTER FOURTEEN

ARIADNE

T he hall was alive with joy, and Ariadne loved every second. She could barely hear herself think, but she reveled in the crowd's roar, as it made her forget the imposter knight and the pure hate in his eyes when he'd looked at her. If she thought about it too much, it might just shake her to her core. She'd thought she would have been ready for her first fight outside of training, but she had been horridly wrong. Her limbs ached, and her head throbbed, but the wine and healing tonics numbed the pain nicely. She would need to work more and train harder. But that was a thought for another day. Tonight, she would forget her responsibilities.

She was already two full goblets of wine in and feeling much happier when the desserts arrived. The faint buzz of her limbs and mind made her feel easy and relaxed. And she couldn't get enough food. Her stomach rumbled even though she'd had two full helpings of dinner. Ariadne eyed the tray of apple tarts.

"It's the tonics," Mirah said when Ariadne mentioned how hungry she was. "Your body healed so fast it needs to replace that energy." Mirah shoved a mug of water at her, but if Ariadne drank anymore, she would need to run to the privy.

"Lyrion hasn't taken his eyes off you, by the way" Mirah said, nodding toward him.

Ariadne followed her gaze and caught Lyrion's eye. Her cheeks burned, but that was most likely from the wine. He looked good with his hair slicked back, and the navy tunic brought out his eyes, even from across the hall. He had been at the High Table during dinner, but moved when the acrobats performed, wanting a better view.

Ariadne smirked at him. "Why do you think I wore this dress?" she said to Mirah, who laughed.

"You two have grown closer since I've been gone."

Ariadne tore her eyes away from Lyrion and turned to her friend. Her hair was pushed away from her face by a twisted gold band that matched the necklaces around her neck. Her cheeks were also slightly flushed, but her brown eyes were soft as they always were. Ariadne pondered Mirah's words. She and Lyrion had grown closer. Ariadne found herself with him more than anyone else while Mirah had been away. Although their meetings were brief and often followed by guards or knights, their relationship had gotten a bit more serious. Perhaps they should declare themselves officially courting soon. Even if Ariadne did not want to rush a wedding for herself. If she was courting Lyrion, it would help to keep other proposals away. At least for a time.

"A bit," Ariadne said and took Mirah's hand. "I've missed you, though." She wasn't quite comfortable talking about her and Lyrion's relationship just yet, though.

Mirah laughed and gave her hand a squeeze. "I've missed you too. Mayhaps you should slow down on the wine."

"But it's so good! And I feel amazing."

"That's the adrenaline, most likely. Mixed with the healing tonic. I wish I was half as powerful as Lady Vivienne. Her magic healed you instantly!"

"You only just started learning under Merlin," said Ariadne. "You'll get there. You're already the best healer and tea maker in the city. Your mother would be proud."

Mirah's eyes glistened with tears. "Thank you," she whispered.

Ariadne gave her a playful nudge with her elbow. It had only been a couple of years since Mirah's mother, Nazrine, had passed away. She, too, had been a talented healer, and when a remote village had been struck with the plague, she immediately went to help. Unfortunately, the plague had also taken Nazrine before Sir Jabir could reach her.

Mirah cleared her throat. "We should dance," she said, nodding to the now packed dance floor.

Ariadne grinned, downed her wine, and took Mirah's hand. They pushed themselves to the middle, where a dance had already started, and jumped in, not missing a beat. Ariadne twirled and stepped and jumped with Mirah and other dancers, including Anwil and Yvanne, laughing, sometimes tripping, and forgetting about the day's earlier events. She felt so full with energy she almost feared she would burst. She wanted to spin and yell and maybe run laps. She had never felt so free. Though she knew she was lucky to have the freedoms she did have. Guinevere had given her far more than most daughters, especially royal daughters, but that royalty came with a price. Privacy was out of the question. Everything she did had repercussions. She couldn't speak freely without offending someone or having her words twisted. She had duties she couldn't ignore. But tonight, she could and would. Even Brionna wasn't hovering as close to her as usual.

"I thought you were supposed to save one for me?" someone said in her ear.

Ariadne spun around and knocked into Lyrion's chest. His gaze was intense and his eyes dark, and it made Ariadne's stomach flip. She grinned and took his hands.

"The dancing isn't over yet," she said and dared to steal a quick kiss before spinning away from him and into the next step of the dance.

"Someone is feeling bold," Lyrion muttered, clapping with the other men. He held up his hand, and Ariadne met it with hers, and they stepped around in a circle. His skin was warm against hers.

"I've missed you," said Ariadne, looking up at him through her lashes, and Lyrion's eyes darkened even more. In some sober part of her mind, she felt silly, but the wine took away most of her cares. They finished the song, and as soon as the musicians started the next, Ariadne took Lyrion's hand and pulled him out of the hall.

She pushed open the doors and was met with a rush of cool air. She hadn't realized how hot it had been in the hall. She took in a deep breath pf the cool night air and took Lyrion into the shadows.

"Ari, where are we—"

Ariadne pushed Lyrion against the wall in a small alcove, hidden behind a tapestry of the kingdoms of Briton, and pressed a kiss to his lips. His hands slid to her waist, and he turned them around, lifting her against the wall. She wrapped her legs around his waist, her skirt hiking to his thighs, and he moved to her neck, paying special attention to a spot just above her collarbone. She moaned, her skin tingling against his lips.

"Did you wear this dress for me?" he whispered against her throat, and Ariadne shivered. She let her head drop, giving him more access, and he moved down, fingers playing with the strap at her neck until footsteps echoed, halting their actions. They both held still, barely breathing.

". . . a madman," said a deep voice as the footsteps grew louder. "I've never seen such disrespect."

"There is always truth in the madness," came a reply. Ariadne did not recognize that voice either. "Perhaps the queen did have his wife executed?"

Anger boiled in her veins. How dare they even suggest such a thing! Lyrion gave her a warning look and shook his head.

"The only woman to be called for execution was her own sister, and that order was never carried out. You can't say you believe him?"

"I didn't say that. I said I wish to look into it. Many still do not believe the prince and princess are Arthur's, and if this man knows anything of it, I'd like to find out more."

Lyrion put a finger to his lips and she gripped the fabric at his shoulders, shaking.

"But they look—"

"Just like Arthur. I know, I know. I've heard it for years . . ."

The voices faded away, and Ariadne slid down Lyrion, glaring at the dark space over his shoulder. Ariadne hadn't heard exactly what the imposter knight had screamed when the fight was over. She hadn't been able to concentrate on anything except the pain in her head and wrist. Mirah had explained a little about the accusations while Ariadne bathed, but she hadn't thought to dwell on it. The rumors that she and her brother were bastards popped up every now and again, but most didn't pay them much mind. Or so she thought.

"Ari?"

"I need some air."

Ariadne didn't give him time to reply before she flung the tapestry aside and hurried down the corridor. Her heart pounded against her chest, and as soon as she made it to the courtyard stairs, she plopped down on the top stair and let her feet dangle over the steps as she let herself fall to her back. She wasn't sure why this was bothering her so much. She'd never put much stock in the rumors before. Her entire life, she was told so often how much she looked and acted like Arthur that the rumors of her not being his daughter had never had much effect on her. But what if they reinforced that she was like her father because she wasn't? No, she couldn't believe her mother would do such a thing. Guinevere had loved Arthur, and the affair with Lancelot was nothing more than a rumor. It had been her sister who courted Lancelot, not Guinevere. Her mother had never lied to them, so Ariadne had no reason to believe otherwise.

So why then did those two men talking upset her? Perhaps because if enough people believed those rumors . . .

"Are you all right?" Lyrion's face appeared over hers.

"I don't know," she mumbled. "Sorry."

Lyrion sat next to her and rested his arms on his knees. "Don't apologize. I'm sorry you had to hear that. Ridiculous. I don't know how you deal with it."

"I try to ignore it," she said, now looking up at the gray tiles of the stone archway's ceiling. "Some days it's harder than others, though."

Lyrion was quiet for a long while and she was grateful for it. Her head spun and there were too many thoughts swirling around her mind. She squeezed her eyes shut and rubbed her hands over her face.

"You shouldn't have fought that knight," Lyrion mumbled and Ariadne's eyes shot open. "Once of us should have. It was embarrassing. He never should have been allowed to compete either."

Ariadne pushed herself up on her elbows and narrowed her eyes at him. "You heard the crowd. What were we supposed to do?"

"Let us-the knights, handle it."

Ariadne stared at Lyrion, trying to wrap her buzzed mind around his words. "It was handled."

Lyrion got to his feet and held a hand down to her. "Come on. We should get back."

Ariadne hesitated, but took his hand and followed him back to the hall.

CHAPTER FIFTEEN

ANWIL

Yvanne yawned for the third time in a row and rested her head on Anwil's shoulder. It was late, and some guests had already headed back to their rooms. The musicians had stopped playing, and others now huddled in smaller circles or had fallen asleep in their chairs. The fire in the hearth had died down to an ember glow, and Merlin's floating candles were slowly going out one by one. Anwil had retired to a seat at the High Table long before, just needing to sit. Yvanne had danced most of the evening and had even pulled him into the revelry as well. He was not an excellent dancer, but no one had noticed, as many were too drunk to get the steps right anyway. He had taken off his cloak and flower crown hours ago, but with the heat from all the lights and bodies, it barely made a difference.

He couldn't wait to go back to his comfortable linen tunics. One day in the heavy embroidered fabrics was enough for him. Even in the winter months, they were more uncomfortable than warm.

Lohengrin, who sat Guinevere's empty seat, smirked. "Looks like your bride is ready for bed."

"Don't start," Anwil warned, but it only made Lohengrin laugh. To Anwil's surprise, Lohengrin had joined him not long after he sat down. It seemed Lohengrin, who was usually the first one to let loose at a party, was barely feeling any effects of drinking, even though it had been he who suggested Anwil have fun. But Lohengrin was not one to shirk his duties. Anwil could see the crease in his eyes all night, scanning the room. The imposter knight had made him more uneasy than he was letting on. Lohengrin took his duties as Knight of the Round Table as seriously as Anwil took his own. When it came to work, there was no goofing or slacking off.

"I'm surprised you're still here." Lohengrin sipped at the water in his mug. "You get the entire king's chambers all to yourself now. I'd have been up there hours ago, a trail of clothing—"

"Stop." Anwil shook his head, but Lohengrin laughed again.

"Take your wife to bed, you ninny," he said.

Anwil sighed and gently nudged Yvanne. "Would you like to retire?"

"Mmm, yes, please." She yawned again. "I'm so tired."

"Come on." Anwil helped her to her feet and let her lean on him. He ignored the wink from Lohengrin and silently prayed he could sneak them out with no one noticing. But, of course, his prayers went unanswered as Sir Ulrich raised his mug and cheered. Some of the other guests followed, and Anwil's cheeks burned. Yvanne buried her face in his shoulder, and he picked up his pace, giving a quick wave to his mother before hurrying out of the hall.

The guards closed the doors behind them, and Anwil was hit with the silence. He closed his eyes and let out a breath. Moonlight streamed through the windows and a cool breeze swirled around them.

"Are you all—all—" Yvanne yawned. "My goodness. I can't stop!"

"Do you, er, do you need your ladies . . . or?" Anwil stumbled, realizing he should have asked earlier. He, too, had wanted to leave—even hours earlier—but Yvanne was having so much fun, and he hadn't wanted to pull her away from the festivities.

"No," she said, taking the flower crown off. Strands of her hair got caught in it, and she tugged them out. "I just want to go to bed as quickly as possible."

"Me too," said Anwil.

Yvanne slid her hand into his. "Lead the way, please?"

Anwil swallowed and took her through the dark corridors. He was vaguely aware of the guards following behind, but he ignored them, careful to make sure Yvanne didn't trip on her

161

gown. The wall torches had already been snuffed out, and the only light among the corridors was the moonlight streaming in from the top windows. They were silent on their trek, and Anwil was grateful for it. His head couldn't take any more noise for the night. He'd love to hide away for a week and not speak to anyone.

Anwil paused at the door to his old rooms, nearly forgetting they were not his anymore. It was an odd feeling, almost uncomfortable, and somehow, it didn't feel right.

"What is it?" Yvanne asked as the guards took their places along the hall.

Anwil shook his head. "Nothing." He led her to the door across the hall and pushed it open. The first thing he noticed was the smell was different. The king's chambers had always smelled of his mother—of flowers and fresh linen. But now, there was no smell, save for the smoke from the fire already burning in the hearth.

Anwil took a breath and stepped inside. He didn't recognize the chambers. A large four-poster bed sat against the wall in the very center of the room, with thick red velvet curtains tied back. Silk pillows of gold rested at the head, and red blankets with fluffy white furs were neatly laid over it. Two wardrobes sat on either side of the larger window, open and full of their clothes. His own writing desk sat under the other window, the quills and parchment he had used the day before resting on the desk. The armchairs from his room were positioned in front of the hearth, along with a small sofa and end tables. Carpeted furs covered the stone floors near the bed and hearth. The washroom door was open, and a very faint scent of lavender wafted through it. A privacy divider was folded in the corner. It looked nothing like it had before. Nothing of his mother's touch was left. It was odd, but a good thing. He'd not be able to stay in the chambers if it still reminded him of his mother.

"It's lovely in here." Yvanne crossed to the bed and brushed her hand along the furs. "Much bigger than my room at home—well, my old home now."

"Er, I'll get the privacy wall up," Anwil mumbled, but as he passed Yvanne by, she grabbed his arm.

"Can you help me with my dress, please?" She turned around and pulled her hair over her shoulder. Her dress was fastened with gold lacing and a clasp at the neck. Anwil undid the strings with shaking fingers, and she shrugged her shoulders, letting the fabric fall to a pool on the floor around her feet, leaving her only in her white shift. Anwil swallowed.

"Oh, that's so much better. It was so heavy." Yvanne turned around, a small smile on her lips. He kept his eyes fixed on her face. "I'm nervous too," she whispered, putting a hand over his heart. He was sure she could feel it pounding. It echoed in his ears.

She leaned into him, nudging his nose with her own, and his breath hitched in his throat. He could smell the wine on her breath, and the scent of the flowers she'd worn in her hair all day lingered. His eyes fluttered closed on their own account.

"You, er—" Anwil swallowed again. She was so close. "You said you were tired . . ."

Yvanne let out a breathy laugh. "I am, but . . . we are married now."

"Yes," Anwil breathed, and he closed the gap between them.

Yvanne gasped but wrapped her arms around his neck. Her lips were so soft, and he could taste the berry stain she had used to color them and the wine she had. His hands slid to her waist. The linen of her shift was so thin he felt the heat of her skin. His heart pounded harder in his chest, and she tilted her head, giving him better access to her lips. She pulled him closer and moaned as her hands slid from his neck down to his chest and to the belt at his waist. She undid it quickly, and it fell to the floor with a thud.

Anwil gripped at her hips, and she moaned again, arching into him. She pulled her lips from his to grab his tunics and yank them over his head. She let out a soft growl when the thick undertunic got caught, but she gave it a pull and tossed it across the room. That little growl did something to Anwil, and he tugged her to him, his hands rubbing up and down her back, gathering the fabric of her shift in his fists. He kissed her neck, and she gasped and moaned, and Anwil backed her toward the bed, where they both tumbled onto the soft furs.

CHAPTER SIXTEEN

NIMUE

The King's Road was quiet, but Nimue kept to the tree line anyway. Her black cloak blended into the shadows, and she had gotten rid of her horse at the last village. It was a beautiful creature but too noisy for what she needed to do. She may go back for it eventually. She had always had a soft spot for animals, but even with most of the country distracted by the wedding, she couldn't take any chances. Thieves would watch the roads for nobles, and she did not have the energy or time to deal with them. She needed to get to Glastonbury while it was less guarded. The Lady of the Lake and Merlin would be plenty distracted by all the commotion and magic in Camelot that if she worked quickly and with little magic, she could get what she needed undetected.

Nimue's ear twitched as a faint sound behind her caught her attention. She dipped into the trees as the sounds grew closer. The swish and clanking of armor echoed, along with the heavy footsteps of near a dozen horses. She crept behind a bundle of small trees where she could monitor the road without being seen.

The grumbling of horse hooves on the cobbled stone and dirt road grew louder as they approached. As they came into view, her stomach tightened. The metal of their armor gleamed in the moonlight, and the red tabards were hard to miss, even in the night. Camelot guards. An entire patrol. Nimue recognized the man leading them as Sir Jabir, a gifted mage for a human. He might recognize her. Or at least recognize that she was not human. She barely dared to breathe in case he sensed her magic. It was harder to hide from other magic users, even if they were human.

"It's unusually quiet on the roads," one man said. "I thought we'd encounter more thieves."

"Everyone worth stealing from is already inside the city," said Sir Jabir in his deep voice. "Thieves will crawl these woods when they return home."

"You'd think they'd learn by now," said the man. He had the arrogance and naïvety of youth. Nimue had to keep herself from scoffing out loud. "They can't get away with it with us on patrol."

"Doesn't keep them from trying," said an older guard. "And don't underestimate them. Some are clever." She rolled her eyes.

"Why are we on patrol, then, if no one is out here?" By the goddess, he was whiny human. How did the others put up with him? She would have done away with him already.

"It is our duty, Master Anfri," said Sir Jabir. "Our mere presence is a deterrent. And we provide safety for those who could not attend the festivities, such as the monks who needed to stay behind at the Tor. We shall check on them next."

Shit. Nimue inwardly cursed. Of course they would be headed to the Tor as well. She would have to come up with a new plan.

"Surely they are sleeping?"

"You keep questioning orders like this and you won't be a guard much longer," said another man.

"I cannot speak my mind? What happened to Camelot taking everyone—"

"You're not speaking your mind. You're whining," said the other guard.

Before the young man could reply, Jabir held up a hand and halted his horse. The men stopped behind him. Jabir's eyes traveled along the tree line and settled right on her. She knew he saw her when his eyes narrowed.

"We have company," he said, his dark eyes not leaving hers.

She cursed and sucked in a deep breath, spinning into a spell. The wind gusted, and her hair whipped around her face. She disappeared from their view as she spun faster and faster and came to a stop across the road. Her legs wobbled a bit, but she kept herself steady. Her eyes burned with white light, and the horses closest to her panicked, their whinnies echoing in the night. Nimue threw out her arms with a yell, and the tree branches above her grew and struck a few of the guards. They cried out in pain as they fell from their horses. The rest pulled out their weapons as the guards on the ground rolled away from frantic hooves. Arrows shot at her, but she batted them away with her arm. She grunted in pain, but raised her arms again, the earth rumbling under her feet.

"Show yourself!" Jabir's voice boomed. "Who are you, and why do you harm us?"

She answered by slamming her hands into the dirt, gripping the grass. Vines from the ground shot out toward the men. They wrapped around the whining man, who screamed as he was lifted into the air, the vines twisting like a boa constrictor around its prey.

Sir Jabir jumped from his horse, his hands engulfed in glowing white flames. He raised his arms, his eyes flashing, but before he could hit her with anything, she transported herself a couple of yards behind them. She dug her fingers into the gravel, and with the force of her energy, the road shook and the cobbles fell away, dropping into sinkholes. Horses screamed and ran away, their riders trying desperately to control them. Jabir shot a white light at the sinkholes, covering them in magic before anyone fell into them. More arrows came at her, and she transported herself again, but not as far as she had hoped. She stumbled into a tree, panting. Her energy was fading, but she was still too close to them, just inside the tree line. She pulled a vial from her bag and popped it open. After murmuring a spell over it, she threw it as hard as she could.

The glass exploded as it hit the stones, and thick, green smoke enveloped the human guards. The men coughed and yelled. A white light burst from the smoke, but she did not stay to witness. Using the distraction to her advantage, she transported herself one more time, this time to the doors of Glastonbury. With the last remaining energy she had, she glamoured herself into an old woman before slipping into unconsciousness.

"Mistress?" came a soft voice. "Mistress?"

Her head pounded, and her eyelids were heavy. Her bones ached from the glamour, and she blinked her eyes open. The sunlight was bright through the small window, but a face hovered over her. A short bald man in brown robes smiled down at her.

"Good morrow, mistress," he said. "You are at Glastonbury Abbey, and it is a few hours after sunrise. We found you in rather poor shape last night, passed out at the door."

She tried to sit up, but her joints cracked.

"Ah, ah," said the monk. "Rest all you need. I am Father Micel. I brought you some hot broth and bread. You are welcome here as long as you need, mistress."

She put a smile on as he stood from the stool he had been sitting on next to her cot.

"If you need anything, please do not hesitate to ask. We have healers and plenty of food."

"Thank you," she said in a gravelly voice that was not her own. The glamour. "You are kind."

"As our Lord God says in Ephesians, 'Be kind and compassionate to one another, forgiving each other, just as in Christ God forgave you.'" The man bowed his head and left her room, closing the door softly behind him. The smile instantly fell from her face and she grumbled about hypocrites.

Nimue pushed herself off the cot and crossed the small room to the window, where she had a fantastic view of the Tor. She smiled again.

CHAPTER SEVENTEEN

GUINEVERE

G uinevere hadn't had afternoon tea with the ladies of court in years. Ever since she was appointed regent, she'd barely had time for it. Now she was surrounded not only by the normal courtiers, but the kings' wives and guests from the wedding. Lady Eudocia, the Byzantium ambassador's wife even joined them. She had kept to herself since arriving, even though the ambassador and Guinevere had met several times. They were to stay in Camelot for a while as they set up negotiations between the two countries. Though, judging by Eudocia's face, she was not too happy about it. Guinevere, Blanchefleur, and Lady Lynette had all tried engaging her in conversation, but they were met with short clipped replies. Even her translator looked apologetic. Guinevere was already brushing up on her Greek in hopes that it would help the woman feel more comfortable in time. Perhaps it would be best if she and her two sons left for their home while Lord Leontius stayed in Camelot. With Merlin's mirror, Leontius could see his wife every night if he so wished, and Eudocia would be more comfortable at home. Guinevere made a mental note to bring that up at the next council meeting.

The talk of tea, of course, had settled on the excitement at yesterday's tournament. Guinevere had tried to steer the conversation to Anwil and Yvanne, as it was their wedding, but the ladies kept going back to the imposter knight, as they had dubbed him. Guinevere listened as they prattled on and guessed how he'd managed to get into the tournament. She would've liked to know that herself. Camelot guards were the best in the country. It was embarrassing that this man had slipped past them so easily. She would need to have word with Percival soon. Gawaine and Percival had returned to the dungeons earlier that morning to interrogate this man further. Hopefully, they'd been able to get useful information out of him.

Guinevere had ordered an extra patrol of guards to roam the city and keep an eye out for anything unusual or suspicious. Dindrane had also spoken to her network of spies to find any information they could. Guinevere needed to know how he knew. She had been so careful when—no, she still couldn't even think about it. The guilt was too much. And if Morgana was still alive, it would be bad for them all. Would she want revenge? Blackmail? But this didn't seem her style. Morgana would have shown herself. She wouldn't have had others make her threats for her. She had no need. But then, how did the knight know? Guinevere had thought she and Morgana had been friends. They were family. Despite the rumors, Arthur and Morgana had a close relationship. Morgana had never done anything to hurt Arthur, but maybe Camlann had been the turning point. Arthur had killed Morgana's son. His own nephew. If Arthur had survived, he most likely wouldn't have been able to live with himself. Arthur had cared for Mordred, deeply, and when Mordred betrayed him...

"Your Grace?"

Lady Ilsa peered at her over her teacup. Guinevere blinked and realized that Lady Ilsa was not the only one looking at her.

"Yes, my dear?" Guinevere put a smile on her face, one she'd practiced well. Guinevere had hoped Ilsa would have left early this morning. She had never liked the young girl or her ambitions to marry Anwil. Ilsa reminded Guinevere too much of her sister, Gwenyth—too deceptive, too clever. Ilsa hoarded information to use against others, just as Gwenyth had. Perhaps Ilsa helped the imposter knight?

"I asked what you planned to do with that awful cheat from yesterday." She tilted her head so her dark brown hair fell over her shoulder.

"He is in the dungeons," said Guinevere, setting her cup down. "And that is where he will stay until his trial."

"Trial?" said Lady Lynette, Sir Gaheris's wife. "Is one even needed after what he did to our Ari?"

"Camelot law states that everyone has the right to a fair trial," said Guinevere. "No matter how any of us personally feel."

"Well, *I* personally feel that Ariadne fought admirably yesterday," said Lady Ellyn, Lord Roland's daughter and one of Ariadne's close friends. "She must be so excited to have competed in her first proper fight."

Lady Tessa, Ellyn's mother, shot her daughter a look, and Ellyn blushed.

"She did indeed," Guinevere agreed, a smile tugging at her lips. "No matter how hard I tried to steer her away from the sword, she is a natural fighter. Just like her father. I am very proud of her. Of both my children."

"Speaking of children," piped up Lady Laudine. She sat next to Lady Ilsa, who did not seem too happy with the arrangement. "It's nearly evening, and I hear that our two newlyweds have not left their chambers all day."

Guinevere sputtered and coughed into her tea as giggles and murmurs echoed around. While, of course, she was privy to their whereabouts, she was certainly not going to dwell on *that* sort of speculation about her own son. Although, the look on Ilsa's face was rather amusing. Guinevere mentally scolded herself for that thought. She was too old to think like that.

"Neither has Ariadne," said Guinevere, wiping her hands on a soft cloth. "Both deserve a day of rest, shouldn't you agree?"

"I give it less than a year," Lady Laudine loudly whispered to Lady Ilsa, and Guinevere wondered if Laudine knew Ilsa's feelings on the matter. She most likely did. The woman knew more about what was happening in the castle that Guinevere did sometimes. "For our new princess to fall with child."

A sinking feeling erupted in Guinevere's stomach. She hoped as well. Perhaps too much. She wanted nothing more than for Anwil and Yvanne to not have to struggle with producing heirs as she had.

"Have you discussed Ariadne's marriage?" asked Lady Lynette. "She's high past age now."

"She and I have discussed it, and we have agreed to hold off on any prospects for her. Her heart is set on becoming a Knight of the Round Table."

"That seems cruel," said Lynette, and Guinevere's eyebrows shot up. "Letting her become a knight, only to marry her off."

"Ariadne will not marry a foreign royal," said Guinevere. "That is not her wish. She and the young lord Lyrion have grown rather close as of late."

"Seems a waste." Lynette gave a shrug. "She would bring forth powerful alliances."

Guinevere took a breath to calm herself before responding. Lynette meant well, but it was always an argument with her. While she had a point, Guinevere would not break her promise to her daughter. But before Guinevere could answer, a young page boy dashed into the gardens, frantically calling for her.

Guinevere met him halfway, falling to her knees and catching the boy by the arms. "What is it, child?"

He stuttered, trying to catch his breath. He was no more than nine or ten. "The . . . guards. In the . . . infirmary. Lord Gawaine said . . . to get you!"

Guinevere didn't bother excusing herself from tea and took off straight for the infirmary. She ignored the calls of the ladies as two guards hurried to catch up with her. She ran nearly all the way to the infirmary, her heart racing. Gawaine and Percival hovered just outside the door and turned when they heard her footsteps. They were both pale.

"What happened?"

Gawaine shook his head. "An entire patrol was attacked near Glastonbury. Sir Jabir . . . Guin, it's bad."

They stepped aside for Guinevere to see, and she clutched a hand over her heart. The infirmary was filled with injured guards lying on cots, and the court physician, Master Cassius, hopped from one patient to the other alongside Mirah and Lady Vivienne. The few priestesses that had traveled with Vivienne were also there tending to wounds. Merlin was even there, but he caught Guinevere's eye and crossed the room, careful to not get in the way.

"It would seem," said the wizard in a grave voice, "whoever attacked the abbeys came face-to-face with this patrol. Their wounds are infected with a magic I have never seen before."

Guinevere turned sharply to Gawaine. "Glastonbury—the abbey!"

Neither Gawaine nor Percival said anything as they ran off, and Guinevere watched them go, tears threatening at her eyes. She had spent most of her childhood summers at Glastonbury, peacefully tending to the gardens there with the nuns and studying under the monks. It was more of a home to her than her old kingdom, Cameliard, had been.

"We need to act," said Guinevere. "Tighten security. No one in or out of the city. And Merlin . . ." Guinevere pulled the wizard from the earshot of the room. "Merlin, could *she* still be alive?"

Merlin furrowed his bushy eyebrows. "She?" Merlin gripped his staff with both hands. "Morgana?" He shook his head. "This is not Morgana's work."

"How do you know?" Guinevere whispered. "You said yourself that she was more powerful than you. Could she disguise herself? Her magic?"

Again, Merlin shook his head. "This is not Morgana. Of that, I am certain. But perhaps . . ."

"Perhaps what?" Guinevere questioned.

"I need my books," he said. "Excuse me." He brushed passed Guinevere, leaving her confused. She called out to him as he left, but he ignored her.

Word about the guards spread quickly, and Guinevere found herself at the Round Table surrounded by unhappy kings of Briton. The hall had already been stripped of wedding decorations and put back to normal. The Round Table sat in the very center, and the walls were lined with shields and banners of the kingdoms of Briton and Arthur's original Knights of the Round Table. A guard was posted at every entrance and column.

"Enough is enough!" Bors slammed his hand down on the table. "My men are ready to take down this attacker."

"We don't even know who it is!" Constantine shouted over him.

"We know they're magic and have broken the Fae Treaty!"

"Are they magic, or are they a human who can use—"

"It matters not!"

"How can we trust Camelot when that cheater wormed his way into the tournament under our very noses?" Bors sent a glare to Guinevere.

"I don't seem to recall you objecting," said King Caewlin. "In fact, you said you rather enjoyed it. What was it you said? 'Who cares? Let the man compete?'"

"My lords!" Guinevere snapped, having enough. "Please, see reason! Bickering is unbecoming of all of you."

Eyes shifted to her, and she gestured for the ones standing to sit. They did so reluctantly.

"Thank you," said Guinevere, sitting straighter in her chair. "Now, I understand your grievances. I am just as angry as you are. But we must work together." She paused when Cerdic scoffed, but when he didn't say anything, she continued. "Now, Lord Merlin and Lady Vivienne shall be leaving for Avalon soon to gather their own forces. If this person, or persons, is of the fae, then we alone cannot fight them."

"I do not want help from Avalon," Bors growled. "Fae are not to be trusted. Who's to say they won't just rally together and take us out?"

"Merlin and Lady Vivienne have always had Camelot's—"

"*Camelot's.*" Bors rolled his eyes. "No, they have the *Pendragons'* interests at heart. Not Camelot's, not Briton's."

"The Pendragons *are* Briton," Guinevere hissed before she could control herself. "Your grandfather and father both served under Uther and Arthur. You well know we have Briton's best interest at heart! Now sit down, my lord, before I have you escorted out!"

Bors glared at her a long while, and she held his gaze until he finally plopped down into his chair. She would not be bullied by the spoiled son of a great knight. His father and grandfather would be ashamed. She stared him down until he looked away.

"Now," said Guinevere. "Merlin and Vivienne are leaving as soon as they can for Avalon to gather forces and take care of this once and for all. Whoever is behind this will see their punishment."

"Then it is an act of war!" Bors shouted. Guinevere shot him another hard look. His face was turning purple and Guinevere was sure he would burst at any moment.

"We do not know enough yet!" Constantine snapped. "We cannot jump to conclusions when we don't know who it is we are fighting!"

"We know who we are fighting!" Bors once again stood from his chair and turned his glare to Guinevere. "My men are ready to put a stop to this. If we must do it alone, then so be it!"

"It is against the law to engage in war without the approval of the High Throne!" King Elyion stood from his chair as well, gripping the sides of the table with white knuckles. "You will commit treason if you do so, sir!"

"Then I am a traitor," Bors spat and stormed from the room. Silence fell as he slammed the doors behind him, rattling the shields on the wall.

Guinevere sighed and pressed her fingers to her forehead. This was not good. She did not blame the kings' anger. She was angry herself. Livid, in fact. Camelot's forces were supposed to be better than this. And yet, another attack and still no idea who or what is behind it all.

It was silent a long moment until Constantine said, "Wait until he finds out you ordered the city on lockdown."

CHAPTER EIGHTEEN

NIMUE

Nimue remained glamoured as an old woman to rest and recuperate. She barely had the energy to leave the room she was given, so she stayed there, sitting by the window to feel the air on her face. The monk that had woken her brought her more food and tried to ask her questions, but she refused to answer. She didn't feel like making up some story. They wouldn't be alive for long anyway.

These Christian abbeys were spreading lies and convincing humans to harm, capture, and even kill the fae, and Glastonbury was the worst of them all. The Tor had once been a sacred place where the two worlds merged. It had vibrated with magic, but the Christian zealots had ripped through and massacred the priestesses. She could still feel the raw power the Tor held. It aided in her healing. Her magic would be more powerful here. But she would have to wait to retrieve the item they had hidden away until she was fully recovered. Then she would turn the abbey to ash.

As she figured, she was fully rested and recovered by nightfall. Nimue waited until the monks were all fast asleep before she removed the glamour from herself, the magic sliding from her body as though she had emerged from water, and snuck out of her room. She kept to the shadows in the corridors, hands on the stone, feeling for signs of energy and vibrations. It was here somewhere, and with how important it was to the Christians, she was surprised there weren't armed guards around. The stories said that Sir Galahad, the knight who found the Grail, had taken it with him in death, but she knew it was brought here by Sir Percival after Galahad's death many years ago. She had watched him do it. She'd been with the other priestesses of Avalon that had escorted Percival, his sister, and another knight back to Briton after they lost Galahad on their quest. Nimue paused in the dark corridor, shaking the thoughts from her head. That life was in the past, so much so that it barely felt as if it had been her own once.

The swish of fabric and footsteps echoed down the hall, and she pressed herself into the wall, closing her eyes and asking the shadows to hide her. They blanketed her with their warmth, and she held still. The monk that had cared for her hurried down the hall, his dressing robe billowing out behind him as he cradled a bowl in his hands. She waited until his footsteps faded and thanked the shadows.

Nimue continued on her way down the halls, and her heart skipped a beat when she came upon a door. The familiar hum and scent of apples filled the air. She would recognize her sister's magic anywhere. The door was locked, but she pressed a finger to the lock and it clicked open. She pushed on the door and slipped inside, careful not to make any noise.

The room was empty save for some rushes and hay on the floor. There were light parts on the walls, showing that there had been something pressed against them for a long time. There wasn't even a window. That did not matter though; she could still see in the dark. She closed her eyes and breathed, focusing on the vibration of the magic and where it pulled her. Her fingertips tingled, and she felt a tug on her left hand. She crossed the room to the left wall and rubbed her palms against the stone.

When her hands passed along a cinder block that was more jagged than the others, she grinned. Pressing her fingertips into it, she let out a huff of air, and the cinder block and the immediate surrounding ones disintegrated. But it came with a price. She vomited on the floor, and her body convulsed. Her sister's barrier. It took Nimue a long moment to regain her composure. She slid herself to a sitting position against the wall and breathed slowly to settle the shaking in her body.

Sweat dripped down her forehead, and she wiped it away, then pushed herself to her feet.

There it was. Sitting in a hollowed-out portion of the wall was the thing the Christians of the island had been abuzz about for over two decades. A golden chalice they called the Holy Grail. They said it contained the blood of their god, and if that was true, it would be the ultimate power she needed.

With shaking fingers, Nimue reached for it. Her fingers hit something hard—an unseen force blocking her from touching it. She let out a low growl and pushed her hand through it, gritting her teeth through the sensation of dragging her skin across a thousand sharp splinters. Finally, with blood coating her hand, she gripped the chalice and yanked it out of the hole. She breathed a sigh of relief but stilled. She switched the chalice to her other hand. Nothing. There was no hum, no sensation, no scent of magic or divinity on it. Nothing.

White-hot anger bubbled in her blood, and she threw it across the room. It hit the wall with a loud clang, and white light burst from her. She screamed, and the room shook, stone dust falling from the ceiling. She fell to her knees and screamed until she couldn't anymore. Dust coated her, turning her black hair gray. Shouts and voices sounded, and she grabbed the stupid cup and stuffed it in her bag, then ran out of the room and right into a man's chest.

The man was tall, with black hair sprinkled with gray and a goatee. *Shit.* She should have been more careful in her rage.

She would recognize this man anywhere. Gawaine of Orkney, eldest son of her old friend, Anna-Morgause. Gawaine's face shifted from shock to fury.

"Nimue?" he growled, and she backed up a few steps, clenching her fists. "Has it been you all along? When we thought you dead? Have you come back to finish what you started then?"

Nimue didn't answer. She shoved her arms out, and Gawaine flew backward, hitting the wall with a loud thud and a grunt of pain as he tumbled to the ground. She ran down the opposite corridor before he could get back up but was cut off by two Camelot knights. She recognized one as Percival but did not know the younger one. She shot out her hand again, and they, too, were lifted into the air. They hit the ceiling and then the floor with loud clangs. Her vision went blurry, but she blinked it back into focus as footsteps sounded behind her, and this time, when she shot out her arm, flames flew from her fingers. The knights screamed as the flames engulfed them. She shot out more flames, burning the doors and anything wooden she could find in the stone abbey.

Nimue staggered through the smoke and flames, coughing and fighting to stay conscious. Her hand throbbed, and she stumbled around the fallen beams. The flames were spreading fast, and shouts sounded all around her. When her feet found the grass outside, she could clearly see the group of Camelot guards in the bright moonlight. One of them spotted her and pointed her out to the others. Her limbs shook, but she pushed herself to her feet and disappeared.

Nimue collapsed as soon as she appeared inside the foyer of the old Roman manor. She ached all over, and her head spun. She had spent all the energy she'd saved, and the Tor had barely granted her any extra. The magic was leaving the lands. If she didn't act soon, it would be too late.

"Nimue!" Whispers swirled around her, and a warm hand gently lifted her head. A female with dark brown skin and pointed ears much longer than her own hovered over her, her bright violet eyes wide with concern. "Nimue?"

Nimue groaned and let Melara help her sit up. Her pale green hair washed over Nimue's face, and the clean scent of moss and grass filled her nose.

"You're bleeding. Come."

Nimue tried to stand, but her body gave way. Melara called for help, and another fae appeared. He carried Nimue to a sofa in front of a roaring fire in a pit in the middle of the wide room. The furniture was mismatched, and the mosaic tiles on the floor were broken or faded with age.

"Fetch Thistle," Melara said, carefully taking the bag from Nimue.

The male fae nodded, and his gossamer wings fluttered out behind him as he hurried away.

"Melara!" Nimue rasped.

"I am here," said Melara, a tight smile on her red lips. She pressed a hand to Nimue's forehead and hissed. "You're burning up."

The words were barely out of her mouth when a small female leapt through the open stone doorway, her fuchsia curls bouncing on her head. Her green skin was paler than usual, and she dropped to her knees next to Nimue. She carried a large bag with vials bulging the leather from inside.

"My lady," she said, her voice like a soft breeze. "You mustn't keep doing this to yourself." She dumped her bag out on the floor, the vials clattering on the tiles. The male fae that had fetched her brought in a large water basin and clean cloths. His dark gray lips frowned as he set it down. Nimue tried to smile at him, tell him she would be all right, but she couldn't muster the energy. She hissed as Thistle dumped a vial over her hand, the clear liquid stinging.

"Sleep, my lady," Thistle ordered, and Nimue gladly obliged.

When Nimue awoke, she was in her bed in her private room at the manor, and judging by the sunlight streaming through her window, it was late afternoon. Talk and laughter from outside wafted in, and Nimue closed her eyes again, savoring the small moment of peace. A soft knock sounded at her door, and she opened her eyes again, annoyed at the interruption. The door opened, and the male fae from the day before entered, carrying a tray with a pitcher and a teacup. His skin was silvery gray, his hair and lips almost black. His clothing looked to be spun of cobwebs.

"Thank you." Nimue pushed herself to a sitting position as he set the tray on the bedside table that had been woven from vines.

He smiled and gave a brief bow, then made movements with his hands.

"Yes," Nimue answered. Recently, a group of humans had cut out his tongue, claiming he had placed curses upon their families. "I am much better. Thank you."

Were you successful in your task? he signed.

"That depends," said Nimue, swinging her feet around the bed. She was in a chemise and had been cleaned of dust. "Can you find Melara?"

He bowed and left her alone. She poured herself some tea. It wasn't long before Melara appeared and helped her dress. Nimue's limbs were stiff, and her head pounded, but she could at least walk around. She needed to check on the others.

"I put your bag with the others," Melara said as they made their way through the manor. Half the roof was destroyed, and remnants of statues and painted murals remained on the cracked walls. It had been easy to hide away; no one had lived there for nearly two centuries, and it had been forgotten to any living human memory. It didn't take much magic to conceal it from the outside world. "The chalice . . . It was . . ."

"Fake," Nimue growled, hugging her shawl closer around her shoulders. Despite the warmth, she was cold. She would be until she regained her full strength, if that were to ever happen again. Ever since she had returned from the In-Between—the place between life and death—her magic hadn't been the same. She rarely tired before. Being full-blooded fae, magic came naturally to her. She didn't tire like magic-touched humans or half-fae. But something had happened to her in the In-Between, and now, every spell drained her more and more.

"I do not think there is a Holy Grail," Nimue said. "And it certainly wouldn't be a golden chalice. Their god was a humble carpenter, as they say in their teachings. Why would he have had a gold chalice made for kings?"

"What will we do?"

They stepped outside where the air was warmer with a gentle breeze. It was always the perfect weather under the bubble of protection Nimue had created. Occasionally, she let the rainfall in to water the plants and vegetation, but they needed the sun.

All around were fae of all shapes and sizes, eating, laughing, playing, and relaxing. Many, though, sported wounds and disabilities. All of them had been beaten or nearly killed by humans. She took them all in, just as she had for centuries in Avalon with her sister, Vivienne. She was sure Vivienne still tended to wounded fae, but many came to her when she returned, and more arrived every day.

"If the idiot humans believe that cup is the Grail, it should still have some power." Nimue watched a small sprite buzz around a flower patch. "We shall wait a few days. If word spreads that their Holy Grain has been stolen, then it will do. Their belief should sustain the power we need. Especially as we have the other treasures as well."

"If you say so," Melara said.

Nimue raised an eyebrow at her old friend. Melara had been a priestess with her in Avalon but had joined in her rebellion against Vivienne when the Lady of Avalon had grown weak against the humans. She had also joined Nimue in banishment.

"Do you doubt me?" Nimue asked.

Melara sighed and clasped her hands in front of her. "I fear the repercussions," she said. "It is a dark and forbidden spell."

"We have to try. I am not strong enough alone. We need him on the human throne."

Melara gave her a disappointed look but did not reply. She crossed the stone footpath and into the garden. Melara had always been her voice of reason, but Nimue would not budge on this. There was too much at stake, and she would not fail again. A small brownie ran up to her, jabbering away in its own language. It wore a mushroom cap like a hat and mismatched stockings. One of its eyes was missing but had healed over. It tugged on her gown, and she knelt down. It placed a button in her hand and ran away. She watched it scurry into the vegetable patch, chattering away to itself, and put the button in her pocket.

"My lady?" Nimue looked up to see a sprite hovering over her head. Her wings buzzed, and her golden face was full of worry. "There are humans approaching."

Nimue and Melara waited just behind the moon gate. From the outside, no one could see them, but they could see everything that passed by. A company of human men approached on horseback. Nimue knew their leader well. And hated him.

Cerdic of Wessex slid off his horse and approached the moon gate. He bowed, and she waved her hand, letting him inside the barrier. After securing the barrier so his men couldn't get through, she led him back to the manor and into the drawing room, where he helped himself to some wine.

"Well?" Nimue asked as he handed her a cup of wine.

He huffed. "No *Hello, how are you?* or *Good to see you?*"

Nimue glared at him. "I don't have time for pleasantries, and I don't think you do either."

Cerdic let out a breathy laugh and took a long drink of wine. "You sure did a number on that patrol, didn't you?"

"If you are not here with information—"

"Camelot's gearing for war," he said, plopping down on one of the moss-covered sofas. "Bors of Gwent has men ready, and he's not too happy with Guinevere at the moment. You should speak with him."

"Bors is a bullheaded Christian. I cannot ally myself with my enemy."

"Isn't the enemy of your enemy a friend?"

Nimue rolled her eyes. "Is that all you have?"

"No," said Cerdic. "Avalon is lending aid."

Nimue sank down into the chair across from him. "She hasn't aided humans in a long time," she said. "I'm surprised she is helping them now."

Cerdic snorted. "I'm not. She needs her precious Pendragons on the throne, and you're a threat."

"Vivienne vowed not to aid humans after Camlann." Nimue swirled the wine in her goblet. "But I shouldn't be surprised. She has a habit of breaking her vows. Well, Camelot now knows it's me, so we have even bigger problems."

Cerdic froze. "How do they know it's you?"

"I ran into Gawaine at Glastonbury."

"Why are you lounging about here, then?" Cerdic yelled.

Nimue narrowed her eyes. "Do not shout at me. I am recovering and planning. What of Hywel?"

"That idiot?" Cerdic drained the last of his wine. "Got himself locked up. Tried to kill the princess."

"The princess?"

"Aye, she championed for her brother," Cerdic explained, pouring more wine. "He drew blood as he was supposed to but got carried away. Tried to kill her, and now he's rotting in the dungeons."

Nimue gripped her goblet so hard it exploded. Cerdic threw his hands over his face to block the wine splashing at him.

"*Idiot*," Nimue hissed. "He had specific instructions and outright defied me!"

"He has a trial in a month."

"He can die now today for all I care," said Nimue, leaping to her feet and pacing. "He had one job—to get Pendragon blood—and he failed."

"What can I do?" Cerdic asked.

"Start crumbling them from the inside," Nimue snapped. "You said Bors of Gwent wished for a new king. Ally with him. Leave the boy to me."

CHAPTER NINETEEN

ANWIL

News of losing nearly an entire guard patrol the day after his wedding was not how Anwil had expected his new life to start. But he had grown accustomed to expecting the unexpected, and he threw himself into his duties right away. King Bors had thrown what could really only be described as a tantrum after trying to leave the city only to be stopped by guards. Anwil had been tasked with trying to help calm him and was almost punched. It had taken Bors's wife, who was usually silent, threatening to drag him by the ear for him to finally agree to return to his rooms in the guest wing. And just barely after the Bors situation was handled, Anwil had worked with Sir Malcolm to organize extra guards around the city and castle. They worked late into the night, and Anwil didn't even bother to change his clothes when he crawled into bed with Yvanne.

The next two days saw him in the throne room with his mother and sister, getting paperwork ready for Anwil to transition into power and hearing report after report of finding nothing about who the imposter knight was working for, nor of any suspicion within the city.

"My spies have found nothing. *Nothing*!" Dindrane scoffed as she tossed papers onto the table. "Ten years of near perfect performances, and nothing. Whoever is behind this knows how to cover their tracks, that's for sure. Has the prisoner talked?"

"No," said Anwil. "He keeps repeating that he cannot."

"Maybe he actually can't," said Ariadne, trying to wipe ink from her fingers. "He used magic in the tournament. If this person is as good as you say, mayhaps they put a curse on him so he can't reveal who they are."

"That's not a bad theory," said Guinevere.

"I still say you should torture him," said Dindrane. "That gets anyone talking."

"Torture brings more false confessions than true," Guinevere snapped. "There are better ways to interrogate." Anwil agreed with his mother. He did not like torture. It was inhumane.

Dindrane scoffed but didn't push the matter as Yvanne stalked in, her face flush with anger. Lohengrin followed behind her and gave Anwil a look that said, *It's been a day*. She walked right up to Guinevere, hands balled into fists at her sides. Anwil wanted to rush to her, but she didn't even look at him.

"May I speak freely, Your Grace?" Yvanne asked Guinevere, who sat up straight in her chair.

"Of course, my dear. Always. What is it?"

Yvanne took a breath, and then: "King Bors is the *most* vile and despicable man I have ever had the misfortunate to meet! He deserves not the kingdom of Gwent or any kingdom of Briton, and I feel terribly so for his wife, who has to put up with him!"

There was a beat of silence, and then Ariadne snorted and pressed a hand to her mouth, failing to keep herself from laughing. Yvanne sent a glare her way, and Ariadne waved her hands apologetically.

"What has he done?" Anwil asked, a surge of anger bubbling in his gut. If Bors had hurt her . . .

"The way he speaks to me—to everyone!" Yvanne shrieked. "He is like a bratty child, and yet he is nearly ten years my senior!"

Anwil stood so fast from his chair that it nearly toppled over. "What did he say to you?"

He ignored the looks of surprise from his mother and sister. Lohengrin shot him a grin, but he ignored him too. Yvanne shook her head.

"Nothing I couldn't handle," she said. "Thank you for your concern, though. I just . . . do not wish to ever speak to him ever again."

"I'll handle him," said Dindrane. "Don't you worry your pretty young head anymore. I know how to deal with that man."

Yvanne's shoulders sagged in relief. "Thank you, my lady." The words had barely left her mouth when Sir Malcolm entered, looking upset. Anwil's stomach dropped at Malcolm's puffy red eyes.

"Your Graces," said Sir Malcolm, his voice heavy with tears. "Lord Gawaine has returned."

When Anwil and the others arrived at the courtyard, Gawaine was sliding off his horse. The knights were accompanied by two oxen-pulled wagons and quite a few monks. The first thing Anwil noticed, however, was the person-shaped blanket in the middle of the five monks. Anwil's breath caught in his throat. He scanned the faces of the knights. Gawaine, Percival, Xiang . . .

Servants and guards ran up to help with the horses and monks. The monks looked worse for wear, and a couple needing help to walk.

"What happened?" Anwil asked Gawaine.

Gawaine winced. His hands were wrapped in makeshift bandages, and there was dried blood at his hairline. The rest of the knights did not look any better. They sported various injuries and makeshift bandages.

"Glastonbury is gone," Gawaine said in a hollow voice. "It was Nimue, the Lady's own sister. We lost—"

Guinevere stepped up to him. "Gawaine," she breathed.

"I'm sorry, Guin," he said, his voice shaking. "The abbey . . ."

Guinevere let out a shaking breath and glanced at the wagons. "Who have we lost?" she whispered. Gawaine turned around and nodded to Sir Xiang. He pulled away the blanket on one wagon, revealing two bodies so burnt they were unrecognizable.

"Gaheris and Ulrich," Xiang said quietly. Spots of ash were scattered about his face, and his eyes were red and puffy.

"No," Lohengrin uttered. "No!" Lohengrin had been Ulrich's squire and it was Ulrich who led him to be knighted.

Guinevere let out a sob and clasped her hands over her mouth. Anwil put an arm around her shoulders and squeezed her bicep. He held back tears. While they hadn't been as close to Gaheris as they were with Gawaine, he was family, and Ulrich was just as good as. He had been a Knight of the Round Table since they were little and had aided in Anwil's training. Ariadne sniffled and wiped at her eyes just as Lady Lynette, Sir Gaheris's wife, ran into the courtyard, the hem of her skirt muddy. She looked at Gawaine, then to the bodies in the wagon, and screamed. The agony of the scream pierced through the air, and her knees gave out, but Guinevere and Ariadne caught her.

"No, no!" she yelled through tears. "No! It's not him. Please, no! Please, God, no!"

Gawaine let out his own sobs and knelt down next to them, taking Lynette in his arms.

CHAPTER TWENTY

MERLIN

The rain had ceased hours ago, but the dense forest was humid, and the ground was sloppy. It was not, however, an unwelcome sight as Merlin, Vivienne, and her company of priestesses approached the entrance at the lake shore. Merlin welcomed the sight and smells of the marsh and mist, the magic swirling around him like a calming breeze. He had not been to Avalon in a long time, and he missed the isle. He closed his eyes and listened to the trees' whispers of welcome. He had always had a special connection to the trees. They were his home and playgrounds as a boy and kept him safe from any who'd wished him harm. He was thought to be the Devil's son as a boy, and many had tried to kill him, but his mother and the trees were his sanctuary.

"It is good to be home." Vivienne dismounted her horse and gave it a pat on the neck. "Parisa has missed you, Merlin."

Merlin smiled. "She must be fully grown by now," he said, recalling the small faerie child that had taken a liking to him the last time he was in Avalon.

"Her wings are beautiful," said Vivienne softly and glanced over her shoulder. "Alfdis?"

The priestess in front slid off her horse and joined Vivienne on the shore. Merlin took hold of the reins of Vivienne's mare and watched as the women stepped knee deep into the lake. The lake was covered with a thick fog, but Merlin knew the beauty that lay beyond. The two women raised their arms, and the wind shifted the wrong way. The horses whinnied and neighed, and Merlin's skin crawled, and the hairs on his neck rose. Something was not right.

"Vivienne!" he called, but the wind picked up, whipping his hair about his face.

Vivienne whirled around, eyes shining pure white. A priestess behind Merlin cried out in pain, and she fell to the ground with an arrow sticking out of her breast. Two more arrows came out of the trees, but Vivienne shot out her hands, and the arrows disintegrated. Alfdis ran out of the water to her fallen sister. Merlin gripped his staff, the crystal glowing a bright blue. A gossamer shield surrounded him and the priestesses, protecting them.

"Show yourself!" he boomed, his voice amplified. The wind stilled and nothing moved, not even the leaves. Then leaves rustled, and a cloaked figure stepped onto the shore just outside the shield. Merlin froze. *No, it couldn't be.*

The figure pulled their hood down, and Vivienne gasped. "Nimue? You're alive?"

"Surprised to see me, sister?" Nimue said in a stiff voice. "It's been a long time."

Vivienne slowly left the water, her eyes wide. "It cannot be. Surely I am dreaming."

Nimue did not move as Vivienne approached and waved her hand in front of Merlin's shield. It melted away and Merlin silently sent a warning to Vivienne, but she ignored him.

"My sister," Vivienne whispered, reaching out to Nimue.

"You ceased being my sister when you banished me from my home," Nimue growled and Vivienne froze.

"Nimue-" A flick of the wrist was all it took to send Vivienne flying backwards. Merlin held out his staff to catch Vivienne before she landed hard on the rocks. Her body gently turned upright and she landed on her feet. The priestesses surrounded Nimue, but thorns shot out from the bushes, impaling the priestesses. Vivienne screamed, and a white light erupted from her hands, barreling toward Nimue. It hit her, and she flew backward before slamming into a tree. Vivienne ran to the priestesses as Merlin hurried after Nimue. He found her pushing herself to her feet, covered in leaves and dirt.

"Stay away from me!" she growled.

"Nimue," he said, pointing his staff at her. "What happened? How did you return?"

"I was never dead," she spat. "You left me in the In-Between for years! My soul ripped itself apart only to heal over and over again!"

Merlin's breath hitched in his throat. "Nimue, I'm—"

"You're not sorry," she hissed, brushing the leaves from her hair. "You were never sorry. Not when I was banished, and not when you tried to kill me." She threw out her arms, but Merlin deflected the shooting branches easily.

"Vivienne!" he called over his shoulder. "Run!"

Nimue threw a ball of fire at him, but he threw a shield around him and it sizzled out.

"We met on the *battlefield* at Camlann, Nimue. I was defending myself. I never meant to harm you." Merlin gripped his staff with white knuckles. The memories flooded his mind. Nimue breaking her oath, her banishment, Camlann, the guilt that he felt for not doing enough for her.

Nimue laughed, high-pitched and forced. "Didn't mean to? Still lying, I see, Merlin."

"You broke your oath, Nimue. You harmed and killed. Those were sacred vows that you broke!" Merlin had hung his head and was silent all those years ago when Nimue had begged him to do something to help her. But he was of of Avalon, he held no sway over Vivienne's decisions.

"I couldn't and wouldn't stand by whilst humans did worse to my people—*our* people. But you forget that, don't you? You'd love to be human."

"I am half-human." He thought of his mother. His loving but frail mother, who had protected him, and taught him kindness and compassion, and that there was more than just physical strength.

Nimue scoffed. "Keep telling yourself that, old man." She glanced over his shoulder and threw out her arms. Merlin spun on his heel, catching her bolt of magic with his staff just in time before it hit Vivienne.

Vivienne let out a breath. "Sister!" she called. "Stop this! Your anger-"

Nimue's jaw dropped. "Anger? You *betrayed* me! Your own sister! You betrayed our people, your title, your duties! This is more than just anger."

"You are putting your own guilt on me, sister." Vivienne's voice was even, but her fingers shook. "You broke the sacred vows—"

"I am not the only one to do so," said Nimue. "But you can do no wrong, can you?"

"Nimue, cease this insolence!" Vivienne snapped. "You will come to Avalon with me and return to the Otherworld to face your trial."

Nimue scoffed. "I will not face any trial. But you, sister? You will."

"Nimue, be rational—"

Nimue threw something at Merlin, and he deflected it with his staff, but as soon as it made contact, the world twisted around him, and his throat constricted. There was no air. He couldn't breathe. He tried to cast a spell, anything, but his body wouldn't move. Nimue hurled something at Vivienne before all he saw was black.

CHAPTER TWENTY-ONE

ANWIL

They gave Gaheris and Ulrich a warrior's funeral. Mirah and Master Cassius had wrapped the bodies and dressed them in knight's attire, swords laid on their chests and their hands folded over the handles. Father Ifan led them in prayer, and a Druid priest gave a blessing in Merlin's absence. Ariadne stayed close to their mother throughout the service. Guinevere was taking the deaths hard, but none more than Gawaine and Lady Lynette. Lady Lynette was held between Gawaine and his wife, Lady Reya, as sobs racked her body. She had already lost their daughter a few years prior and now her husband. Silent tears streamed down Gawaine's face during the entire service. Yvanne had held Anwil's hand the entire time, her presence like a rock. She had not known Gaheris and Ulrich, and was able to keep Anwil steady when his own tears fell during the prayers.

The remembrance feast afterward was somber and a stark contrast to his wedding. There was no entertainment save for the musician, Captain Stout, strumming on his lute and singing of Gaheris's and Ulrich's triumphs. A few of the kings had stayed in Camelot as the roads were unsafe for travel, and the guests who did not use Merlin's mirrors had opted to stay as well. The company was stretching their expenses, but Guinevere had fortunately opened an emergency fund a while ago, and they could thankfully pull from there. Though Anwil hoped they would not run out of food, especially as autumn drew near.

The next morning, Anwil entered the war room, an extensive study Gawaine also used as an office, where the Knights of the Round Table and the kings that had stayed were gathered. They were already arguing, but Anwil noticed Sir Jabir was present, and his heart soared. He was one of the few sitting down, and a cane leaned on his chair, but he was healed. Sir Jabir caught Anwil's eye and winked at him, and Anwil couldn't help but smile through his exhaustion.

"I do not appreciate being lied to!" King Elyion slammed his hand down on the table, scattering maps and knocking over his drink. "I care not if that blasted grail is a fake. We should have been privy to that information. Look what has now happened!"

"That is my fault alone, my lord," Percival said, looking exhausted. "I did not tell anyone—"

"Then you have betrayed your oath, Sir Knight!"

"Here," someone whispered in Anwil's ear. His sister. He hadn't noticed she was in the room. She hovered near the corner, where a drink cart had been placed. "You'll need this today."

Anwil took the cup she handed him and took a sip. "Oh!" He sputtered at the bitter-tasting drink. "What is this?"

"It's one of your wedding gifts," Ariadne explained as the kings carried on. "From East Africa. A bean from a fruit that you roast and turn into a hot beverage. It makes you more alert and helps wake you up. It's delicious. Try it with sugar."

The sugar did help, although Anwil wasn't one for desserts. The more he drank though, the more he rather liked it. "What do they call it?"

"Coffee?" Ariadne said, sipping at her own. "I believe that is a rough translation. We were given plenty to plant and even a little book on how to care for and use it. I added some cinnamon to mine."

Anwil nodded. "How long have they been arguing?" He gestured to the kings and knights.

"Most of the morning," she said. "It's not been pretty."

"Where is Mother?"

"With Lady Lynette. She has been inconsolable. She wishes to retire to their estate, but neither Gawaine nor Mother think traveling is a good idea right now."

"It's not," Anwil agreed. "Especially once Nimue figures out the Grail she took is not *the* Grail at all."

Ariadne shook her head. "Ridiculous. I honestly can't blame the kings for their anger. They made a big fuss about Sir Galahad and his vision from the Christian God, all for nothing. And then to keep it at Glastonbury and not even tell anyone! Not even half the monks there knew about it."

Anwil sighed. "I should join them." He topped off his coffee drink. If it helped keep him alert, he would need all he could get. He slid between Lohengrin and Gawaine at the table. Lohengrin pushed a scroll towards him, notes he had been taking in Anwil's absence.

"We have sent word for the Druid High Council," Gawaine was saying. "They are on their way here now."

"The Christian leaders will not like you choosing sides," said King Elyion.

Anwil did not have any experience with battles or war, but he listened intently and monitored how the kings reacted. Caewlin and Constantine were their usual calm and collected selves, but Bors's face flushed with anger, and Elyion tapped his finger with impatience. Cerdic had returned to Wessex for the time being to retrieve his father for the imposter knight's trial. All kings would need to be present to cast their vote.

"We are not choosing sides," Gawaine growled. "How else are we supposed to fight magic, if not with magic? The Druids can help us more than the Christian priests."

"What does Nimue want?" said Constantine. "She has taken prized Briton treasures. What is she doing with them?"

"We don't know," said Sir Percival. "We didn't get any answers from the prisoner, Hywell, either. She didn't tell him anything."

"Smart move on her part," muttered King Bors, who was also sipping on the coffee drink. "I wouldn't be surprised if he was nothing more than a decoy. A distraction."

"Unfortunately, we think that is exactly what he is," said Percival.

"My patrol was attacked the day of the wedding," Sir Jabir pointed out. "And Glastonbury not long after. It seems the distraction worked."

"How much iron do we have?" Constantine asked.

"Plenty," said Gawaine. "I have already ordered armor and arrowheads to be made. We will equip all guards and soldiers with it, and you are more than welcome to our supply."

Constantine nodded. "We have a good supply as well."

"Do we know where Nimue is and if she is building an army?" asked King Elyion.

"My daughter and I will see what we can do to locate her," said Sir Jabir.

"And how will you be doing that?" Bors snapped.

"Scrying is a very useful magic. With the two of us, we might locate her. With your permission, Your Grace, Mirah and I can get started now?" Sir Jabir looked at Anwil.

"Please," said Anwil. "Do anything you can."

Sir Jabir bowed his head and with help from Lord Roland, stood from his chair. Ariadne helped to escort him out.

"We need to end this soon, Gawaine," said Bors. "Nimue must be brought down, or else face a civil war."

"Is that a threat, my lord?" said Anwil before he could help himself. Bors was growing more and more frustrating by the second. And Anwil still had not forgiven him for the disrespectful way he had treated Yvanne.

"Not a threat," said Bors, turning his watery eyes on Anwil. "Nimue is attacking Christian holy places. If she is not stopped, the Christians will rebel and replace you with a strong leader of their own choosing. One who would not tolerate the fae."

Anwil did not miss the jab at him. "The fae have a right to be here as much as we do," he said, anger growing in his belly. "In fact, perhaps more so. They are the children of the gods and built these lands."

"Gods we Christians do not believe in," Bors hissed, tapping the table with his finger for emphasis.

"Just because you do not believe in them does not mean they do not exist." Anwil was normally not one to argue with the kings, nor was he overly religious himself, but he had a respect for this land and the people who gave it life. All people, fae and human, should be treated equally and with respect.

Bors scoffed. "You are incredibly stup—"

"It sounds as if you are threatening the crown, Lord Bors," said Lord Roland, his chest puffed out. "Might I remind you that threats can be perceived as treason?"

"We have a right to speak out if we think the crown is not doing its best to protect its subjects," Bors growled back. "And, as we are seeing, it is not. Nimue is one person; she should have been stopped ages ago. Why has Merlin not handled this? Is he not all-powerful?"

"Merlin tried as much as he—"

"So not all-powerful, then?" Bors interrupted, and Anwil had never wanted to smack a man across the face so badly before. "Never thought so. Same as any other Druid. But of course, the great King Arthur's wizard had to be special—"

"You didn't even know Arthur—" Lohengrin started, but Bors interrupted him.

"Neither did you!"

"Enough!" Anwil burst out. The shock of Anwil's outburst caused silence to fall over the room. His cheeks burned, but he cleared his throat. "Enough arguments, my lords. We need a plan. Now that we know who and what we are up against, it is time to work together and come up with a solution. Lords Gawaine and Percival will take the lead on this. They are more

213

experienced in dealing with magic and Nimue than anyone else in this room. So please, my lord kings, no more wasting time."

No one said anything for a moment, but Bors did roll his eyes. Lord Roland cleared his throat. "Very well said, Your Grace," he said. "Lord Gawaine, what say you, then?"

Gawaine looked down at the maps in front of him. "We need to know what Nimue is planning. Scouts and spies will be sent out, as well as a patrol to Avalon to get word to Merlin. We will need him back much sooner than expected."

Anwil listened intently as Gawaine laid out the plans for the next few days until they all agreed—some hesitantly—and Anwil dismissed them. As the kings left the room, Gawaine put a hand on Anwil's shoulder.

"Nicely done, son," he said, before slipping from the room himself. He had been quiet all during the remembrance feast and had turned in early, barely speaking to anyone.

"Does King Agravaine?" Anwil asked Percival quietly, suddenly remembering Gawaine's other brother who ruled over their northern neighbor, Lothian.

Percival paused gathering maps. "Gawaine sent a letter, but they haven't spoken in years."

Anwil didn't press the matter, as he knew relations between Gawaine and King Agravaine were not good, and left Lord Roland and Percival to clean the table as he went to find Yvanne.

He found her with her ladies-in-waiting in the gardens. They were strolling around the fountains, making small talk with the nobles and gardeners. When Yvanne noticed him, she left her two ladies by the fountain, and he met her halfway. She kissed his cheek in greeting.

"How did it go?" she asked quietly.

Anwil shrugged. "More arguments," he said. "They're all frustrated. I can't blame them. How is everything out here?"

"There's talk." Yvanne glanced around. She pulled him to a quieter spot away from most of the people in the gardens. "There's already talk of the Grail missing and being a fake."

Anwil closed his eyes and sighed. "I shouldn't be surprised. Nothing stays a secret."

"Well, thankfully, many can't seem to make up their minds on the matter. I've been trying to settle the rumors down, as your mother instructed, and have been listening to the talk. I even had Sybilla and Elowen walk the city to listen to the gossip. I didn't realize how much of a spy I'd play as queen. I have to admit, though, it's sort of fun." She let out light laugh.

"Anything of use?" Anwil asked, daring to be hopeful, but it was dashed when Yvanne shook her head.

"Not really," she said. "Have we heard anything from Lord Merlin?"

Anwil shook his head. "No, but he's known to disappear for a time."

215

Yvanne nodded, and they were silent for a moment. Anwil used that time to close his eyes and try to ease the tension from his body. He'd never thought the very beginning on his reign would be like this. They'd had peace for so long, but now the old enemies of his parents were coming back from the dead. He hoped letting Gawaine and Percival take the lead wasn't seen as a weak position on his part. They had the experience. To him, it was the smart move. He was still learning. But he would need to face this head-on if he was to be a good king.

"Well," said Yvanne. "We should get back to Lord Roland. He has more paperwork for us to sign."

"Of course he does," Anwil mumbled, eliciting a giggle from Yvanne.

CHAPTER TWENTY-TWO

ARIADNE

A riadne had never been to a trial before, and it had been years since Camelot needed to hold one. Ariadne had been dealing with anxious feelings on top of her grief in the week leading up to her trial. She already missed Ulrich's roaring laugh on the training fields and Gaheris' calm presence. Gawaine was a shell of himself, barely sleeping by the looks of the bags under his eyes. But he had thrown himself into finding Nimue. Ariadne had never met the Lady of the Lake's sister, but knew of her banishment from Avalon and that she had been married to Mordred, leading next to him at the Battle of Camlann. Nimue was said to have been powerful, almost as powerful as her sister, Lady Vivienne. Both had been born of the mother goddess and a faerie father. Of course Camelot was having such trouble stopping the attacks. Because of Mordred, Nimue knew how Camelot operated. And if she was nearly as powerful as her sister...could they stand a chance?

Ariadne was oddly calm, though, when she met Yvanne and Mirah in the corridors outside the great hall doors. Yvanne was dressed in a red overdress that opened at the skirt, revealing a dark yellow underdress. She wore a sheer veil over her hair with a gold circlet to keep it in place. *She already looks like a queen*, Ariadne thought as she approached. Mirah was the first to hear her and turned around. She wore a Persian dress and pants in green and yellow jeweled tones.

"Where's Anwil and Mother?" Ariadne asked, looking around.

"Inside already," said Yvanne. "Along with what looks like the entire court. Some people from the city are even here."

Ariadne looked to the closed doors. That imposter would get what he deserved. "Shall we, then?"

Yvanne slid her arms through Ariadne's and Mirah's, and together, they entered the hall. A low rumbling murmur of various voices filled the hall. Ropes were drawn, keeping the city's population toward the back, and the courtiers sat on either side of the hall, leaving a long wide aisle down the middle. The Round Table was gone, replaced by a long square table on the dais. Many had brought fans and were already fanning themselves and dabbing their faces with handkerchiefs. Ariadne wished Merlin were there to put a cooling spell over the hall.

Anwil sat in the direct middle with Guinevere to his left and an empty seat at his right. All the kings, even Caradoc from Wessex, filled the table. Ariadne hadn't seen him in years, and he looked ancient. His hair was now pure white, and it clashed against the gold of the thick crown across his forehead. The council and knights sat in tiered seats to the table's right.

With an exchanged look, the three young women made their way down the aisle toward the High Table. Anwil stood from his chair and rounded the table to escort Yvanne to her seat, and Ariadne and Mirah took seats with the council. Mirah sat next to her father and Ariadne next to Lord Roland. It was already hot, despite the cool air coming in from the windows near the ceiling. Many of the women were fanning themselves, and Ariadne wished she had brought hers.

They did not have to wait long. The doors opened once more, and Percival, leading a flank of guards, brought in the imposter knight. His hands and feet were chained together, and he had been given the opportunity to bathe and a change of clothes. His eyes were set in a glare on Guinevere, and a bubble of anger erupted in Ariadne's stomach. She couldn't wait until he was read his punishment.

Percival stopped in the middle of the room and bowed. He stepped aside and let the imposter knight have the middle of the aisle, but the guards behind him kept their hands on their swords, and Ariadne spotted Brionna in the crowd with her bow.

Lord Roland stood from his chair and went to stand directly in front of the table and faced the room, unraveling a scroll. He loudly cleared his throat, and the crowd hushed.

"Hywell of Brecheinoc," he read, "is hereby charged with treason for the attempted murder of Princess Ariadne Pendragon, the falsification of royal documents, and breaking the rules of a royal tournament. How do you plead, sir?"

Hywell lifted his chin. "Not guilty."

Whispers slithered around the hall, but Guinevere put her hand up, and they ceased.

"Very well," said Lord Roland, rolling up the scroll. "That is documented. As your right by the law, you may now state your defense to the kings of Briton and the High Council of the Round Table." He stepped aside, and Hywell clenched his fists. His eyes narrowed at the High Table.

"I am not guilty," he hissed, "because I have not committed a crime against the crown—the true crown! That woman"—he pointed with both hands to Guinevere, who kept her face neutral, and Ariadne wished she had the endurance to do that—"murdered my wife to beget children! She and her demon wizard used magic, just as Arthur and Uther had before them! The Pendragons are false monarchs and murderers! They tricked you and are still tricking you!"

The crowd erupted in gasps and talk, and it took Lord Roland a long moment to calm them down. Ariadne's heart raced, pounding against her chest. She wanted to fight him again, to beat him into silence. She laced her fingers together, squeezing until her knuckles turned white. Guinevere raised a hand again, calling for silence.

"And where, pray tell, did you hear such things about Her Grace, the Queen?" King Caewlin asked, his hands steepled together in front of him.

Hywell's face twisted as if he were trying to pry his lips apart but couldn't. He did this for a long moment, before bursting, "Ask her yourself!" Spit flew from his mouth and dribbled down his chin. "She will tell you! She needed to conceive, but the magic wouldn't give life without taking another!"

The crowd whispered and mumbled to each other. This time, Guinevere had to bang on the table to get them to quiet down. "Sir, you will contain yourself to a respectable volume and calmly explain your defense. If you cannot do that, it will be dismissed."

Hywel's face twisted again, and his skin changed from red to purple as he glared daggers at Guinevere.

"Are you ill, Master Hywell?" said King Constantine.

"I am fine!" Hywell spat. He shook his fist, the chains rattling. "I tell the truth! Ask yourselves. You must break free of the spell!"

King Constantine put a hand to his forehead, and King Caewlin sighed. "So, that is your defense? You claim the queen killed your wife for a child, so you came to kill hers in revenge? Is that what you are saying?"

"Did he even have a wife?" said King Elyion, looking at the others before Hywell could answer.

"Aye," said King Caradoc. He handed a piece of parchment down to Elyion. "My son did some research. Apparently, his first wife fell ill and died of a fever twenty or so years ago. Which, coincidentally, is the same time the queen announced she was with child."

Ariadne nearly leapt from her chair. What was he implying? Anwil glared at him, but Guinevere, again, did not react.

"That proves nothing," said Constantine, shaking his head. "It is an unfortunate thing, but people frequently succumb to harsh illnesses. It is he who is on trial here, not Her Grace. There is no reason in discussing his accusations against her."

"Aye," said King Caewlin. "So let us get back on track. Treason and the falsification of royal documents."

Murmurs of agreement sounded from the crowd, and Ariadne sat back, but her heart still pounded, and she gripped the arms of her chair. She glanced at Anwil, who sat straighter in his chair and stared down at Hywell. Ariadne could see the clench in his jaw and the subtle twitch of his left eye.

"I enacted the right to a challenge!" said Hywell. "Of which is perfectly legal!"

"If I may," Caradoc leaned forward in his seat. "As I was not present, may I have an explanation as to what happened?"

Lord Roland cleared his throat again and recounted the tournament.

"So, you changed the rules of a fair challenge?" said Caradoc, looking at Anwil. "This man felt he was wronged and came to seek justice for it, and we are now punishing him?"

Guinevere turned her head to Caradoc, and her jaw twitched. It was subtle, but Ariadne saw it.

"This man falsified royal documents," said King Elyion. "And he came with the intent to kill His Highness and almost succeeded in killing the princess. Any plot to kill a monarch is treason."

"*Is* Anwil our monarch?" said Caradoc, and the refusal of deference didn't miss anyone's notice.

King Constantine leaned on the table to glare down at Caradoc. "Anwil Pendragon is High King by his birth. You were there, *Lord* Caradoc, when we voted on the matter. Anwil would be High King, but Queen Guinevere would rule as regent until he is of age. So yes, technically, *King* Anwil is our monarch, and any plot or attempt to kill the king or usurp the throne is, by law, treason."

Caradoc shrugged off Constantine's tone. "The princess needn't have accepted."

Ariadne's jaw dropped, and a hand landed hard on her shoulder. Gawaine. His grip pulled her back into her chair.

223

She hadn't even realized she was halfway out of it. Yes, she needn't have accepted the challenge, but it would have been seen as unchivalrous to do so. No knight had ever turned down a challenge in Camelot's history, the most famous of which was Gawaine and the Green Knight. It was a moral obligation to never turn down a challenge. Caradoc was once a Knight of the Round Table. He knew the rules.

"That is beside the point." King Caewlin rolled his eyes. "This man has made his intentions quite clear. He does not wish for Anwil to sit on the throne, and his intentions at the tournament were not just. They were purely to kill our king. That is treason in the books!"

Talking broke out again amongst the crowd, and Ariadne took in a breath to calm herself.

"Any last words you wish to add, Master Hywell?" Lord Roland asked.

Hywell spat in Anwil's direction, and the crowd gasped. If Ariadne could grip her chair any harder, it would surely break.

"Very well," said Lord Roland stiffly. "We shall vote. Your Grace." He bowed to Anwil, who stood.

"Hywell of Brecheinoc, you have been charged with treason and the falsification of royal documents," he said. "The sentence for treason is death. The kings of Briton and the High Council of the Round Table, all those in favor?"

Hands from all the kings except Caradoc's rose, as well as the council's. Ariadne didn't breathe.

"And those opposed?" Anwil said. Caradoc's hand was the only to rise. "The votes have been counted, and all you here bore witness. Hywell of Brecheinoc, you are sentenced to death for treason. Your hanging will be at first light tomorrow."

Hywell burst into a fury of curses thrown at Anwil and Guinevere. Spit flew from his mouth as he tried to fight off the guards, but Percival wrestled him to the ground. The guards had to carry him out by each limb, but even then, he did not stop fighting. His yells echoed even when the doors had closed behind him.

CHAPTER TWENTY-THREE

ANWIL

A nwil would never forget the harsh crack of bones as Hywell's neck snapped. The man was a criminal, and his punishment was just, but Anwil's stomach twisted, and he couldn't bring himself to look at him. A sizeable crowd had gathered in the square to watch, and for the life of him, Anwil could not understand the draw of hangings. He never wanted to see another man die ever again. Both Ariadne and Yvanne hovered close to him, and he felt he may have bruised Yvanne's hand with how tightly he held it.

After the hanging, Guinevere lifted the lockdown on the city, and most of the kings were, thankfully, eager to leave.

Bors and Caradoc were the first to go, but Constantine stayed behind with Caewlin. King Elyion lingered, but he returned home to Northumbria after a couple of days. Guests left in droves, and Anwil was relieved the castle was back to normal as summer turned into autumn. He was busier than ever, working to transition into full power and gearing the army for war.

Mirah and Sir Jabir had no luck finding Nimue or any information about what she was doing, nor had they heard from Merlin or the Lady of the Lake since they had left for Avalon just days after the wedding. Anwil hoped they were working on their own, especially as no new reports of burnt abbeys or stolen relics were heard. But it made Anwil nervous. Why had Nimue stopped suddenly? Everyone was growing more frustrated by the minute, but no one more than Guinevere. The trial had taken a toll on her, and Anwil and Ariadne both avoided her as much as they could for fear of being snapped at. Although the allegations against her had been dismissed, whispers still filled the city, bringing up old wounds.

After a long day of no reports about Nimue, Merlin, or anything else, Anwil sat in his favorite study in the private wing of the castle. He nursed a goblet of wine, staring into the flames of the hearth but not really seeing them. Yvanne had gone to bed hours ago, while he had tossed and turned and given up after a while. He was not looking forward to the day his mother no longer had any ruling power. There was so much work to do and not enough hours in the day to do it. He hadn't been to the library in weeks. How his mother had managed for so long, he'd never understand.

The fire cracked, and a broken log fell. He got up to fix it, but just as he grabbed the poker, a light from the city caught his eye through the window. The moon was bright and clear in the sky, but there was a separate golden light emanating from the city. Anwil peered out the window to get a better look. It was then he noticed the smoke.

He took off from his study, racing down the halls, yelling, "Fire in the city!" to every guard he passed. The castle came alive in a fury as he ran into the courtyard, a trail of guards, servants, and nobles following behind him. He skidded to a halt at the castle gates. Heat blasted on his face. The market was on fire. Screams echoed; people ran about—it was insanity. Anwil's heart pounded against his chest as he took in the blaze. The flames were raging as if they had a life of their own.

"To the springhouses!" he shouted at a group of guards and people. "Grab buckets. Open the taps. Get the water flowing!"

Anwil ran into the city's cobbled roads, straight toward the fire. People knocked into him, trying to escape the flames. He paused for a moment, trying to regain his boundaries, but someone grabbed his arm. An older woman, shorter than him, tugged on his sleeve.

"My granddaughter! My granddaughter!" she screamed, tears glistening on her face.

"Where?" said Anwil.

She pointed, and he followed her finger to the second story of the blazing butcher's shop. There, in the window, was a little girl clutching a blanket and crying. Without a second thought, Anwil ran into the building, ducking under flaming beams. He coughed and held an arm over his mouth, but it didn't do much to help. His lungs burned from the smoke. The stairs were encompassed in smoke, but thankfully not yet aflame. Anwil ran up, narrowly avoiding a falling beam. Sweat dripped down his face and back as he scrambled to find the little girl. The apartment was one large room and empty, but Anwil spotted a closed door with a burning beam leaning against it. Anwil kicked the beam aside and shoved the door open. The girl jumped, but he scooped her up and ran back downstairs with her in his arms. They had almost made it when one step fell away. He faltered, grabbing the railing, then yelped out in pain as the wood burned his skin. The girl squeezed his neck, screaming into his ear, but he forced himself out, stumbling into the street.

He toppled to his knees, coughing, as the girl still clung to him with all limbs. A woman came over to them, not the grandmother, and tried to pry her from Anwil, but the girl wouldn't let go. She screamed for her mother, but as the grandmother hurried over, the child reached for her.

"Oh, my love." The grandmother sobbed, grabbing the girl. "Oh, my Lizzie. Thank you! Thank you."

"Go to the castle," Anwil ordered through rasping breaths.

The woman took her granddaughter and disappeared into the frenzied streets. Anwil pushed himself to his feet and wiped sweat from his face with the back of his sleeve. He was covered in smoke and ash and his hands stung and burned. Men ran past with buckets and tossed them on flames that barely registered the water. Anwil's heart sank. They'd never be able to get ahead of the flames. Not without a miracle. Where was Merlin when he was truly needed? Or the rain? How could it rain all the time but not now? And what had started the fire? How long had it been burning to get this bad? Anwil had a sinking feeling he knew what, or who rather, was behind it.

Someone grabbed his shoulders. A line was forming, and people were passing buckets down. Anwil joined in, ignoring the pain in his hands, but it wasn't long until screams filled the air and loud crashes boomed. Anwil left the line, frantically looking for the source. A grain tower had fallen and spilled over the streets. People were scrambling not to be buried by the grains rushing down like crashing ocean waves.

Anwil's chest tightened. What could he do? It almost seemed hopeless. He'd barely had time to process what was happening when his vision filled with red curls.

"Anwil!" His sister threw her arms around his neck, nearly knocking him over. "Oh gods, you're all right!"

"Ari," he croaked, weakly wrapping an arm around her waist and looking over her shoulder. "Camelot."

"I know." She pulled away and followed his gaze, then cursed under her breath. "Come on." She grabbed his hand and pulled him through the streets. They weaved through the terrified crowd. "We're moving everyone to the castle," Ariadne yelled over the chaos. "But it's filling fast. Mother and Yvanne are helping to find places to sleep. All the rooms have already been filled. We sent messengers to Avalon for Merlin."

"We'll have to send people to the dukedoms," said Anwil as they came up to the castle gates where people flooded in. A woman bumped into him, clutching at the fabric of his tunic.

"Please!" she said. She was covered in ash, and her dress was singed. "My baby! I can't find my baby! Please! Please help me!"

"Where—" Anwil started, but the woman dragged him off. Ariadne called out after him, but the woman took him toward the height of the fire. Anwil's heart sank. There was nothing left of the market except for piles of coals. "My lady. I don't think—"

A sharp pain like no other exploded in the back of his head, and he fell, slipping into unconsciousness.

CHAPTER TWENTY-FOUR

ARIADNE

Ariadne watched as a woman dragged her brother back into the city. She cursed and ran after them, trying not to lose sight of him in the crowd. She called after him, but he couldn't hear. She was almost to him when he paused and fell backward. The woman who had pulled him away caught Ariadne's eye for a split second before grabbing Anwil's hand again. Ariadne made a lunge for him but caught nothing. He and the woman disappeared right before he hit the ground.

"Anwil?" She turned in circles, looking for Anwil or that woman. "Anwil!" But he was gone. "No! No, no, no, no, no! Anwil!"

Ariadne shoved through people, screaming her brother's name over and over. She slid on coals and fell to her knees. She cried out in pain as her kneecaps and palms collided with sharp stone. "Anwil!"

An older man dropped to his knees in front of her. "Your Highness?" He took hold of her hands. They were bloody and covered in ash and dirt. "You are hurt!"

"She took him," Ariadne said, her voice shaking. "She took him!"

"Took who?" the man asked. Gray ash covered his black braids, and his shirt was ripped in various places. "Who took who?"

"She took Anwil."

The man did not answer. "You should get back to the castle," he said. "Treat your wounds." He helped her to her feet and left to help throw water on flames. Ariadne stumbled through the streets, picking up speed as she went. She wiped her hands on her dress, but it only caused her more pain.

Ariadne made her way back to the castle, shoving through people as she did. She frantically searched for anyone she knew but couldn't make anyone out in the darkness and smoke. Ariadne found her mother in the great hall handing out blankets and food to the crowd of people lying in the rushes on the floor. Ariadne ran right up to her, grabbing her arms and almost tipping them both over. Her hands burned, and she smeared dirt and blood on her mother's sleeves.

"Ariadne!" Guinevere exclaimed, grabbing hold of her daughter. "What is it?"

"Anwil!" Ariadne cried. "Anwil, he's gone!"

Guinevere froze. "What?"

"He's gone. He disappeared!" said Ariadne. "He fell and then just vanished! And there was a woman. She disappeared with him. She took him!"

"Slow down, slow down! What happened?"

Ariadne gulped. "Anwil vanished with some woman in the city."

"What do you mean, *vanished*?"

Ariadne let out a frustrated growl. "Vanished! Disappeared! A woman dragged him away, and then they disappeared into thin air!"

Guinevere's face melted into cold fury. "Nimue," she growled.

"Nimue? I didn't . . . She's behind this, isn't she?" Ariadne's hands slid off her mother's arms. "Do you think she started the fire?"

"I wouldn't doubt it," said Guinevere. She looked out over the people in the hall. Many were elderly, children, or people not quite hurt enough to be in the infirmary. "The knights are all out in the city, but Jabir is not. He is with Mirah. Ask if they can use anything of Merlin's to find Anwil. I don't care what it takes."

"What else can I do?" There had to be more she could do. She let her brother slip through her fingers and he was gone.

"Take Yvanne with you," said Guinevere. "I need to inform the kings. If you see Gawaine, send him my way." Without waiting for a reply, Guinevere stormed from the great hall, regal even in her plain wool dress.

"Can you find him?" Yvanne asked, wringing her hands as she sat on a stool in Merlin's workshop. She, Ariadne, Mirah, and Sir Jabir were gathered around a table, various books spread open before them. Ariadne had tried to look through them, desperate for anything to do, but she couldn't concentrate on the words. Her mind was all over the place. Her own hands were now clean, wrapped, and smeared with salve, courtesy of Mirah. Her leg bounced against the chair and Sir Jabir put a hand on her knee, stopping the bouncing.

"Breathe," he told her quietly. Deep breaths."

She did as he was told, but it was a struggle. Her breaths were shaky and rattled against her chest.

Sir Jabir turned to Yvanne. "Nazrine, my late wife, could see things through water and fire. It is called scrying. She taught me how a long time ago. Mirah and I have had much practice as of late, trying to locate Nimue, but with little luck. I cannot guarantee we will find her this time."

Ariadne's heart sunk. This was all her fault.

"I've heard of witches seeing visions in fires," Yvanne said quietly. Bags shone under her eyes, and her blue wool dress was wrinkled in places.

"Yes," said Sir Jabir, his voice gentle. "Fire is the most common to use. However, Merlin has enchanted mirrors that are much more powerful." As he said this, Mirah carefully set a mirror encased in gold on the table. Blood stained her dress, and her curls stuck out from the scarf tied around her head. She had been working in the infirmary when Ariadne and Yvanne had come for her.

"We haven't been able to see her before," said Mirah, taking the seat across from her father. "Though, perhaps if we are looking for Anwil instead?"

Sir Jabir hummed and nodded his head. "It is worth a try. Perhaps she did not place the same wards on him. At least not yet."

Ariadne didn't quite understand what they were talking about, and she sat back and let them work. She was used to it, having sat in on many of their lessons. She never interfered, but would instead read the books from Merlin's shelves. She especially loved the ones about magical creatures and animals. She had never seen a fae animal herself. They did not come near the cities and Ariadne never traveled far from Camelot. Every once in a great while, a faerie would come and visit Merlin, and he liked to use tiny pixies to send messages to Avalon. Ariadne had met one once and learned they were mischievous little buggers who liked to pull hair and leave dead things under pillows. But they loved Merlin.

Mirah turned to Yvanne. "Do you have Anwil's shirt?"

Yvanne handed her the red tunic she was told to grab from their chambers. "His favorite. It's dirty, though."

"That's actually better," said Mirah, flattening it across the table. "More of him on it." She reached across the table and took her father's hands. They whispered in a smooth language Ariadne did not understand but had heard Merlin use before.

The air in the room swirled about like a gentle breeze, and Ariadne could smell hints of sage. Whispers filled the room, bouncing off the walls. Yvanne gasped and grabbed on to Ariadne's arm. Shapes formed in the mirror, but Ariadne could not make them out. She squinted her eyes as the shapes formed together—a vague gray circle surrounded by fuzzy green spots. The whispers grew so loud, Ariadne's ears hurt, and Yvanne let go of Ariadne's arm to press her hands against her ears. The wind gushed through the room, and Yvanne screamed.

For a second, Ariadne saw an archway in a dense forest before Mirah let out a hiss of pain and the mirror burst, throwing shattered glass everywhere. Ariadne yanked Yvanne down to the ground with her and covered her neck and head as the glass fell around them. The glass shattered on the floor, and then everything went still. Yvanne's sobs broke the silence, and Ariadne looked up. Jabir was holding Mirah to his chest, her eyes squeezed shut.

"What happened?" Ariadne asked, climbing to her feet.

"I don't know," Mirah said in a pained voice.

"We were thrown out," Jabir explained, smoothing Mirah's hair. "We were caught looking."

"Nimue?" Ariadne asked as she helped Yvanne off the floor, careful to not step on any glass.

"Most likely," said Jabir as Mirah pulled away from him. "I saw *something*, though. A moon gate in a forest."

"What's a moon gate?" Yvanne asked in a small voice, huddling into Ariadne's side.

"A circular archway," said Jabir. "Made naturally in nature or by magic. Many are gateways through the realms."

"She has Anwil in the Otherworld?" Ariadne whispered, her breath catching in her throat.

Jabir sighed. "Unfortunately, I believe so."

CHAPTER TWENTY-FIVE

MERLIN

D arkness. Endless darkness was all around him. It consumed him. He could not lift his arms or legs—could not feel them, could not feel a body at all. He was floating in nothing. He tried to reach with whatever this sense was. Tried to find something in the dark. He pushed and reached and pushed until something flashed. And then it was gone. He wanted to scream, but he didn't have a mouth to move. But something in the darkness . . . wasn't so dark anymore. A light. Something faint. He pushed toward it. It grew brighter ever so slowly. He reached and reached. Then whispers. All around him. Whispers that grew louder and louder. He could almost make out the words. The glowing light was like a star in an inky black sky. The whispers grew louder. He could make out voices. Who were they? He should know them, and yet he couldn't place them. He wanted to. He *knew* them. He pushed and reached again. The whispers were now voices. He could just barely make out words.

I need her.

She is not yours.

Enough of this siege! Innocent people are dying!

I love her.

This is not love, Uther.

Gorlois is dead. She will be my queen.

There will be a boy. Give him to me.

He pulled the sword!

He is Uther's son?

Long live the king!

My wife and . . . my boy. He is so small. So small.

There is another match . . . you know her father, King Leodegrance.

It's so soon. And she is so young.

A beautiful wedding.

Who are you?

I am Morgana's son.

Magic comes at a price. Do not use it lightly.

She has rebelled against us. She wishes to fully open the realms to one another. It will be destruction for all. Faerie and human will never live in peace.

He betrayed you with the queen. Or ... did the queen betray you with Lancelot?

I would never!

She is guilty!

No!

My own sister? How could you?

Burn her!

How convenient, a look-alike sister. Hiding treason, Uncle? I thought you were just and fair. Have we gone back to one law for the people and another for the king?

We ride to Camlann.

Arthur, be careful.

I shall, Merlin. Have no fear.

The king is dead.

The baby is coming!

There's another!

Twins?

They shall be the salvation of Camelot.

Or the downfall.

An image. A city was burning. A grand castle in ruins. People screaming. Someone called a name. His name. He needed to help.

Breath painfully filled his lungs, and Merlin gasped for air. The darkness was still there, but he was breathing, even though every breath felt like knives. He was aware of a body, a body screaming in pain with every movement. Eyes. He needed to open his eyes.

It was still dark, but it was not a consuming darkness. Light poured in from somewhere near his right. Stone was all around him, and the air was filled with the scent of salt water. He turned his head, his neck creaking as he did. More stone. He squeezed his eyes shut and rolled on his side. It took him a few attempts to gather the strength to sit up. He had to prop himself against the stone wall, and then he finally realized where he was. A cave. A large cave.

Outside, he could make out the edge of a green cliff and a waterfall spilling over it. He closed his eyes and leaned his head back against the wall. He was thirsty and would need water soon. He sat there for a while, just breathing and remembering. Nimue. It had been Nimue all along. He should have guessed, but he had truly believed her to be dead. It all made sense, though, why he could not trace her. She was just as powerful as Vivienne—*Vivienne*! She was not with him. Where was she? With great effort, Merlin pushed himself to his feet, holding on to the wall for support as he slowly made his way to the cave entrance.

Merlin stepped into the light. The sea air rushed over him as he stood at the edge of Briton. Bright blue water splashed onto the sand and rocky shoreline, and gulls flew overhead. He knew this place. Tintagel. He stepped forward but ran into something hard. He rubbed his face, perplexed. There was nothing in front of him. He stepped again but was thrown backward. He landed hard on his backside, the realization hitting him just as hard as he'd landed.

He was trapped and did not have his staff.

CHAPTER TWENTY-SIX

ANWIL

A nwil woke with his head throbbing. It took him a long moment to gain the strength to open his eyes, and when he did, he did not recognize his surroundings. He was in a small room with open windows, lying in a four-poster bed that was almost as big as the room. He shoved the covers off and saw that he wore a simple undyed wool tunic and pants. The stone was cold on his bare feet, as was the entire room. He crossed to the door, but found it locked. He pushed hard on it and pulled, but it wouldn't budge. He sat back down on the bed and ran his hands through his hair, going over what he remembered last.

Camelot had been on fire. He had run into the city to help. He'd burned his hands.

He looked down at his hands, only to find them completely healed. No burns, no scarring. Where was he? He peered out the windows to find a dense and colorful forest. Birds and bugs flew about, with an occasional squirrel or rabbit, but no people were around. He attempted to climb out of the windows, but as soon as he got his leg onto the ledge, a shock shot through his body and he was thrown backward. He landed hard on his back on the tile floor, the breath knocked out of him. He lay on the floor until he regained his breathing and pushed himself back to the bed, rubbing his back.

A creak startled him, and the door opened to reveal a woman who looked a great deal like Lady Vivienne, except her features were rounder and younger, her skin a more pale, silvery gray, and her eyes were a more purple than Lady Vivienne's. Her black hair was pin-straight and reached well past her waist. Long pointed ears stuck out of her hair, and she wore a shimmering blue cloak over her silver dress.

"Anwil Pendragon," she said. Her voice was deeper than he expected. "Welcome to my refuge."

"Refuge?" he croaked. "Who are you?"

"My name in your language is Nimue." She folded her arms across her chest and leaned against the doorframe.

Anwil's breath hitched in his throat, and his blood ran ice cold. Nimue. She was going to kill him. She started the fire in the city to kill him. But why? Why him? He scooted back against the bed frame.

"Did you bring me here?" he whispered, failing to keep his voice steady.

"No," she said. "I am not allowed in Camelot. My companion, Melara, did."

"To kill me?"

Nimue scoffed. "If I wanted you dead, you would be already. I needed to speak to you alone."

"You couldn't have just asked?" he said before he could stop himself and immediately regretted it as she turned a glare on him. But the glare faded, and Nimue put on what looked like it was supposed to be a sweet smile, but that only unnerved him more. She was toying with him.

"If I would have," she said, stepping into the room, "I would have been denied."

"Because you've been killing hundreds of innocent people and stealing precious artifacts!" That, he did not regret, even though it earned him another glare.

"Your *precious artifacts* belong to the fae! I am merely taking back what is ours."

"And killing harmless monks and nuns in the process?"

Nimue's laugh was so cold that it reached under Anwil's skin and gave him chills. "Those monks and nuns have been slaughtering my people and anyone who refuses to believe in their god for years." She bent down so her face was level with his own. "Or have you decided to ignore that? They're killing your people too. Humans. Those they deem heathens for not believing in some Christ god that preaches hypocritical messages. I am only protecting my people. Can the same be said for you?"

Anwil didn't answer. She was lying. The monks were peaceful. And it was illegal to kill anyone for their religious beliefs. Arthur had seen to it before he passed. He declared that all religions would live in peace in Briton.

"What about the knights on patrol at Glastonbury?" Anwil snarled, unable to contain himself. "What you did to them—"

She lunged to him and grabbed his face, jerking him hard. Her fingers were like ice, so cold her touch almost burned. "You're very mouthy," she hissed, her gaze piercing. "If you wish to see your precious city and that new wife of yours again, you'll watch your tone."

Anwil yanked his face from her grip, and she let him go. "Don't you touch her."

"I wouldn't dream of it." Nimue batted her eyelashes. "As long as you play nice. Now come."

The door opened on its own, and Nimue swept from the room. Anwil hesitated but followed her out the door. The tile floors were cold under his bare feet, and he had to be careful to not step on the broken ones. He followed her to an open corridor without a ceiling but with pillars and archways all about. The first thing he noticed was how warm it was, despite the autumn forest that surrounded them. Green vines and flowers wound around the pillars, and the floor was a faded and cracked

Roman mosaic. He caught sight of Nimue passing through a door across the way.

When he stepped through the same doorway, he had not expected to see a cozy room with large furniture and a crackling hearth. Nor had he expected to see others. Others that weren't human. A thin figure with pure white skin and yellow eyes looked up at him and hissed. Their limbs were long, and one of their shimmering wings was broken. Another figure, more humanlike with dark brown skin and green hair, sat at the hearth grinding herbs in a mortar and pestle.

The winged figure spoke to Nimue in a language Anwil did not understand. After a moment, the two other fae left the room, and the white figure glared at Anwil the entire time.

"A human broke his wing," Nimue said, standing against a long table. "Shot him down with an arrow as he flew back to his home to feed his children. He'd never approached humans before that. Never did anything to them. They tried to kill him for simply existing."

"Are you trying to gain my sympathy for your eye for an eye?" said Anwil. Although he would never tell her that he did feel for the poor fae. Humans were supposed to leave them alone. If he ever got back to Camelot he would find out more and put a stop to it.

"I'm trying to make you finally see," Nimue said. "Come here."

Anwil hesitated, but eventually, he crossed the room. Various items were scattered about the table: a drinking horn, a large knife, a cauldron, an elegant red coat, a wooden chalice—the Treasures of Briton! But it was the sword that caught Anwil's attention the most. He felt drawn to it. It was a simple sword, made in the old Celtic style. But there was something about it. A tonal sound rang in his ears, and he hadn't realized he'd crossed the room to reach for it until Nimue grabbed his wrist.

"So it recognizes you," she said, giving him a slight push.

He stepped back and knocked into an armchair. "What?"

"It's Excalibur." She crossed to the hearth, where she picked up a decanter and poured wine into a goblet. "Sit." She nodded to the armchair, and he did as she said. "Good boy. Now, let's chat, shall we?"

CHAPTER TWENTY-SEVEN

NIMUE

The boy regarded her with wide eyes. He was a small thing, nothing like the build of Arthur or any of the knights from Camelot she had ever met. Except perhaps her nephew Galahad. He had been slim, but this boy was just so tiny. Even his presence was small, as if he'd rather sink into a wall than do anything else. But she could see the intelligence behind his eyes, and perhaps she could reason with him. It would be far easier for her if he was compliant.

"Chat about what?" he asked.

"Everything." Nimue poured another goblet of wine and handed it to him. He was rather pale under the freckles. She

250

would need to remember to feed him. Healthy blood was best. The boy hesitated but took the goblet. He didn't drink it as she sank down in the chair across from him. "What do you know of the fae?"

The boy blinked. "Anything specific?"

"Did you know that the fae were here long before you humans?"

He nodded. "Yes, I did know that. The gods walked the lands before anyone else, and the fae are the children of those gods."

"Yes," said Nimue, surprised. She was right; he was intelligent. "So you will understand that we are ... frustrated, to say the least, that humans have been forcing us from our own lands and homes, and have stolen our magic and precious relics. Briton is just as much our home as it is yours." She paused, letting the words sink in a bit. She sipped her wine and leaned toward the boy. "Now, I have another question for you. What do you know of me?"

"You are the Lady of the Lake's sister. You were a high priestess of Avalon. You were Sir Mordred's wife—"

"*Wife* is a human construct. But yes, we were committed to each other."

"And you were banished from Avalon for breaking oaths and participating in war with Mordred."

Nimue snorted. "Breaking my oath." She shook her head. Vivienne was such a hypocrite, telling everyone Nimue broke her oaths when Vivienne only ever followed them when it suited her. "I was thrown out of Avalon for daring to stand up to the humans and have them answer for the crimes they committed against us. Vivienne wanted to forget it ever happened and enjoy 'peace.' But I could not forget, and I could not forgive. So since I couldn't play by Vivienne's rules, she banished me."

"And then you and Mordred waged war on my father."

"Mordred waged war on Arthur, not I," said Nimue. "They had personal issues, and what do men do when they disagree? They fight. They declare war. Mordred's human side got the better of him, and they both paid the price for war, did they not? I did, however, see an opportunity if Mordred won and took the throne. He and I both wanted to restore this land back to the fae. If he were king, *my* cause would have been a lot easier. But he was stupid. He had already been declared Arthur's heir, but he had to fight with Guinevere, causing her to go to Morgana for a spell. And next thing we know, she's pregnant."

She was rambling, but she just couldn't hold it in. The goblet of wine shattered in the boy's hand, and wine splashed all over the floor, staining the tiles. Nimue raised an eyebrow. His hand was dripping, but not from blood. It was only wine. He possessed magic. She would use that information later.

"So it was you who told the imposter knight that ridiculous rumor!"

Nimue laughed. "Rumor? Oh, dear boy, I did not think you were *that* naïve. Though Merlin is known for his lies and half-truths. I'm not surprised he covered up what Guinevere did."

"No!" The boy shook his head.

"Yes. Your mother went to Morgana for a fertility spell. It's quite common, honestly. Many women do it. Though, the spell Morgana gave her was much more powerful considering Arthur was infertile."

"What?"

"Arthur was born from magic," Nimue explained. "He was never supposed to exist. When life is produced by magic, it cannot reproduce, and of course, there was Igraine's curse. When Uther convinced Merlin to glamour him to look like Gorlois, Merlin created a spell to ease his own guilt." Nimue watched as the boy's face paled even more. "That spell was Arthur's conception. I remember it well. Merlin hated himself for agreeing to let Uther rape Igraine, and he said a good had to come of it and created Arthur. I supposed Arthur *was* good in the humans' view. He was kind to us fae, and his death created a peace treaty between—oh, I'm rambling again, aren't I?"

She relished the look of horror and anger on the boy's face. Human men were so emotional and easily manipulated.

"Am I not . . ."

"You're Arthur's," she said. "Technically. The potion was for him. It gave him fertility. There was nothing wrong with Guinevere, but of course, men cannot fathom something being their own fault and not a woman's. You're probably more

Arthur's than Guinevere's, honestly. You look exactly like him. And have you never noticed how sensitive you are to magic? How you can recognize it? How *good* it feels?"

The boy shook his head and buried his face in his hands. Good. He was getting overwhelmed. Soon, he would come to her for answers and eventually comfort. If she could create an ally in him, it would only help her all the more.

"Anwil," she said in what she hoped was a gentle tone. Humans were so emotional. "I am sorry. I didn't realize you didn't know. How about you get some rest? Or perhaps a hot bath? I can have Melara draw one up for you. Or hot soup? I hear soup is good for humans when they aren't feeling well. Melara!"

The faerie with dark brown skin was there in an instant, carrying a tray with a bowl of steaming soup. She set it down next to Anwil, who didn't even look at it.

"You should eat," said Nimue. "It's been a full day since we brought you here."

"You mean kidnapped?" He looked at her, and she could have sworn she saw fire in his eyes. "I don't know what game you are playing, nor do I care. My knights will find you if I don't kill you first."

Nimue let out a soft snort. "We shall see."

CHAPTER TWENTY-EIGHT

ARIADNE

A riadne threw herself into training. She worked with Brionna every morning despite Brionna's protests that she was on the verge of working herself too hard. But she couldn't stand still. Everyone was working hard to locate Anwil and assist in repairs to the city. They had lost so many knights and guards over the last couple of months that Gawaine had canceled the Trials and already knighted those who had been selected. If she had been better, Anwil would still be safe, would still be home. She should have seen through that woman. Gawaine and Percival would have. Brionna would have. If she had any hope left to become a knight after her failure, Ariadne needed to spend all her time training.

"Ari, you need to sleep," Brionna said after Ariadne had gotten dizzy, and Brionna's blade came too close to her face. Brionna shoved a waterskin in Ariadne's hands. "No more training for a while. I will not have you hurting yourself."

"No! I'm fine!" Ariadne tossed the waterskin back to her. Brionna caught it with one hand. "Let's go again."

"Ari, no."

"But I need to be better! If I were better, Anwil would still be here! I need to—"

Brionna grabbed hold of Ariadne's shoulders. "You are already a good fighter," she said gently. "Your brother's disappearance is not your fault."

"Yes, it is!" Ariadne's voice broke. "I was right there! *Right there!* And I couldn't stop them. I couldn't save him."

Brionna put a finger under Ariadne's chin. "Look at me," she said, her eyes locking on Ariadne's. "And *listen*. There was no stopping Nimue. She would have taken him regardless, whether you were there or not. You need to stop blaming yourself for something that you could not control. It is a lesson we all must learn, especially as knights. We cannot save everybody all the time."

Tears stung at Ariadne's eyes. "Then what is the point?" She choked back a sob. "I couldn't even save my own brother."

Brionna pulled Ariadne to her, and Ariadne let herself cry into Brionna's shoulder. She was a failure before she had even began. She'd never be a knight now, not when she had failed the most important test. They stayed there until Ariadne ran out of tears.

Brionna wiped the tear tracks from her cheeks. "No training tomorrow. You need to rest. I know that is hard right now, but if you are too exhausted, your body will break down and you will be no use to us or yourself."

Ariadne reluctantly nodded and sniffed. She gave Brionna her sword and left the training fields and headed for her rooms. She soaked in a hot bath for a while, trying to heed Brionna's words and relax, but she could not quiet her mind. Her thoughts about Anwil, the city, her mother, and the chaos would not leave her alone. What if Anwil never returned? She had never thought about a life in which something happened to Anwil. While progressive laws had been made to undo the laws Vortigern and Uther made to favor only men, a new High King could and most likely would change all of them. The petty kings were old and reluctant to change. They would vote on a new king right away, and then what would happen to Ariadne and her mother? They would be made to retire somewhere in the country with no power and barely any titles. Ariadne would not be a knight and would have to marry a high-ranking lord to care for herself and her mother. A knight's salary was not enough for them. Of course, Guinevere had more than likely planned for this and would have some savings put away, but they would need the protection of a title. Ariadne would be stuck as a wife—a life she'd worked so hard to avoid. She would not let that work be in vain. She would find her brother and bring him home.

⁎⁎⁎

"She is most likely hiding between realms," said Gwenc'hlan, the chief Druid. He looked older than he was, with his chest-length gray-and-white beard and equally long hair. "You will want to look at rivers, caves, and moon gates, as Sir Jabir has seen. Unfortunately, with her knowledge and power, no one will see her with the naked eye. You could look right at her and not see her."

The Druid High Council had arrived early in the morning and were escorted straight to the Round Table. Food, tea, and the new coffee drink were served as they held their meeting. Ariadne had poured herself a large cup of coffee sprinkled with cinnamon . She would need it after weeks of bad sleep.

Her stomach sank at Gwenc'hlan's news. She had been hoping the Druids would be of more help. They were more knowledgeable in magic than any other human. Some were almost as powerful as Merlin or the fae themselves.

"Is there any way at all to find out where she is?" asked Gawaine, shuffling maps. The table was littered with maps of Briton, Lothian, Ireland, and Gaul. Markings had been made on each, pinpointing possible whereabouts. "There has to be some way. We've never come across this many roadblocks before."

"We would have to know what spell she cast to undo it," said another Druid, Ballar. He was younger than Gwenc'hlan and still had brown in his beard. "Magic is a complicated science. Even we do not fully understand it."

"So there is no finding Anwil?" Ariadne said more harshly than she meant to. But she was growing hopeless.

"It will be difficult," said Gwenc'hlan, turning his gray eyes on her. "But not impossible, my child. In fact, I do have an idea, but it would be dangerous." He turned to Guinevere. "And one you may not be willing to agree to, Your Grace."

Although her velvet blue dress was immaculate, Guinevere had never looked so exhausted. Her hair, usually covered by a wimple, was wound in a simple braid around her head, and she wore no jewelry save for her wedding ring and a simple gold circlet.

"What is it?" she asked in a hollow voice. Ariadne had accompanied her mother throughout the days when she wasn't training. Her mother never cried, but the emptiness in her eyes and the extra guards she stuck Ariadne with were telling.

"Since Their Highnesses are twins, they share a special bonded connection, unlike regular siblings. The princess may be the key to finding His Grace."

Ariadne sat straight in her chair, and Guinevere narrowed her eyes. "How?" Guinevere asked.

"There are a few spells that we could cast upon her to act as a sort of beacon," Gwenc'hlan said. "It could enhance her connection to her brother to the point where she could sense him."

"I'll do it." Ariadne nearly stood in her seat. They should go now! There was no time to waste.

"Wait," said Guinevere, holding out a hand and sending Ariadne a look. "What are the consequences?"

"The spell would not harm the princess," said Gwenc'hlan hurriedly. "She may feel a bit . . . odd, as her senses would heighten, but other than that, she should be fine."

"And you'll need to take her?" said Guinevere. "Out of Camelot?"

"The closer we are to His Grace, the better," said Gwenc'hlan. "We would travel along the King's Road and follow Her Highness's lead."

Ariadne looked to her mother, silently begging her for permission. With Anwil gone, Guinevere had full power as regent once again and could order Ariadne to stay. But if this was their only hope for finding Anwil . . .

Guinevere did not respond right away. She wrung her hands together and looked down at the table.

"It is a promising idea, my lord," said Gawaine before Guinevere could respond. "But I am concerned for Ariadne's safety.

If Nimue catches wind of this, she will desolate us all. I've seen what she can do."

Guinevere shook her head, and Ariadne's heart sank. "If there is no guarantee, it is too risky. I cannot risk my Ari too."

Ariadne shook her head. No. She had to! She had fix this!

Gwenc'hlan bowed his head. "I completely understand, Your Grace."

"Mother!" Ariadne exclaimed. "If this is our only chance, we should take it! Anwil has already been gone too long. He could be dead by now! I want to help."

"Darling, I know you do, but I cannot risk—"

"And I can't risk losing my brother if I can do something about it! I'm the one who lost him! I *need* to find him."

Silence fell around the table as Ariadne and Guinevere stared at one another. Ariadne could not read her mother's expression.

"Ari, I don't—"

"Mother, please," Ariadne pressed. "The longer we take, the closer Anwil is to being dead. If there's a way I can help find him, I will do whatever it takes. I've proven that I can fight. Let me serve our family as I was born to do." Ariadne's voice shook on the last word, and Guinevere looked at her a long time.

"Very well," Guinevere whispered and then turned her gaze to Gwenc'hlan. "But if anything happens to my daughter, I will hold you personally responsible."

"We won't let anything happen to her, Guin," Gawaine said, and Ariadne breathed a sigh of relief. Finally.

CHAPTER TWENTY-NINE

NIMUE

Nimue watched the Druids enter Camelot through her scrying bowl. She spied one of Caradoc's Druids in their midst, but it did not bring her any comfort. If the Druid High Council was aiding Camelot, she wouldn't have much time. They were powerful in their own right and could break through the wards she'd put around the lake shores at Avalon. Nimue couldn't wait for Samhain any longer. She would have to cast the spell now.

Nimue found Melara in the gardens gathering herbs with a few of the other faeries.

"It is time," said Nimue.

Melara's eyes widened. She shooed the other fae away and whispered, "It is not yet Samhain. We have a few more days."

"We do not have the time," said Nimue, shaking her head. "The Druid High Council is aiding Camelot now."

"Have you convinced the boy?"

Nimue shook her head. He was stubborn, which she had not quite expected. She'd tried to get him to see. She had spoken to him every day, taken him throughout the refuge, meeting the wounded fae, but he was dismissive and cold towards her. He had met with the fae folk on his own accords almost daily, despite the coldness they gave him, yet he would barely speak with her. He had tried to escape once, resulting in him injuring himself. She'd had to send Melara to tend his wounds, as no one else would. Nimue didn't blame them. "I'll have to give him an ultimatum. We are out of time."

Melara hesitated but nodded. "I shall get everything ready."

Nimue hurried off to the boy's room. He was sitting up in the bed, reading one of the books she had given him. She had gotten him to say that he liked to read. She had plenty of books written by the fae folk, and she'd eagerly given them to him, hoping to catch his sympathy. Nimue had found that it was exhausting being nice. His curls were wild, and the purple under his eyes was more prevalent than ever. He was not sleeping, but she did not comment on it. She hated that she needed him. Perhaps she would have had better luck with the girl, but Melara's reports were that she was even more stubborn and extremely hotheaded.

"Come to chat some more?" he said without looking up. "Or have you finally come to kill me?"

"You are no use to me dead," Nimue answered honestly. "Besides . . . I need your help." The words tasted awful in her mouth.

The boy regarded her with wide eyes, as if he couldn't believe what he'd heard. "*You* need *my* help?" He laughed. "What could you possibly need my help with?"

Nimue curled her hands into fists but said calmly, "A spell."

He snorted. "Fat chance."

Nimue entered the room and sat next to him on the bed. She took his hand in hers and put on what she hoped was a sweet smile. Melara had told her to act nicer to him, so she would try. "I need your help with something important. You were made of magic. You are human, but the fae made you. You are the perfect being to help the fae. We are dying, slaughtered by the humans. Your kind. If I can get this spell to work, we can live peacefully in the Otherworld."

He stared hard at her. She could practically see the thoughts swirling around in his mind.

"I don't trust you," he finally said.

She tossed his hand away and flew off the bed. "Look." She put her hands on her hips. "You are going to help me whether you like it or not. Don't you wish for all this to be over?"

"I don't trust you," he repeated. "Kill me if you must, but I won't help you."

265

Nimue clenched her jaw. "No," she said through gritted teeth. "I won't kill you. I'll kill your wife, then your sister. And after that, your mother. And I'll make you watch as I slit their throats and they bleed out on the floor, choking on their own blood."

He glared at her, but he must have known she was not bluffing, because he snapped the book closed and got off the bed. "If I help you, you will return me to Camelot unharmed and repair the damage you've done to my city."

Nimue knew she would never be allowed close enough to the city to do anything to it. She could promise to return him unharmed, and if something happened to where she couldn't . . . well, that wouldn't be her fault.

"Fine," she said. "But if you back out at any point, my earlier threat still stands."

"I wouldn't assume otherwise."

Nimue stuck out her hand, and she could already feel her fingers tingling. "Then we have a deal."

The boy looked at her hand, then took it. Tendrils of smoke-like magic wrapped around their clasped hands, and the boy hissed as they tightened around their skin. Nimue smiled.

CHAPTER THIRTY

ARIADNE

Ariadne was up and dressed in her armor by dawn the next morning. She was anxious to get going and had only slept because of Mirah's valerian root tea. Brionna had assisted with her armor, though Ariadne tried to wave her off. Brionna wouldn't budge, however, and stayed close to her side as they made their way down to the courtyard where the horses were waiting for them. Gawaine and Percival were already there, speaking with Gwenc'hlan. Ariadne had never seen a Druid without their robes. But he was dressed in a thick tunic and trousers, and a cloak wrapped around his shoulders. He looked like an ordinary old man rather than the Druid High Chief.

Mirah and Jabir joined them not long later along with the rest of the Druids and knights and her mother. They were a rather large party, and Ariadne thought they'd draw more attention that way, but when she voiced her opinion, Guinevere only glared at her. Gawaine had shrugged and mumbled about following her orders, and Ariadne let it go for the time being.

Once Ariadne said her goodbyes to her mother, Jabir and the Druid chief placed their hands on the top of her head and whispered words in another language. The spell made her feel odd, as if she were not asleep, but toeing the line into dreamworld. She had to be helped onto her horse and it was hard to concentrate on the road in front of her. They'd barely made it out of the city before Ariadne steered her horse off the path without realizing. So now she was flanked closely by Jabir and the Druids. Mirah tried to stay close, but Lyrion hovered as well, and any time Ariadne tried to make some distance between herself and the others, Lyrion was there to cut her off.

"He's only trying to protect you," Mirah said quietly as they made camp on the first night.

The Druids had lifted the spell so Ariadne could sleep peacefully—or as best as she could—throughout the night. Ariadne bit into her apple as she plopped down on the dirt in front of the small fire. Mirah wrapped the blanket tighter around her shoulders and sat next to her. Brionna hovered behind them, bow in hand.

"He's pissing me off," Ariadne said through a mouthful of apple.

"We're all just scared," said Mirah. "That's all. Lyrion loves you. He's going to worry. Just be patient with him."

Ariadne glanced over at Lyrion, who had just returned from scouting the area with a few of the others. He caught her eye and made to come over to her, but Ariadne looked away. She needed to be alone for a moment. Or at least, as alone as she could get.

"You know I have no patience," Ariadne mumbled.

Mirah snorted. "Don't I know it."

"Do you think we'll find him?" Ariadne whispered, tossing the apple core into the flames.

"I have hope," said Mirah.

The tracking spell took them toward the Forest of Dean, just north of Avalon. They had been traveling for a few days now and had already turned off the King's Road to get deeper into the forest, despite Gawaine's protests. They passed through an abandoned Roman village and had to trek through a few marshes until they came to an ancient Briton road that was not used anymore. Nature had taken over most of the stones, and it was difficult to get through. The knights voiced hesitation, but the pull was strong, so Ariadne urged them to keep going. it was the right way, she was sure of it.

"Wait," Ariadne said suddenly as the sun was setting. She pulled Nerys to a halt. White light had shot out between two trees. Her stomach twisted like cramps. "There." She pointed toward it. "Something's there." Nausea crept up her throat, and she squeezed her eyes shut. Lyrion hurried over to her and grabbed Nerys's reins. Mirah and Jabir were not far behind him. Sweat pooled on her body and her stomach twisted again. Her breathing was shallow against the pain.

"Stay there," Gawaine told her, and he and Percival dismounted. Jabir followed them into the trees.

"I feel nothing here," said Gwenc'hlan, glancing to Ariadne. "Are you sure, my lady?"

"There's something with those trees," said Ariadne, not taking her eyes off them. "But something feels wrong." She could not explain it, but a wave of dread washed over her. She had a flashing image of Anwil's dead body lying in the grass covered in blood. She cried out.

"Ari! What is it?" Mirah reached for her, but Ariadne had already lost her grip on the horse. Lyrion and Lohengrin were fast, catching her before she fell.

"What do you mean?" Gwenc'hlan asked, dismounting his own horse and hurrying over to Ariadne.

"I don't know." Ariadne pressed her forehead into Lyrion's shoulder. The pain in her stomach grew worse, and she could not rid herself of the vision of Anwil. "I don't know. Something is *wrong*. I don't feel so good." She was sweaty under her leathers, yet her skin was cold.

Lyrion touched a hand to her forehead. "She's burning up!"

"I'll release the spell." Gwenc'hlan took her face in his hands. After a moment, the nausea faded, and she took a deep breath. She blinked her eyes, and no longer felt as if she were in a dream state. The ball of white light was gone, but Ariadne still felt clammy. Mirah pushed a waterskin into Ariadne's hands and ordered her to drink.

"How are you now?" Gwenc'hlan asked her quietly, genuine concern in his eyes.

"Fine," Ariadne mumbled after sipping the water. "I think. But can we try again? Anwil is—"

Gwenc'hlan shook his head. "It's too risky. That reaction . . . It was not good."

Ariadne opened her mouth to argue more, but Lyrion took her hand and gave it a slight tug. She clenched her jaw shut and yanked her hand from his grip. Mirah put a hand on her shoulder.

"Ari, what is it?" Mirah peered into her eyes, giving her a look that said she knew there was something more. Ariadne would tell her later.

"Take a bit more water," Gwenc'hlan said and then looked out over the brush. "Lord Gawaine, do you see anything?"

"Nothing unusual!" came his reply. "Wait! There's—what is that?"

Ariadne went to go for them, but Lyrion grabbed her arm as Gwenc'hlan and Brionna went to Gawaine and Percival. Ariadne whirled on Lyrion, glaring.

"Will you stop it?" she snapped.

"Stop what?" he said. "Trying to keep you from running off and doing something stupid?"

"I beg your pardon?"

Lyrion reached for her again, but Ariadne stepped back. "Ari, don't do this."

"Don't do what?"

"Don't—just—will you please just listen and do what you're told?"

Ariadne wanted to smack him. "I *always* do what I'm told," she hissed. "If I'm not following my mother's orders, I'm following Anwil's or Gawaine's or Brionna's! Because that's my *duty*. That's what I was born to do. I'm a princess, a *girl*. I was born to look pretty and stay quiet."

Lyrion shook his head and opened his mouth, but she cut him off and kept going.

"But I can't do it anymore. My brother is missing and it is my fault! Everything we've done so far has gone to shit, and this may be our only chance of finding Anwil, and I'll do whatever I can to do it!"

Lyrion stared at her, jaw open. But he just shook his head and walked away, mumbling to himself. Ariadne watched him leave, breathing hard. She turned on her heel and brushed past Mirah. She didn't get very far before someone called her name.

"What?" Ariadne snapped, whirling back around. "Who—" Her name was called again, this time behind her in the trees. No one in the party had called her name. Someone else was here.

Mirah suddenly braced and stood alert, as if listening for something.

"What is it?" Xiang asked her.

"Someone's here," Mirah whispered. "Someone's watching."

Ariadne's hands immediately went to her sword, and the knights followed suit. She looked through the tree line and over the brush, but could not see anyone. They were hiding.

Ariadne.

Ariadne looked to Mirah and did not like the way her face paled. Mirah clenched her fists, looking in the direction her father had left in. But he, nor Gawaine or Percival, were anywhere to be seen.

"Did you hear that?" Ariadne asked Mirah, and she nodded.

Brionna appeared at Ariadne's shoulder, bow nocked and drawn. "What did you hear?" she asked. Lyrion and Lohengrin were not far behind her. Xiang stuck close to Mirah, sword already drawn.

"What is it?" asked Lyrion, pulling his sword.

Ariadne!

Ariadne whirled on her heel again, yanking her sword from its sheath and holding it in front of her with both hands. She gripped the handle so hard her knuckles turned white. "Who is there?"

"I see no one," said Lyrion, looking around.

Ariadne's heart pounded, and a rustle echoed in the brush. Lyrion jumped in front of her, brandishing his sword with one arm and the other holding Ariadne behind him. Lohengrin joined them, guarding Ariadne's back. She tried to push Lyrion's arm away, but he wouldn't budge. She huffed out an angry breath of air and glared at him.

"Baba?" Mirah called, but no answer.

"Ariadne!"

"Who's there?" Lohengrin called, now stepping in front of both Lyrion and Ariadne. "Show yourself!"

"Ariadne, is that you, my dear?"

A man stepped out of the brush, and Brionna aimed her bow. The man looked right at Ariadne, and a wave of relief fell over his bearded face. He wore fine clothes: chain mail under a red tunic and a matching red cloak clasped with a gold chain of office. He looked vaguely familiar, as if she should know him. She adjusted her stance, holding her sword before her.

"Thank the gods, you found her." He took another step toward them, but Brionna stepped forward, pulling on the bowstring.

"Do not come any closer," she growled. "Who are you?"

The man, who was middle-aged with white in his red-blond hair, cocked his head, as if confused. "Do I know you, my lady?" he asked, but his gaze fell over her shoulder. "Ah, who is this young witch? A friend of Merlin's, perhaps?" Ariadne looked to Mirah, who held her chin high and narrowed her eyes at him. "Don't listen to him. He is made of magic. His lies will consume you. He is not real."

Ariadne's heart raced in her chest, and she gripped her sword tighter. If he was magic, Nimue must be near. Would Anwil be with her? Could they hold her off on their own? They had the Druids this time.

"Not real?" The man opened his arms and took another step, but Brionna pointed her bow right at his face.

"Stay back!"

"Come now." The man tried to push Brionna's arrow away with his hand, but she didn't budge.

A crack of thunder echoed overhead. Ariadne jumped and knocked into Lyrion. The sky was a clear blue. She held up her sword in front of her, almost like a shield. But then the air shifted, and silence consumed Ariadne. She couldn't breathe. The air was too heavy. She couldn't hear a thing. Her vision blurred, and her head swam. A loud piercing shrill erupted, and she cried out, falling to the ground on all fours. As sudden as it had come, it was gone. She let out a breath and nearly vomited onto the dirt.

"Ariadne, daughter!" Hands took hold of her shoulders and pulled her to her feet. She staggered, grabbing on to the arms that held her without thinking, and she froze. She stared into the face of that strange man. But he was older now, his hair almost pure white and wrinkles prominent on his face. "Are you well?"

Ariadne looked around. The Druids and Mirah were gone, as were Brionna and Lohengrin and Lyrion. Gawaine and Percival were there, but they looked different. Gawaine's hair was longer, and he was no longer poised and stoic, but carefree and walked with a slight swagger she had never seen in him before. Percival was more or less the same, but there was something off about him, something she could not place. She let go of the man and stepped away from him. Her hands went to her sword, but it was not at her hip. And it was not on the ground where she'd fallen either.

"Who are you?" she whispered. "Nimue? Were you sent by Nimue to kill me? Is that what you did with my brother?" She shoved the man, and he stumbled back, but Gawaine and Percival caught him before he fell.

"What in God's teeth is the matter with you, girl?" Gawaine growled at her, his eyes piercing. "How dare you treat your father so?"

Father? Ariadne shook her head. "No. No, my father is dead." She backed up some more. "You're fake. You're an illusion! Mirah!"

"Have you hit your head?" the old man asked. "Daughter, come—"

"Don't!" Ariadne spat at him. "Don't you look at me or speak to me!" A dagger was still attached to her belt, and she could feel the smaller one still in her boot. They weren't iron, but they were still sharp.

"This is why we shouldn't have brought her, my lord," said Gawaine. "Women are not cut out for battle."

Gawaine must have been an illusion too, as Ariadne knew well that he did not believe such a thing. He'd fought hard to change the law to allow women to become knights. Ariadne needed to leave. Somehow. She was in the same place as before, but even the nature was different. Had she somehow gone through a veil? The old man stepped toward her, and she had her dagger at his throat in an instant.

"You put that down right now, young lady!" he snapped.

"You are *not* my father!" she yelled back. "I don't know who or what you are, but my father died before I was born. You're an imposter! *You're not Arthur!*"

The man's face went from shock to anger, and he reached for her, but she slashed her dagger at him, catching his wrist. He called out in pain, grabbing on to his wound. His face twisted into a snarl, and he lunged at her. Ariadne yelled out as he tackled her to the ground. Her dagger flew out of her hand. She tried bucking him off, but he was strong. Stronger than the Black Knight at Anwil's wedding. She twisted and turned, trying to get a firm hold for a move Brionna had taught her, but he would not let go of her wrists. The knights didn't move; they just watched with blank eyes.

Ariadne fought against the man's hold, getting enough room to lift her knee and knock him hard in the groin. He yelped, but all it did was make him angrier, and his hands went to her throat, squeezing. She couldn't breathe. Her body panicked. In her struggle, her eyes caught Brionna's, who stepped through an invisible veil. She forced her body to relax and wove her hands within his arms and yanked them down and away from her, hard. He released her neck, and his palms fell on the ground on either side of her head. She coughed and punched at his face. It was weak but enough of a distraction. Ariadne shoved her other hand into his throat and brought her leg up and into his chest and pushed him away. She scrambled away, still coughing, but got back on her feet and grabbed her sword from the ground.

An arrow whizzed past her ear and buried itself in the man's chest. He screamed, and the sound that came from him was piercing. Brionna was in front of Ariadne now, her bow nocked and pointed right at the man. He screeched again and yanked the arrow from his chest. Spurts of blood followed, and he turned his glare to Brionna. She loosed an arrow again, but this time, he dodged it with a speed Ariadne could barely believe. He grabbed Brionna by the throat with one hand and tossed her like a rag doll.

"Brionna!" Ariadne yelled. The man turned to her again, and barely thinking, Ariadne grabbed the dagger from her boot and threw it at him. He caught it by the blade, and blood streamed from his fist. *Shit.*

An arrow struck him in the back of his hand. His skin blackened as if burned, and he howled. Brionna loosed another arrow. This time, it landed in his throat and pierced it straight through. He gurgled, stumbling, the skin on his neck singeing black. Ariadne backed away, bumping into someone. She froze, but when two hands took hold of her shoulders, and the smell of sage filled her nose, she whirled around, coming face-to-face with Mirah and Jabir. Jabir's eyes were set on the fake Arthur, his sword drawn and a white light engulfing his free hand.

"Step away," Jabir growled and ran for the man. But the fake Gawaine came back to life and swung his sword at Jabir.

"Mirah, what happened?" Ariadne said, her eyes locked on the fight.

"You disappeared!" Mirah gripped Ariadne's arm. "There was a horrible sound, and you were just gone! But I could hear you. Father and I broke through. Ari!"

Ari whirled around just in time to see the fake Arthur coming for her. Jabir tried to intervene, but the fake Gawaine would not let him. Ariadne yanked the dagger from Mirah's belt and shoved it into the man's diaphragm just before he could grab her.

He froze and gasped. He looked her in the eye. The entirety of his eyes turned pure black, and he fell to his knees. Ariadne let go of the dagger, and he tumbled over and fell still. The Gawaine fighting Jabir also disappeared, as well as all the other fake knights, as if they had never been there in the first place. The air cooled, and the wind switched.

"Ari!" Brionna's arms were around her, and Ariadne's vision was clouded by her thick black hair. Ariadne tried to move her arms, but she couldn't. Her limbs shook, and her breathing was ragged.

"What the fuck was that?" She panted into Brionna's shoulder.

"Watch your language!" Gawaine snapped, but he pulled her from Brionna. He held her tight against his chest, his armor cool against her cheek and poking at her stomach. He swore in Gaelic. "Scared me half to death with you disappearing." His arms shook, and Ariadne let herself return the embrace. She relaxed in Gawaine's arms, the real Gawaine.

Jabir knelt next to the fake Arthur, who no longer resembled the late king. He now bore bluish-gray skin with long ears and pointed features. A changeling. Ariadne pulled away from Gawaine as Mirah and Jabir took care of the changeling and laid it to rest.

Ariadne stepped away from the group, plopping down in the dirt and laying her arms on her knees. She closed her eyes, tilted her head up, and just breathed. Nausea churned her stomach again, but it wasn't as bad as before. She would need to get her bearings straight before they continued. It had been a close call with the illusion and changeling. Why had it changed into Arthur? Did Nimue hope to mess with her mind? Did she assume Ariadne had always wanted her father, that she would go willingly with him?

A shadow passed over her, and she blinked her eyes open. Lyrion stood over her, a stiff look on his face. He was probably angry at her outburst earlier, but she did not care.

"You're hurt," he said, his eyes on her neck.

She put a hand to her throat. Her skin was tender, and she hadn't processed that her neck still ached until now.

"We should head back to Camelot," he said, looking over his shoulder. "I'll tell Father—"

Ariadne jumped to her feet and yanked him back to her. "Absolutely not."

"Ari, you were almost killed!"

"I don't know if you realized," said Ariadne, pointing to where Jabir and Mirah had taken the changeling's body, "but I embedded that dagger in his chest! I can keep myself safe."

"You shouldn't have to!" Lyrion took her hand. "You should be back at Camelot, where you are safe with the other ladies, as is your place."

Ariadne's blood ran cold. She was vaguely aware of Lohengrin calling for his brother and Mirah calling her name, but she ignored them.

"My *place*?" Her voice shook with fury, and Lyrion went pale, his eyes wide.

"No. No, that's not what I meant," he said, shaking his head.

"Yes, it is," said Ariadne. "Or you wouldn't have said it."

"No, I meant—I meant—" Lyrion stumbled. "You're the princess. You shouldn't have to worry about things like this! That is *our* job."

"A knight's job?"

"Yes."

Ariadne huffed a laugh. "So what did you think I've been training for these past few years, then?" she said. "That I've been doing it for fun? Because I was bored?"

"I didn't think you'd actually fight!"

Ariadne opened and closed her mouth a few times, barely believing what she'd just heard. Out of all people, she never would have thought Lyrion believed such things.

"Well, surprise," she said, the words barely audible, and brushed past him, ignoring his calls for her.

⁂

They found a nearby village and made camp for the night just on the outskirts. Gawaine and Percival met with the villagers while the others set up for the night. Ariadne kept her distance from Lyrion, even though he kept shooting her looks. She barely spoke to anyone, needing to to be alone. She took her time with Nerys, letting her drink from a stream and cooling her off with the water.

Had everyone thought the same? Had they just been humoring her and hadn't expected her to actually participate? Is that why she hadn't been chosen for the upcoming Trials? Ariadne leaned her head against Nerys's neck and patted the mare's nose. Nerys huffed and leaned into Ariadne's touch. What else did she have to do to prove herself?

"You're a girl, Nerys," she mumbled to the horse. "And yet you and the other mares keep the males in line. What's your secret?"

"Knowing your own value." Brionna's voice startled her. The female knight crossed the path over to her. "I've never doubted you, Ari. You must stop second-guessing yourself and letting others make all your decisions for you."

"I don't—" Ariadne started, but truthfully, Brionna was right. She made it seem as if she did what she wished, but Ariadne always followed her duties, always did what was asked of her.

"I know you take your position quite seriously," Brionna said gently, "but you are letting it consume you. You are in the perfect position of power but have little royal expectations. You can do great things, Ari, of your own choosing, but first you must take control of yourself."

Ariadne didn't know what to say. She hadn't realized how far down the rabbit hole she had sunk herself.

"And Lyrion . . ." Brionna said. "Is still a boy. And insecure. A terrible combination when up against a confident and strong woman. Weak men tear women down to make themselves feel powerful. Do not let men make you doubt who and what you are."

Ariadne stared at her for a long while. Brionna was right. She was always right. Ariadne nodded, her throat tight. Brionna winked at her, and they walked back to camp. After Ari secured Nerys, she strode over to Gawaine, who had brought rabbits to cook over the fire.

"Tomorrow," Ariadne told him, "we ride to Avalon and get Merlin. Then, we find Anwil and bring him home."

Gawaine blinked at her, and the camp went quiet. After a long moment, Gawaine's lips cracked into a smile. "Aye."

CHAPTER THIRTY-ONE

ANWIL

Nimue took him to a small clearing in the dense woods. A fire was already crackling inside a ring of stones. The other priestess was already there, along with a few fae and a body-shaped blanket next to the priestess's feet. The other fae were no where to be seen. Nerves bubbled in his stomach and his every instinct was screaming at him that this was a bad idea. But what else could he do? He couldn't fight her on his own and his escapes were futile. If he played her game, he might have a chance.

"Who is that?" Anwil asked, pointing at the body shape, but Nimue ignored him.

She went straight to a makeshift table—a stone slab sitting on top of two thick tree stumps—that held the Treasures of

Briton she had stolen. Nimue picked up the Grail and Excalibur and returned to him. The sword sang to him again, and his arm reached to take it from her. This time, she gave it to him and held out the goblet. His grip on the sword was weak, but it vibrated in his hands, a comfortable warmth spreading over his skin. An ethereal tonal pitch reverberated in his ears.

"Just a minor cut on your hand will do," she said.

Anwil looked from her to the sword and to the goblet. He shouldn't do this. He should take the sword and kill her now and run, but he would surely be dead before he took his first step. The few fae that had gathered glared at him, and he turned back to Nimue, her expression unreadable. Despite his body's protests, he cut his hand and bit his lip to keep from making any noise. He let the blood drip into the chalice. The other priestess snatched the sword from him and shoved a cloth into his hands as Nimue pulled the Grail away.

He tied the fabric around his hand as Nimue stepped up to the fire and murmured words in another language. The fire grew with a loud whoosh, and Anwil took a step back, the heat too warm on his face. Melara picked up a ring and a vial of dried herbs and placed them into the goblet as Nimue's chants grew louder. The wind whirled around them, and Anwil's stomach turned. Melara dropped some of her own blood into the Grail, and then Nimue dumped the contents of the goblet into the fire. It hissed, and Nimue yanked the blanket away. It *was* a body. A man with dark hair and a clean-shaven face. He looked to be sleeping, but something was off. His skin was too smooth, too hard, as if he were carved from stone.

Nimue kept chanting and laid a hand on the sleeping man's forehead as the fire sizzled and hissed. A crack of thunder echoed overhead. The ground shook, and a gust of wind knocked Anwil off his feet, his knee cracking on something hard. He cried out as the wind roared in his ears, and he thought he heard someone scream. The fire, as if alive, stretched flames toward him. He scrambled away, tripping over a tree root and slamming himself on the ground just as a flame roared overhead. Although the flame didn't touch him, the heat burned his face, and he felt the same panic he had when he'd run into the flames in Camelot. He covered his face with his arms. The fire roared so loud it cut out all other sounds. He had no idea for how long. It felt like ages, when suddenly, it stopped, and everything went still.

Anwil slowly lowered his arms and pushed himself up. Melara was slumped on the ground, her eyes wide and glossy. Nimue leaned over the man, her forehead resting on his. The man no longer looked as if he were a statue. His skin was flush with color. Nimue whispered to him, but Anwil couldn't make out the words. He tried to push himself to his feet, but as soon as he put weight on his knee, a sharp shooting pain erupted, and his knee gave out. Anwil let out a groan as the man took in a huge breath and opened his eyes. Nimue pulled away from him, and the man looked up at her. He raised a shaking hand, and she grabbed hold of it and placed it on her cheek.

"My love," she whispered as tears fell down her face. "My love."

Love? Oh no. Anwil shuffled himself backwards, his knee stinging in pain with every movement.

"Nimue," the man whispered. "You did it."

Nimue let out a sob, and the man groaned as he sat up. Of course she had lied! There was never a veil to open. Anwil backed away more, but his movement caught the man's attention. His gaze locked on Anwil's, and he gave Anwil a look of such hatred it made his blood run cold.

"He still lives?" he hissed at Nimue.

"It took the wrong one," she said with a sob.

The man glanced at Melara's body on the ground, and Anwil realized what the spell had actually been for. The man had been dead. It was to bring him back to life. A life for a life. Anwil had a sinking feeling he knew who this man was.

"Then kill him," the man growled.

"I can't," said Nimue, gasping for breath.

The man cursed and pushed himself to his feet. Anwil once again tried to get on his own feet, but his knee screamed in protest. *Run, you daft idiot!*

The man picked up Excalibur and approached Anwil. Anwil froze on the post as the man hovered over him. He should get up and fight. He'd lose, but at least he wouldn't die a coward.

"It's as if I'm looking at Arthur himself." The man grabbed Anwil's arm and yanked him to his feet. Anwil hissed in pain, and the man's grip tightened. "I'll enjoy killing you. Fight me!" He shoved Anwil away. Anwil stumbled, catching himself on a broken tree. The man laughed.

"Perhaps you are not Arthur's son," he said, his eyes wild. "You look like him, but lack all his mannerisms. *Can* you fight?"

Anwil pushed himself to his feet, his injured leg shaking. He had no weapon, but he would face death head on.

The man raised Excalibur, , but another sword blocked it before it could come down on Anwil's head. A large, armored, figure stepped in front of Anwil.

"Let him go, Mordred."

Anwil's fear was confirmed. Mordred. Nimue's lover and Arthur's murderer. That was Nimue's plan all along. To bring Mordred back and finish the fight so Mordred could take the throne.

"Always the heroic savior." Mordred scoffed at the other man. "Looks like nothing has changed."

"And never will."

Mordred lunged at the man and Anwil limped as fast as he could to get away from their fight. He didn't make it far before Nimue caught him and tackled him to the ground. He pushed her away, but she was stronger than he'd realized. He felt a rock under his hand and used it to smack her in the face. She screamed, and her grip loosened enough for Anwil to scramble away.

"You cannot best me, Mordred!" the man yelled, blocking a swing from Mordred easily. "Stop this now!"

"And you cannot harm me while I wield Excalibur!" Mordred laughed and attacked again.

The other man ducked and landed a blow to Mordred's stomach. Mordred let out a cry and stumbled. "Seems that I can," he said.

Nimue got back to her feet and grabbed Anwil by the neck. Her face was twisted with fury and wet with tears. "*You* were supposed to die," she hissed. "You bastard son of a whore!"

A swish of swords rang out, and Mordred fell to his knees with a yell as Excalibur flew from his hands. He roared and made a lunge at the man, but he stuck his sword through Mordred's chest. Mordred grunted and choked on his breath. Nimue screamed and let Anwil fall to the ground, running to Mordred. Anwil swore as he hit his knee again, the pain knocking the breath from his body.

The man pulled his sword, now dripping with blood, from Mordred. He picked up Excalibur and ran to Anwil. "Come, boy!" He grabbed on to his arm, and Anwil tried to follow him, but his knee was in too much pain.

"I can't!"

The man ducked and draped Anwil's arm over his shoulder and half carried him away. Nimue was yelling, but Anwil dared not look back. They made it to a horse tied to a tree. The man sheathed his sword and boosted Anwil onto the horse's back. He stuck Excalibur into a pack tied to the saddle before mounting the horse himself and taking off. Anwil forced himself to not look back.

"They'll follow us!" he called to the man.

"No, they won't," he said over his shoulder. "Not in their conditions."

They rode hard through the forest, away from the roads. The man led his horse easily through the trees and brush as if he traveled through them a hundred times. When they finally slowed, the sun was setting, and they came to a cottage nestled between a tiny pond and an old stone temple that was mostly ruins. A large garden wound around the back, and a fence kept chickens, pigs, and goats inside. The animals made a ruckus as they approached, and a dog barked from inside. The man slid off the horse and held out his hands to help Anwil down.

"Knee injuries are some of the worst," the man grumbled, helping Anwil inside the house. "I dislocated mine in a tournament once. Nearly passed out seeing it sideways. Couldn't walk for months."

Once inside, they were greeted by a brown dog. He barked and sniffed Anwil as the man led him to a wooden chair in front of the hearth. As Anwil sat, the dog barked again, and the man scratched at its ears.

"That's enough, Cafall," he said. "He's our guest. Can you straighten that leg?"

Anwil did and sucked in a breath.

"We'll clean it up and put a splint on you," said the man. "I've got a crutch around here somewhere. You'll want to stay off it for a bit. I'll be right back."

The man left Anwil alone with the dog, who had stopped barking and was now sniffing his legs. Anwil held out a hand for the dog, and he sniffed that too. He scratched the dog's head and earned a few licks.

"Good boy," Anwil mumbled and looked around the room. Mismatched shelves hung about with jars of food and dried meat, along with various tools and dinnerware. Dried herbs hung from the thatched ceiling, and two mismatched doors were at the far end. The room reminded him a bit of Mirah's sheds at the herb gardens in Camelot. A pair of women's brand-new shoes sat next to the hearth, still wet with brown dye.

Anwil ran his hands through his hair and cringed. It was dirty. He needed a bath. He hadn't been allowed many with Nimue. He leaned back in the chair and closed his eyes. He lost track of how long he'd been gone from Camelot. And now because he was stupid, Camelot was in danger. He never should have helped Nimue. He should have known she was lying. He wasn't cut out to be king. This proved it. He put his whole country in even more danger. He'd have to give up the crown before he was given it.

The dog whined, and Anwil scratched his ears again. A noise sounded outside, a dull thud. The dog's ears perked up, and he barked. They'd found him —Nimue and Mordred—but then the man stepped inside and dropped two large leather bags on the floor. He shoved his long brown hair out of his face and sighed.

"Sorry about that," he said. "The animals get excited when I return. One of the goats tried to run free before I could close the gate. Let's look at that knee, shall we?" He knelt in front of Anwil, and Anwil rolled up his trousers. A large purple bruise was already forming.

"No cuts." The man gently poked around Anwil's knee. "Doesn't feel broken. Takes a lot to break a knee, anyway. I should know. Seems just a nasty bruise, but it worries me you can't walk on it. When you get back to Camelot, have Merlin look it over, just in case. I'll get you a cool cloth and a poultice to reduce the swelling."

The man left once again and returned with a small basin, then pulled one of the jars off the shelves. He handed them to Anwil, along with a clean cloth.

"Er, who are you?" Anwil asked.

The man let out a small laugh and put his hands on his hips. "Not sure if I should give you my name. But if I don't, you

won't trust me. And if I do, I'm not sure you'll believe me."
He sighed. "But . . . my name is Lancelot."

CHAPTER THIRTY-TWO

NIMUE

N imue was drained. It had taken all she had left to heal Mordred. That bastard Lancelot was supposed to be dead! She should have known, though. Being Vivienne's son, of course he would not die easily. And he'd snooped where he wasn't supposed to, just as he always had. Him and his savior complex.

But it didn't matter in the end. Mordred lived. She had pulled him from the In-Between—a place not of life, but not of death either. When Arthur mortally wounded Mordred at Camlann, Nimue had tried to keep him alive, but she hadn't the strength to pull him all the way back to the living. When Merlin caught her, in trying to stop her, he'd sent her to the In-Between as well. It had taken her years and most of her power to crawl back to the land of the living. She had sacrificed everything to get back to the living. Even her powers and it had taken her years to regain her strength. But during those years, she studied Camelot and how it changed, found where it was weakest. And now with Mordred returned, he will sit on the human throne, Briton will be returned to the fae, its rightful people, and the humans will be the ones to hide in fear and anguish.

"You're lost in anger again." Mordred slid his arms around her from behind. She had been staring out one window in the lounge overlooking the stream. Many of the fae had fled, fearing that humans could now gain access. She didn't blame them. The stronger ones had stayed, the ones willing to fight with her. She would have to create another safe haven for them soon, especially now that Avalon was lost to her. Vivienne had sealed it off before Nimue could stop her.

"We have much work to do," Nimue said. "Those Christian priests are more powerful than ever. Humans are denouncing the gods for the Christian prophet." There was once a time when the humans worshipped the gods and the fae. Many of the villages still did, but the nobles, the ones in power, were turning fast., and their influence was spreading. They needed to stop it before it was too late.

"I warned Arthur it would come to that," said Mordred. "That if he did not put a stop to it, the Christians would overpower us."

"I don't understand why anyone lets them. The messages they teach—sins, women unholy, an eternity in flames . . ."

"Manipulation and fear," Mordred said. "But do not worry yourself anymore, my love. Once I have Camelot, the priests will be silenced."

"Many of your old allies are gone," said Nimue, leaning her head back on his shoulder. "But Caradoc still stands with you. Though, his son Cerdic will have his throne soon. Caradoc is dying."

"And Lothian?"

"Awaiting our command. Agravaine still worships you."

Mordred chuckled and placed a kiss on her neck. "What of the other Briton kingdoms?"

"Fully allied with the Pendragons, unfortunately." Her eyes fluttered shut at his featherlight kisses. "Bors of Gwent might be easily swayed. He is frustratingly Christian, but a stupid oaf. We should be able to take Gwent easily. Constantine's daughter wedded the Pendragon boy. There is a new king of Ireland, though. One who defeated the Christians in his own lands."

"You have been working hard in my absence." Mordred spun her around in his arms. "You never cease to amaze me." He kissed her, and she melted. She had missed him, this feeling, his smell. He made her feel alive like nothing else had ever done, even magic. Her anger and frustration faded away as he pushed into the kiss, gripping her hips. She ground herself against him needing to feel more. He backed her into the wall, the cool stones digging into her back.

"We need to kill the boy," he whispered against her lips. "Start the crumbling of Camelot now."

He took her leg and hooked it around his hips. She groaned. She didn't want to think of Camelot right now. She fumbled with his tunic, trying to get it over his head. Mordred laughed against her throat, the sound reverberating through her. He pulled away from her and she made a sound of disappointment, but he led her to her bedroom, leaving a trail of clothing on the way.

Moonlight poured over Nimue as she shifted closer to Mordred in the large bed. She basked in the light, feeling the energy and magic surround her. She could feel it swirl in Mordred's veins. Power from his mother, Morgana, and now the Pendragons. He would be unstoppable. His chest softly rose and fell in his sleep and she trailed her fingertips along his bare chest. She had waited for this moment for so long. To just be with him, her match, her equal.

"That tickles," he whispered, eyes still closed. She kissed his throat and he shifted, pulling her to him, and her own eyes fluttered shut as sleep finally took her.

"Guinevere sits on the throne," Nimue said the next morning as she and Mordred packed for travel.

Mordred's eyebrows shot up and he nearly dropped the pack he was filling. "Guinevere?"

Nimue nodded, adjusting her cloak. "Merlin convinced the kings to make her regent after Camlann. She's been ruling with a tight grasp ever since."

"Of course it was Merlin," he said. "But you took care of him, yes?"

Nimue smirked and nodded. Merlin would suffer the same fate as her. A slow and painful death, devoid of magic. She'd crushed his staff and hidden him away where no would would dare look. He was most likely dead already, as was her sister. Although Nimue lost in the fight, she knew Vivienne had drained her powers. She had spent far too long in the human lands. Vivienne would never be able to leave Avalon now.

"Then why are we in this Roman ruin and not under the apple trees in Avalon?" Mordred said following her outside to the horses Thistle and procured for them.

"I cannot open the gateway." Nimue strapped her pack onto the saddle of the gray mare. "Vivienne sealed it shut against everyone."

"Perhaps I can." Mordred climbed onto the tall, brown gelding. "My powers are different now."

"I thought you wanted Camelot?"

"If we take Avalon," said Mordred, "then we'll have more strength to take Camelot. The Druids would be ours to command."

"Oh," she said. She had forgotten the Druids also get their powers from Avalon. "Yes. They would be."

Mordred grinned. "So we head to Avalon, where you shall be made high priestess and Lady of the Lake. You'll have all of Vivienne's powers, and you will be unstoppable."

Nimue matched his grin.

"To a new and brighter future." Mordred reached to take her hand. "To a free world."

CHAPTER THIRTY-THREE

ARIADNE

Ariadne, Jabir, and Mirah led the knights and Druids to Avalon. Lyrion stayed far behind her, toward the back of the company, and Ariadne did not feel guilty about it. She was still angry with him, and herself for not seeing how he felt earlier. If Lyrion was not the only one who thought she was was just playing around, she would show them just how serious she was about becoming a knight. A newfound determination rose in her gut. There was no room for failure in this mission. She *had* to succeed.

When they came to the Tor, Ariadne halted Nerys and stared up in awe. She had never been to Glastonbury and was instantly entranced. The rolling bright green hill—so green, even in autumn—overlooked Briton like a king on his throne. Ariadne wanted to climb it, to see the view from the very top, but they had no time. They needed to hurry to the shores of the lake. They didn't even have time to stop and check on the abbey's rebuild.

As they rode closer to the lake, the air thickened, the sun darkened, and even the trees were less alive the closer they got to the shore. The trees sagged, and the shrubs and plants shriveled. The mist and fog were so dense that she could barely see in front of her. Even her breathing was hard in the thick air.

"Is it supposed to look like this?" Ariadne asked Mirah when they halted. The warm autumn colors were nowhere to be found in the muddy brown of the plant life.

"No," Mirah whispered, her eyes wide and face pale.

Jabir slid off his horse, and Mirah and Ariadne followed suit. The crunch of pebbles and sand under their boots echoed as if they were inside a cave and not on the shores of a lake.

"Stay close together," Gawaine called out to them as the rest dismounted their steeds.

"This is . . . This is . . ." Gwenc'hlan shook his head, stumbling over his words. "This is Nimue's doing. The Lady would never . . ."

"There was a fight." Sir Xiang walked to the shore and squatted to look at the sand. "Here. There's blood."

"That hasn't washed away?" Percival questioned.

"The air is still," said Mirah, an airy tone in her voice. "So still. I can't feel anything. The trees, the water . . . the air. Nothing."

Ariadne's stomach twisted and her instincts were telling her to turn and run the other way. Something was wrong. Very wrong.

"Neither can I," said Gwenc'hlan. "A ward was placed."

"Nimue?" Ariadne asked. She knew a little of wards. Merlin placed them around the city from time to time to fend off enemies or severe storms, but she had always been inside the castle when he did it.

"Mirah," said Sir Jabir. "See if you can open the veil."

Mirah shrugged off her cloak and boots and handed them to Ariadne.

"What—" But Mirah was already trekking into the water. "Wait, Mirah! It's freezing!"

Mirah ignored her and kept going until she was waist deep. She lifted her arms to the sky as if to welcome an embrace and tipped her head back. For a moment, nothing happened. Then the water moved. Gently at first, rocking back and forth, but when the wind whirled, the waves that rose made Ariadne panic and run for Mirah, but Jabir held her back.

"Wait," he said, his eyes never leaving his daughter. He gripped Ariadne's arm tight, and she could feel a hum coming from his fingers.

"Ari!" Mirah called. Her voice bounced off the trees and the ground, swirling around as if it had left her body completely. "Ari, I need you!"

Jabir let go of Ariadne, and she tore off, Mirah's cloak and boots dropping from her hands. She heard Lyrion call her name, but she ignored him and splashed into the freezing water that felt like knives against her skin. Ariadne charged to Mirah, pushing against the strengthening current. Her armor held her down, but Ariadne made it to her. Mirah didn't look at her, but she held out her hand, and Ariadne took it. Her skin was ice cold, but Ariadne held tight. A shock spread up her arm, and she cried out, but Mirah's grip didn't let up. Her eyes were wide and white, as if they had rolled back into her head. Ariadne's body vibrated, and a warmth spread about her chest. Words echoed in her mind—Mirah's voice, but she couldn't make out the words. The water crashed around them, and Ariadne closed her eyes, digging her feet into the sand below. The rocking waves came to a halt, and Ariadne opened her eyes.

The fog drifted away, and the water settled into a calm and gentle rocking, like a caress over her. The sun poked through the clouds, streaming into the water.

The Isle of Avalon was now in sight, and Ariadne's breath hitched in her throat. It was a small island, but lush with green trees surrounding a large stone temple. Gooseflesh emerged on Ariadne's skin, and she felt a sense of home, as if she had known this place her whole life. But she had never been to Avalon before.

Mirah lowered her arms but did not loosen her grip on Ariadne as a boat with a single rider glided toward them. The figure was hidden under a hooded cloak.

"Mirah?" Ariadne whispered. Mirah blinked, her eyes returning to normal. She exhaled. "Are you all right?"

Mirah nodded as the boat approached them. The figure removed their hood and revealed themselves as a priestess. She was tall, with brown skin, short cropped black curls, and long pointed ears. Her eyes were a vivid purple, just like the Lady of the Lake's. Her silvery blue robes glimmered and moved as if they were made from water itself. The priestess regarded them with a sharp stare as the boat pulled up next to them.

"You hold great magic within you," she said. Her eyes turned to Ariadne. "The female Pendragon. I should have known. No one else could have gotten through our wards. Come, then."

Ariadne shared a glance with Mirah and then back to the shore, where the knights and Druids had lined up to watch them. Ariadne caught Gawaine's eye, and he nodded.

The priestess stood in the boat and held out her hand. Mirah took it and stepped into the boat as if climbing stairs. Ariadne did the same, surprised to find steps under her feet. As soon as she stepped into the boat, she was dry and warm. As was Mirah.

They rode in silence, but it did not take them long to reach the shores of the small island. The boat stopped at a rocky shoreline, and they carefully stepped over the boat and onto the path of rocks, through the water, and onto the soft moss.

The air was much warmer on the isle, and the trees were bright green, filled with apples and other fruits. A small vineyard wove through bushes and statues and bright colorful flowers. Wooden huts were scattered about, and a winding stone path led to the temple in the middle.

"This way," the priestess said, stepping onto the winding stone path.

Ariadne and Mirah followed. The hut houses were empty and still. Ariadne thought it odd not to see any animals scurrying about, but they were on an island. Perhaps there truly weren't any animals.

They reached the temple, and Ariadne was surprised to see how much it resembled Stonehenge. But the stone towers were not alone. A small stone building sat behind them.

Ariadne and Mirah followed the priestess up the steps and into the atrium. Instead of doors, there were drapes of silken fabrics and vines. Statues and shrines of the various gods and goddesses were scattered about. Ariadne recognized most of them: Belenus, Ceridwen, Brigantia, Cernunnos, Epona, Morrigan, Mab, Saitada. They were surrounded by candles and small fountains.

The priestess disappeared through a veil, and Mirah took Ariadne's hand as they ducked under the fabric. They were met with a room full of priestesses surrounding an enormous bed.

The area was furnished like a living space, with open windows in the stone walls. Lady Vivienne lay in the bed, her gray skin dull and sunken. Even her hair did not shine.

Mirah gasped. "What happened?"

Ariadne shook her head. No. The Lady of the Lake could not be hurt. She was all-powerful, was she not? She was part of myths and legends, of the gods themselves. How could she be so hurt?

"Nimue," the priestess answered. "We were ambushed."

"What about Merlin?" Ariadne asked.

"Who are you?" a priestess with tanned skin and gold hair asked. Her eyes were the same purple. They all had the same eyes.

"I am Mirah, daughter of Nazrine and Jabir," said Mirah. "And this is Ariadne Pendragon, daughter of—"

"Arthur," the gold-haired priestess whispered. "I see. Why are you here?"

"They ask for aid against Nimue," answered the priestess from the boat.

"What happened to Merlin, though?" Ariadne pressed. Mirah squeezed her hand as some priestesses gave Ariadne warning looks.

"Nimue ambushed us," the priestess explained. "She killed our fellow sisters, sent Merlin somewhere, and tried to get into Avalon. She almost succeeded. Vivienne sacrificed herself to save all of us, to save Avalon. She cast a powerful ward over

Avalon so Nimue, nor anyone else, could enter. We had to send everyone else away."

"Is she . . . dead?" Ariadne whispered.

The priestess shook her head. "No." She sat down on the side of Vivienne's bed. "Not yet. She is holding on, protecting us. But for how long, we do not know."

Ariadne had a thousand questions ready to burst over her tongue. Why had they waited so long to help? The priestesses had sent messengers before. Had they not heard them? Where was Merlin? But she kept her questions to herself.

"Nimue took Anwil," Ariadne said before she could help herself. "And burned the market down. Did you know that?"

The priestesses glanced around at each other. "No," the boat priestess answered for them. "We did not know. Vivienne's wards also kept us in."

"Then how did you hear us?" Ariadne questioned.

"Your combined magic is powerful," she said. "More powerful than anything I have seen in a long time."

"I don't have any magic." Ariadne shook her head, confused, but the priestess smiled at her.

"Oh, but you do," she said. "You just have not found it yet. I am Uira, I will aid you in your task of stopping Nimue. However, the rest of my sisters will have to stay here and guard over Vivienne. If anyone learns that the Lady of the Veils is dying, it would put both realms in grave danger. Now come. If I am to go with you, I will need supplies."

Ariadne was in awe of the island as Uira gathered her supplies. Everything was so much more alive there. She wanted to stay in Avalon forever and eat apples under the trees and swim in the lake, but she didn't have time to savor any of it, as Uira had quickly changed into a woolen tunic and trousers, with a heavy cloak and a bag over her shoulders. It was a complete contrast to her blue robes. If not for her ears and eyes, she would look like any ordinary human.

Uira brought Mirah and Ariadne back to the lake shore, where the knights and Druids were waiting, and relayed the news about Lady Vivienne.

"Who will take her place?" Gwenc'hlan asked, standing from the log he sat on. His eyes were red, as if he had been crying.

"We do not yet know," Uira answered gently.

"We're going to find Merlin," Ariadne interjected before anyone else could start talking or asking questions. She was growing anxious. They needed to move.

"How will we do that?" said Gawaine. "We've come up short locating Anwil."

Uira glanced at Gwenc'hlan. "There is someone who could help who is more powerful than I. More powerful than Merlin," she said.

Ariadne looked at her, confused. Who was more powerful than Merlin besides the Lady of the Lake?

"Absolutely not," Gawaine growled, his face turning red.

"Wait, wha—" Ariadne tried, but Uira interrupted her.

"She could find—"

"*She* cannot be trusted," said Percival, putting a hand on Gawaine's arm. "And I do not think she would help. Not after . . ."

"Not after what?" said Ariadne. "Who?"

No one answered for a long moment. Ariadne even looked to Mirah, who was just as confused as she. If there was someone as powerful as Merlin, why had they not gone to her earlier?

"Tell me now!" Ariadne demanded.

It was Uira who answered. "Morgana le Fey."

CHAPTER THIRTY-FOUR

ANWIL

The cloth slid from Anwil's hand, and he stared at him, open jawed. "S-Sorry?" he said. "Lancelot? *The* Lancelot?"

"I'm the only Lancelot I've ever come across." He pulled up a stool and sat across from Anwil. He picked the cloth up off the floor and brushed it off. "But if you mean Lancelot, disgraced Knight of the Round Table, then yes, 'tis I."

"I thought . . . We . . . You're not dead?"

Lancelot laughed. "No, not dead yet," he said. "Have you done this before?" He gestured to the jar.

Anwil shook his head. Lancelot took the jar and basin from Anwil and began to work. Anwil stared at him, jaw open.

Lancelot was far older than his mother, and yet he was sitting in front of him not looking a day over forty.

"May I ask a possibly insensitive question?" Anwil said as Lancelot mixed ingredients.

His eyebrows raised. "Perhaps."

"You look young," said Anwil. "Younger than . . ."

Lancelot laughed again. "That wasn't a question. But I am far older than I look. That's what having a faerie mother will do. I inherited little magic from Vivienne, but I did get blessed with a long life. May I ask you some questions now?"

Anwil nodded as Lancelot wrapped the cloth and goop of herbs around his knee.

"You are Arthur's son?"

Anwil nodded again, but turned his gaze down at the floor. He never felt like Arthur's son and was even more ashamed now. He made a horrible, dumb mistake, that might cost Camelot its kingdom. And he didn't even try to fight! He was a disgrace. He wasn't fit for the crown and now the Pendragon line would die with him. He failed.

"What were you doing bringing Mordred back?" Lancelot looked up at him and met his eye.

Anwil wanted to look anywhere but at Lancelot's strikingly blue eyes. "Camelot caught fire," he said. "And as I was trying to help, I was captured. She lied to me. She said she wanted to help the fae. She threatened my family."

312

Lancelot nodded. "Nimue has always been good at lying. She used to be like a second mother to me. And happy."

"What happened to her?"

Lancelot didn't reply right away. "A lot of things."

Anwil didn't press. Lancelot was done with the poultice for his knee, and Anwil unraveled his trouser leg down and carefully slipped on his boot.

"I hear you recently married." Lancelot stood from the stool and fiddled around in one of his cabinets. "Congratulations. I am sorry you were taken away from your new wife. We'll have you back soon enough. As soon as I can buy another horse, we'll be on our way. Though, I think I am still banished from Camelot." He ended his sentence with a laugh, but Anwil saw through it.

"You are welcome back at Camelot," Anwil said quietly. "The . . . rumors have died down. Besides, I'm told every day how much I look just like Arthur. So."

Lancelot gave him a look, and Anwil regretted what he'd said. Perhaps he shouldn't have said anything at all.

"You do, though," said Lancelot. "Very much. Hair is curlier, though. Probably get that from your mother." Lancelot cleared his throat and handed him some dried meat. "You said Camelot caught fire. What happened? How bad is it?"

Anwil nibbled on the meat. "Er, most of the market street and adjacent houses. I was taken before . . ." He shook his head. "I shouldn't have let her take me. If I were a better fighter—"

"Don't do that to yourself." Lancelot handed him a cup of water. "Nimue could have bested anyone. Rest now. Don't dwell on anything other than getting some sleep. You can have the bed."

"No, this is your home."

Lancelot chuckled. "And it'll be a bitch to get up off the floor with that knee. I would know. I have a roll I can lay out. Do not fret. Your knee will be fine in a few days. Stiff, but fine. Stay off it tonight, though, if you can."

Anwil drained the water, and Lancelot helped him over to the bed. It did not take long for him to fall asleep.

Something wet touched Anwil's face repeatedly. He groaned and tried to bat it away, but he was met with a solid force and soft fur. Anwil opened his eyes to meet the eyes of Cafall, who was licking his face. Anwil pushed him away and sat up. His head pounded, and he had to relieve himself. Looking around the cabin, he found Lancelot nowhere in sight. He pushed himself off the bed and groaned at his stiff joints. He could put a bit of weight on his knee, although it still pained him to put any weight on it at all. He used the table and walls to help him get outside. The sun was shining just above the skyline in hues of purples and pinks. His breath swirled in front of him, and he was quick to return to the warmth of the house. He did not have a cloak, and the thin clothes Nimue had given him did nothing to keep him warm.

He found the water basin refilled, and he splashed some water on his face. When he sat back down on the bed, the events of the past few weeks came hurling at him. He let himself fall on his back and stare at the ceiling. Camelot had been on fire. He had been kidnapped, and now Mordred was brought back to life? He did not know magic could bring back the dead. But it couldn't be a good thing. Mordred had rebelled against Arthur and had a very well-known loathing for Guinevere. And if he and Nimue were back together, it would be nothing but bad for them. Anwil needed to go home. To see if his mother, sister, and Yvanne were all right and what had happened to the city—how dire the fire was. They needed to put a stop to Nimue immediately.

Anwil pressed his hands to his eyes. He had so many questions. What had Lancelot been doing all these years? Was it even Lancelot? Anwil had been tricked by a glamour before. Perhaps he should sneak out while Lancelot was still away. But the horse was gone, and he wouldn't make it far limping.

The door burst open, and Anwil jumped, hissing at the pain in his knee. Cafall barked and wagged his tail as Lancelot stepped inside, carrying a dead rabbit.

"Breakfast," he said, holding it up. "How about a spicy stew, eh? Do you know how to skin a rabbit?"

"No."

"I'm surprised Gawaine didn't show you," said Lancelot. "Come on, then. I'll teach you how."

Not long later, Anwil and Lancelot were at his table, eating the savory stew. It was packed with herbs and vegetables from the jars Lancelot had on his shelves.

"I'm going to head down to the village today," Lancelot was saying. "The farmer there, Bryn, has a horse he should be able to spare for a bit."

"How far are we from Camelot?"

"Few days," said Lancelot. "We're near Dinas Emrys."

"Where Merlin saw Vortigern's fighting dragons," Anwil said, letting out a breath. "The King's Road doesn't go up this far north. It'll be a hard ride."

"You've been before?"

Anwil shook his head. "No, I like to study the maps, though," he said. "My sister and I weren't—aren't—allowed out of the castle much."

"Are you not the king?" said Lancelot. "Who wouldn't allow the king outside his own castle?"

"I have not yet been officially crowned," said Anwil, swirling his spoon around in the stew. "The coronation is set for the spring, just after Beltane."

"You're still king." Lancelot finished his stew and wiped his short beard with a cloth. "Your mother was voted as regent, and you were blessed as the king when you were born. You may refuse any orders."

"It is for our safety," said Anwil. "Gawaine and Mother see to it. Along with Sir Percival. Look what happened when I ventured into the city."

Lancelot stared at him a long while, and Anwil had to look down at his stew. Lancelot's gaze was too intense.

"Come with me to the village," Lancelot said finally.

"What about Nimue?"

"She'll be distracted with Mordred. We have a day or two to get a head start."

"Mordred is alive, then?"

"I assume no one is dead unless I hear their heart stop beating." Lancelot stood and cleared his bowl. "Besides, too much magic around at that moment for him to die. I just needed to buy some time and get you out."

"What were you doing there, anyway?" Anwil finished his stew with a big gulp. "How did you find us?"

"I'd been spying on that spot for a while." Lancelot grabbed one of the bags in the corner. "I can't do magic myself, but I can sense it. And I sensed it there. Now I know that's where Nimue has been living. She put up wards to camouflage the Roman manor house, so they may be gone now with that surge of power to bring back Mordred. Here." Lancelot tossed clothes at him: a thick green tunic, heavy trousers, and clean stockings.

Not long later, Lancelot was helping Anwil onto the horse since his knee was still stiff.

"What about your dog?" Anwil asked as they headed away.

"A beautiful lass will be home soon to care for him."

"Who?" Anwil asked before he could help himself.

Lancelot just chuckled and winked at him.

CHAPTER THIRTY-FIVE

GUINEVERE

Guinevere was not a crier. Do not let them see you cry. Crying was weak. But she did not know how much longer she could withstand her son missing. She had cried herself to sleep every night since. And now her little girl was out in the dangerous countryside, encountering God knew what. She shouldn't have let Ariadne go. She should have stayed her ground. But Guinevere also couldn't lock Ariadne up inside like a delicate princess in a tower. Ariadne was too much like her father. She was made to be a warrior. And if Guinevere had locked Ariadne in her rooms, she would have found a way out. It was less dangerous for Ariadne to go willingly with Gawaine and the knights. If anyone had a fighting chance against Nimue, it was Gawaine and Percival. They delt with her before, knew how she operated. And with the Druids and their magic, there was a chance...

Guinevere splashed cold water on her puffy face and finished dressing with Blanchefleur's help. Dindrane was busy with her spies and had been for a while, so Guinevere had relieved her of her lady's maid duties. Dindrane had uncovered little about Anwil or Ariadne, but she had heard rumblings of a coup. Guinevere had expected it. She was honestly quite surprised it hadn't already happened. With Bors bursting at the seams and Caradoc's known hatred of her, she'd expected them to have done it already. Or at least tried. Camelot's security was the best in Briton and surrounding countries. With the spy networks and Percival's training, nothing slipped past them. But now with the chaos, the king missing, and the princess gone and the best knights with her, it left Camelot vulnerable. Of course, Sir Malcom in control was just as good as Sir Percival, but he did not carry the same reputation as Arthur's knights.

Guinevere had already given Malcolm word to be ready for a coup and an order to monitor all the kings, even Constantine and Yvanne. She couldn't and wouldn't trust anyone at the moment.

Guinevere and Blanchefleur made their way to the gardens. Guinevere held tea every day with the ladies of court, despite the whispers about her character for it. The city was still cleaning up after the fire, and although many refugees had returned to the city or to the noble lands that had agreed to house them in their villages, having tea was seen as disrespectful. But tea was the best time for gossip, and gossip meant information. Many of the men talked freely in front of their wives without thinking twice, and many women were eager to share what they'd heard. They may have thought they weren't giving anything away, but Guinevere knew how to listen. As did the maids serving them. Dindrane had trained them herself.

"Good afternoon, ladies," Guinevere greeted them as she strode toward her seat. Although the air was cold, Guinevere did love the autumn foliage. It would most likely be the last tea outside, and Guinevere would savor this little peace.

Yvanne was already there, sitting with Lady Ellyn and Lady Tessa. Yvanne had thrown herself into helping with the refugees, caring for them and even helping the healers with their tasks. She reminded Guinevere of herself at her age, though Yvanne carried a sharper wit than she had. Guinevere had been hopelessly naïve as a young girl, but there was clever intelligence behind Yvanne's eyes. Guinevere, of course, had Yvanne looked into, but Dindrane had come up with nothing except that Yvanne was genuinely sad for Anwil's missing presence and that she cared for him. It put Guinevere at ease, at least a little.

"Your Grace," Lady Ilsa said as soon as Guinevere took her seat. "You'll be happy to know that the people arrived safely at my family estate."

"Good," Guinevere said as a maid filled her teacup. "I'll send a thank-you to your father." It did not go past Guinevere's notice that Lady Ilsa had been much more pleasant than usual this week. "Would you top off Lady Ilsa's tea, please?" Guinevere asked the maid quietly.

The maid caught her eye, nodded, and went over to Lady Ilsa, who looked smug to have the queen's favor. But Ilsa, in fact, had the opposite. Guinevere had just ordered the maid to keep an eye on her.

"Your Grace." Yvanne approached and curtsied.

"Darling." Guinevere reached a hand out to her, and Yvanne took it. "You do not have to curtsy to me anymore. We are a family now. Nor do you have to call me Your Grace. Sit."

Yvanne forced a smile and sat between Guinevere and Blanchefleur, who had moved her chair to make room. "Any news?" Yvanne whispered.

Guinevere shook her head, and Yvanne sniffed. Her eyes were red and a little puffy.

"Cerdic, this morning," Yvanne said. "I heard him talking to my father."

"What did he say?" Guinevere had to restrain herself not to seem too eager for the information.

"That Anwil is dead." Yvanne sobbed. "And that we should move on and vote for a new king already."

Blanchefleur reached across the table and took Yvanne's hand. "Did he have proof of this?"

Yvanne shook her head.

"Then don't think too much about his words," said Blanchefleur, but Guinevere could see the worry in her eyes too. Both her boys and husband were out with Ariadne. Blanchefleur was not new to her husband's dangerous quests, but it got no easier.

Guinevere caught the eye of the guard standing near the hedges across from her. She made a subtle shift of her eyes, and he left without a word. Guinevere put an arm around Yvanne.

"Blanche is right," she said. "There is no proof. And until we have proof, we will assume Anwil is alive and that he will come home. All the best knights are out looking for him, and they've never failed on a quest before. They won't fail on this one." Guinevere wished she could believe the words herself.

Yvanne sniffed, and Guinevere handed her a handkerchief.

The rest of the tea brought nothing. Ilsa prattled on about marriage pursuits, and Lady Tessa talked about her dog's new litter of puppies to be trained as companion dogs for those grieving loved ones. It was a rather disappointing tea for any useful information.

"Cerdic is growing louder by the day," Blanchefleur muttered as she and Guinevere walked back to her chambers later that day after tea.

"Once, I didn't think it was possible," said Guinevere. "He is planning something or is just utterly daft."

"Most likely both," said Blanchefleur, and they rounded the corner to the private wing. "Are you meeting with Dindrane tonight?"

"Yes. Looks like she's already here." Guinevere's door was ajar, with no guards on either side. She pushed it fully open, and a gasp left her mouth. Dindrane was indeed in the room, but gagged and bound to a chair with Bors's wife standing over her.

Blanchefleur gasped behind Guinevere as Queen Ingride turned to them. She had always shown herself to be a quiet and fearful woman. Guinevere assumed it was how Bors treated her, but the way Ingride looked at Guinevere now showed that it had all been a mask. Her brown hair was pulled into an elegant braid and a gold crown sat atop her head. Her green silk and gold dress hugged her figure nicely, and she topped it off with gold chains about her neck and waist. She had also touched her face with rouge and berry stain on her lips to enhance her features. Guinevere never would have guessed this could be the same woman.

"Clever," said Ingride, one arm folded across her chest and the other raised to her chin. "The men never would have guessed it was the women. And you used that against them."

Dindrane yelled against the gag, but her voice was muffled, and Guinevere couldn't make the out the words. Dindrane pulled against her restraints, but they didn't budge.

"Of course I figured it out," said Ingride, a painted eyebrow raised. "By now, my husband and Lord Cerdic will have infiltrated the city and called the kings to meet. I have, of course, already gathered allies in the court. Lady Ilsa's father is *quite* wealthy and terribly upset that you passed over his daughter for your son's wife."

Guinevere didn't respond. She needed Ingride to keep talking. Her heart pounded against her chest, but she kept her own face a mask of indifference, unwilling to give anything away. She calculated the information Ingride had already given up. Guinevere wasn't shocked to hear that it was Bors and Cerdic leading the coup. A bit surprised at Ilsa and her father, but not quite a shocking betrayal. If the kings were meeting all together, that was good. They were all in one place. The guards could lock them inside.

Dindrane yelled against her gag again, kicking her feet. Ingride regarded her with mild amusement. "I've always wanted to get her to stop talking," she said, looking down at Dindrane. "It'll be glorious not to have her in the castle when I'm High Queen."

Blanchefleur gasped again behind Guinevere.

"Not Lady Ilsa?" Guinevere raised an eyebrow.

"She'll marry my son." Ingride shrugged. "Now, if you would be so kind as to follow me back down to the throne room. Nothing bad has to happen." Ingride laid a hand to the back of Dindrane's chair.

Guinevere caught Dindrane's eye, and Dindrane gave a curt nod, letting Guinevere know she'd be okay before turning her wrath onto Ingride and trying to kick her. Dindrane yelled against her gag, but Ingride ignored her and crossed the room. That was her first mistake. Blanchefleur stepped around Guinevere, dagger in hand, and raised it to Ingride's throat. She hadn't been married to one of the best knights in the country and not learned anything from him.

"You move," said Blanchefleur, "and you'll lose your life."

Ingride glared at her as Guinevere crossed the room and untied Dindrane. As soon as the gag was out of her mouth, she was spitting profanities at Ingride.

"No one ever suspects the women, right?" said Guinevere to Ingride.

CHAPTER THIRTY-SIX

ARIADNE

A riadne's jaw dropped open.

"I thought Morgana was dead," she said, staring at Gawaine.

Gawaine did not look at her as he answered. "She's alive," he said, his glare instead fixed on Uira. "And has lived in solitude for years. We are not going to Morgana."

"But if she can find Anwil—"

"She won't do it." Percival shook his head. "We have wronged her."

Ariadne rolled her eyes. "Well, *I'm* going to her. And if you lot wish to stay behind, then so be it." Ariadne made to go to her horse, but Gawaine grabbed her arm.

"You can't go running across this country on your own," he said. "Come back to Camelot first."

"No." Ariadne yanked her arm from his grip. "I'm going to find my brother, no matter the cost!"

"Those are heavy words," said Sir Jabir. "Some costs are too great to bear."

Ariadne wanted to scream in frustration. Why weren't they doing everything they could to find Anwil? It seemed as if she was the only one who was willing to do whatever it took to find her brother. But instead of yelling or arguing, Ariadne looked to Gawaine, knowing how to hit him hard, even if she would regret it later.

"What would Arthur have done?" she asked him quietly. "If he were alive and Anwil was missing?"

Gawaine's face fell, and his mouth dropped open. But he said nothing. Ariadne looked around to the others, who bore similar looks. It was a low blow, but she had to do it. All her life she was told stories of how Arthur put himself in danger to save his friends, family, and people. She would do the same.

"That's what I thought," she said and turned to the priestess. "Can you take me to Morgana?"

Uira bowed her head.

"I'll go with you," said Mirah, taking Ariadne's arm. "You won't go alone. I want to find Anwil too."

Ariadne put her hand over Mirah's. "Thank you," she whispered.

"As will I," said Jabir.

Brionna stepped up next to Ariadne. "Is this what you wish?" she asked, and Ariadne nodded. "Then I shall go too. Uira, you may ride with me. My horse is big enough for two riders."

"Ari, Gawaine just said this was a bad idea." Lyrion came up to her and took her hand. "Morgana could hurt you or worse."

"I'll risk it," said Ariadne, and then she turned to speak to everyone. "Those of you who wish to return to Camelot may do so. Those who wish to join us to speak with Morgana, we leave now."

Lyrion protested again, but again, Ariadne ignored him and strode to Nerys. She untied her from the tree and climbed onto her back. She caught Gawaine's eye, and he stared at her for a long moment as the others shuffled around.

"Very well," Gawaine said finally. "Jabir, I'll trust you with them. The smaller the party the better. Morgana won't like an entire company on her doorstep, especially me and Percival."

"I'll go too," Lyrion said before anyone else could move.

"No, lad," said Gawaine. "You're with me."

Ariadne let out a breath of relief. She wouldn't be able to handle Lyrion's overbearing protectiveness.

"Lohengrin, you go too," Gawaine said, then turned back to Ariadne. "Remember what I taught you. Eyes and ears open. Trust no one."

Ariadne nodded. Jabir and Mirah mounted their own horses, and Brionna helped Uira onto hers. Lyrion still stood on the ground, anger and disbelief written in his features. Ariadne looked away from his gaze as Lohengrin trotted his horse over. He said goodbye to his brother, who just shook his head and went to his horse.

"He'll get over it," Lohengrin said as Gwenc'hlan spoke with Uira.

Ariadne glanced at Lyrion, but his back was turned to her. "Let's go."

"Go where?" said an unfamiliar voice.

All eyes looked to the tree line, where two figures on horseback rode out. Ariadne didn't immediately recognize either of them, but the woman looked so similar to Vivienne that it had to be Nimue. The other figure was a male with shoulder-length dark hair and a scar on his face. He was strikingly handsome, but his eyes were cold.

"Mordred?" Gawaine breathed, his face pale. "No. It cannot be."

Mordred? Ariadne looked to Brionna and Uira. Brionna's bow was drawn and nocked, and Uira was glaring at Nimue.

"What a pleasant surprise." Nimue grinned, looking around at all of them. "I'm so glad we waited a bit, or else we wouldn't have heard such wonderful information. My sister is dying. Avalon will need a new Lady indeed."

"You will never become Lady!" Uira snapped. She slid off Brionna's horse, eyes on Nimue. "You betrayed your oaths and tried to kill your own sister! You are not worthy."

Nimue just huffed. "I don't care what you think is worthy or not."

Ariadne's breath echoed in her ears, and her hands itched to grab her sword and dagger. She looked to Gawaine to wait for any command, but he was staring at the man he'd called Mordred, who grinned.

"Gawaine," he said. "You old rascal you. You know, the gray suits you. Makes you more handsome, I'd say. Still charming all the ladies?"

"Another illusion," Gawaine muttered, shaking his head. "Just like the one of Arthur. Don't listen to it!"

"Ari, Mirah, run," Brionna commanded, barely audible. "Now. Go."

Ariadne hesitated. She had Anwil! Anwil could be with them!

Mordred put a hand to his heart and stuck out his bottom lip. "You hurt me, Gawaine. Not happy to see an old friend?"

"Ari," Brionna growled. *"Go."*

Nimue twisted her gaze at them. Brionna loosed an arrow, but Nimue was too fast. She swatted it away and shot her arm out toward Brionna. A gust of wind knocked Brionna and her horse over. Her horse screamed, and Brionna fell to her back. Uira slid to her knees next to them. Nerys reared, and chaos erupted. Jabir and Gwenc'hlan ran in front of Ariadne and Mirah. Jabir lifted his hands, and they exploded in white light. Mordred leapt from his horse and lunged for Gawaine. Ariadne gripped at her reigns, trying to calm Nerys down.

"Take Mirah and run!" Jabir yelled, throwing a ball of white light at Nimue, which she dodged.

Ariadne took one look at the pure terror in Mirah's face and didn't protest. "Come on!" she hissed at her, and it was enough to snap Mirah from her shock. "Ha!" Both horses took off. Nimue was shouting, but Ariadne did not look back. She and Mirah urged their horses into the woods, leaping over fallen trees and dodging around brush.

Something whizzed past Ariadne's ear, and she cringed but ignored it, willing herself not to look back. Mirah was right beside her as they went deeper into the forest.

A crack echoed, and a tree snapped in half in front of them. The horses reared again, and Ariadne and Mirah were both thrown from the saddles. Ariadne landed hard on her shoulder, and Mirah on her stomach.

"Nerys!" Ariadne called, but the horses ran away. "Shit." She scrambled over to Mirah, grunting at the pain in her shoulder. "Mirah."

Mirah groaned, and Ariadne pulled her to her feet. "Come on." Ariadne took Mirah's hand, and they ran. Ariadne was slower than usual, her armor bogging her down, but she kept running, and Mirah kept up. Deep down, Ariadne was angry that she'd run from the fight, but keeping Mirah safe was more important.

An arrow whizzed past them again, and Mirah screamed. "Sh, sh, sh!" Ariadne hushed her and knocked her down in the brush. "Get down!" Ariadne hissed, pushing Mirah to her stomach. Ariadne hovered over her and stilled. She listened and peered through the branches of the bushes. Mirah's short breaths were the only thing she could hear, and Ariadne put a finger to her lips. Mirah put a hand over her mouth to stifle the noise.

"Come out, come out," Nimue's voice rang. "Wherever you are!"

Mirah cried into her hand. Ariadne pushed herself to her feet and drew her sword.

"Where's my brother, you bitch?" Ariadne stepped into the clearing.

Nimue was on her feet, walking toward her. Her long black hair was tied back into a braid, and she wore trousers with a blue cloak wrapped around her torso and shoulders. But she looked tired. Bags shown under her eyes, and her cheeks were sunken. Nimue stopped in her tracks and laughed. "Let's not name call, shall we?" she said, raising a delicate eyebrow. "Now, do you have any last words, Princess? I don't want to be rude."

"Where's. My. Brother?" Ariadne gritted through her teeth. She gripped her sword with both hands, digging her feet into the dirt.

Nimue shrugged. "I'm sure his body has been dragged off by the animals by now. Who knows, really?" Nimue raised her hands, and the ground rumbled.

Ariadne's breath sped up, and her heart raced. "No," she growled, steadying herself on her feet. "You're lying."

"I do not lie," said Nimue. "I am many things, but a liar is not one of them. Your brother is dead, girl." Nimue shot a burst of blue light from her hands, and Ariadne dropped to her stomach just before it hit her.

Another burst of light shot from Nimue, and it hit Ariadne. She screamed. Her whole body burned, but the pain was gone as fast as it had come, even though it felt like much longer.

Ariadne rolled over and got to her knees. She was hit again. And again, the pain was gone in a flash. Ariadne snatched a rock from beside her and threw it at Nimue. She smacked it away as Ariadne scrambled to her feet. Her limbs shook, but she brandished her sword.

Nimue snarled at her. "Why aren't you dying?" She threw another burst of light, but Mirah was suddenly in front of Ariadne, hands out in front of her, and Nimue's light bounced off something invisible and shot back at her. It hit her in the stomach, and she yelled in pain and rage.

Mirah whirled around to face Ari, but before she could open her mouth, Nimue grabbed her and put a dagger to her throat.

"Seems we have a pretty little witch on our hands," said Nimue. Her cold eyes bored into Ariadne. "Drop your sword."

Ariadne didn't move, but Mirah let out a whimper as the dagger pushed into her throat. Ariadne threw her sword down, eyes never leaving Nimue.

"Good girl," Nimue said with a sneer. "Now, I don't wish to kill a witch, but I will if you try anything again."

Ariadne didn't move. Her mind was racing. She had good aim with a throwing dagger, and she had one made of iron in her boot, but if she reached for it, Nimue would slice Mirah's throat before she could get it out of her boot. They were too far from the knights. Ariadne would have to get closer to Nimue somehow. She racked her brain, trying to remember if Brionna had taught her about anything like this.

"What do you want?" Ariadne asked. She caught Mirah's eye and screamed in her mind. *Come on, Mirah. Do something. I know you can do it.* Ariadne pleaded at her with her eyes, hoping Mirah would understand.

Nimue huffed a laugh. "I want you to die."

"Why?" said Ariadne. "I never did anything to you."

"Oh, my dear." Nimue laughed again, jerking Mirah. "It's nothing personal. But the Pendragons must go."

Come on, Mirah. Come on!

Mirah jerked her elbow back, hitting Nimue in the stomach hard, and then slammed down on her foot. Nimue cried out and tumbled, and Ariadne yanked the dagger from her boot and threw it at Nimue, catching her in the shoulder.

Nimue let out an earth-shattering scream. Ariadne grabbed her sword as Mirah ran. Ariadne pulled another dagger from her other boot and threw that too, but Nimue smacked it away with a grunt. Blood seeped through her shirt. The skin of her neck just above the wound blackened. Ariadne had known the fae had an aversion to iron, but she never knew what happened to them. Nimue pulled the dagger from her shoulder with another scream as Mirah hid behind Ariadne.

Ariadne held her sword in front of her, her eyes on Nimue, but her ears were open to the surrounding sounds.

"You will die," Nimue growled. She shot her good arm out, and the ground rumbled. Mirah grabbed on to Ariadne as fat vines shot up from the ground and reached for them. Ariadne sliced at them with her sword, and Mirah pulled her dagger and stabbed at them. Ariadne let out a scream as one of them caught her in the ribs, but as soon as it made contact with her vines shot back into the earth. Nimue looked at them in pure bewilderment. She threw her hands out again and the vines returned.

"Mirah, can you curse her or something?" Ariadne asked, slicing at another vine that came to her face.

"I've never tried before!" Mirah ducked from a vine as Nimue came toward them. Her purple eyes were now black, and her face twisted with pain and rage. "Stay back!" Mirah shot out her hand, and a slight gust of wind emerged, hitting Nimue enough to cause her to stumble.

336

"Don't play magic with me, girl!" Nimue snarled.

The vines stopped and shot back into the earth. Nimue was only a few steps away, and Ariadne wished she had a bow. She raised her sword, but Nimue raised her hand, and Ariadne screamed as the sword in her hand burned. She dropped it, her hands stinging. Nimue grabbed at her face, her fingers digging into Ariadne's cheeks. Ariadne shoved her hard right in her wound. Nimue yelled and stumbled back. Sweat dripped on her forehead. The iron must've been taking a toll on her. Mirah whispered something, and a poof of powder exploded in Nimue's face. She coughed. Ariadne grabbed Mirah's hand and took off.

"What was that?" Ariadne asked as they ran.

"Dried herbs I had in my pack!" Mirah answered, jumping over a large root.

They came to a halt when Nimue appeared right in front of them. On instinct, Ariadne pushed Mirah behind her, then pointed her sword at Nimue.

"Do you really think that'll work on me, girl?" Nimue hissed.

"It's made of iron. I see what my dagger did to you. Your neck is black. And you're struggling. Are you dying?"

Nimue scoffed. "It'll take more than that to kill me." She lifted her good arm again, but a raging scream of pain echoed through the trees. Nimue whirled around, and then she was gone.

"That sounded human," Mirah said.

"The others!" Ariadne gasped. "You can come with me or find a village and get word to Mother that we need backup."

"I'll come with you," Mirah said. "There's no time to send word."

They ran back to the shores, but by the time they'd arrived, they were too late. Bodies lay about the shore, and Mordred thrust his sword straight through Gawaine's breastplate. The tip shot out Gawaine's back, dripping with blood.

"NO!" Ariadne roared and took off, ignoring Mirah's calls. Loathing and rage pumped through her veins as she ran to Mordred, screaming. He turned to her, eyes widening a moment before pulling his sword from Gawaine, pushing him over, and turning on Ariadne.

Their swords clashed, and Ariadne's handed vibrated from the strength of his hit. She swung and swung, seeing nothing but red. Mordred blocked her easily and even laughed, but she kept going. Kept swinging. Her lungs burned, and her heart raced, but she ignored the pain.

"How wonderful." Mordred laughed. "I always told Uncle to let the women fight, that they were equal to men, but he wouldn't hear a word of it! You fight just like him!"

Ariadne yelled again and slashed at his side, but Mordred caught it and grabbed hold of her hands over her hilt.

"You have such fire," Mordred said, his face close to hers. "Such passion. Such rage and power. We could be great allies, you and I."

"Never," Ariadne gritted, trying to yank her sword away, but Mordred barely noticed her pulling.

"Oh, come now," he said in a sweet voice that dripped with poison. "Think about it. How many lies have you been told? How many secrets kept from you? How many have held you back? Your brother saw the truth. He helped us. You can too."

"Fuck you!" Ariadne growled, and Mordred let her sword go. She stumbled back, and Nimue came up beside Mordred, holding her shoulder and looking pale. Mordred did a double take and wrapped an arm around Nimue's waist.

"Think about it," Mordred repeated to Ariadne. "Think of all the lies and how trapped you are in Camelot. When you want freedom, just call for me."

And then he was gone. Disappeared as if he and Nimue were never there. Ariadne stared at the spot where they had been until Mirah called her name. Ariadne whirled around. Jabir was helping Brionna to stand, blood streaming down her face. The Druids and Uira were dead, their bodies scattered about the sand and shriveled as if they had been dead for years.

But the sight that ripped Ariadne's heart from her chest was Lohengrin lying atop Lyrion's body, sobbing, and Gawaine and Percival lying beside them.

Ariadne gasped, her body shaking. "No." Hot tears ran down her cheeks. She dropped her sword and stumbled over to them. "No, no, no, no."

She fell to her knees, hands hovering over Gawaine and Lyrion. Their eyes were still open, glossy and staring at nothing. Her chest tightened. She couldn't breathe. Her breaths came in gasps. This couldn't be happening. They weren't dead. They couldn't be.

"No," she whispered, tears dropping onto her knees. "I'm sorry. I'm so sorry." She laid her head on Gawaine's chest and cried.

CHAPTER THIRTY-SEVEN

MERLIN

M erlin had lost track of the time he'd spent in the cave. He was weak. He had been without food for too long. Water was scarce, but there was a dripping from the waterfall, and he used that to catch fresh water in his hands to drink when he needed to. But he was finding it harder and harder to gather the strength to even do that. Without his staff, he aged quickly. The crystal entombed in it had been a significant source of power for him, enhancing his own magic. He was only half-fae; his mother was purely human. While his father had been a powerful wizard, born of the goddess Ceridwen,

Merlin was limited in his own powers by his human blood. He needed that crystal to stay strong.

He'd fought against the cave's wards for days, perhaps weeks—he didn't know. He couldn't break through. Without his staff, he was useless. And that angered him. He was *Merlin*! Merlin, the most powerful wizard and magic user next to the gods themselves, and he couldn't break through a simple ward. How had Nimue trapped him? There had to be some secret. There had to be an answer!

He pushed himself up off the floor of the cave and staggered to the cave's entrance once more. The sight was magnificent. The waterfall, the shores, the roaring of the ocean winds. It was one of the most magical places in Briton. Nimue must have used that magic to amplify her own. There was no other way she could have been so successful. Or perhaps it wasn't Nimue after all? She had many friends amongst the gods and fae. Or at least, she did.

Merlin fell to his knees and did something he had not done in a long time. He prayed. He prayed to the gods of the land and sky. He prayed to his grandmother, Ceridwen, begging for her to hear him.

Merlin, the wind whispered.

Merlin's eyes snapped open. The cave rumbled. Rocks fell from the ceiling, and Merlin covered his head, dodging the falling stone. The wind whispered his name again, and he followed the voice. Followed it out of the cave . . . and onto the shores, just in time for the cave to close in on itself.

Merlin scrambled away, breathing hard and tripping in the sand. When the quaking stopped, he fell to the ground, his head spinning.

A hand rested on his shoulder. He blinked his eyes open, and a face swirled into vision. A beautiful female face with bright green eyes and golden hair the color of the sun.

"Merlin," she whispered. "My boy. It is time to come home."

Merlin shook his head. "No, lady," he said to his grandmother. "I must . . . I must repent for my sins. I must stay."

Ceridwen shook her head. "The Pendragons no longer need you. You have done enough."

He gasped. "What about Vivienne?"

Ceridwen's smile faltered and she did not answer.

"No." Merlin sobbed. "No, we had so much more time together. So much time . . . lost . . ."

Ceridwen's grip on his shoulder tightened. "Rest now, Merlin."

Merlin's eyes closed, and he drifted away.

CHAPTER THIRTY-EIGHT

NIMUE

Nimue hissed as Mordred cleaned her wounded shoulder. He had returned them to the Roman manor house and immediately gone to work on her. The iron in the dagger had burned her entire body and left her arm useless. She would need weeks to heal.

"I told you to wear armor," Mordred hissed as he bandaged the wound. The blackness had already faded, thanks to the potions and tonics she had made for the other fae. "You're getting arrogant. And you need to stop playing with your food."

Nimue glared at him but did not respond. She hadn't expected to find the knights at Avalon, nor had she expected the Pendragon girl to have such power in her. If Nimue had been at full strength, she would have killed her outright. She *should* have killed her outright. The witch with her had proven to be of no consequence, despite the power in her. She didn't know how to use it properly or fight. Probably Merlin's doing. He never wanted his students to know their full potential. Nimue knew that from experience.

"We need more protection," said Mordred. "I'll ride to Lothian and take the men Agravaine has offered. You should return to the Otherworld and gather forces there."

Nimue hopped up from her chair and winced. Her arm throbbed. "No, I'm not leaving you. Not again." She slid her hands up his chest. "I just got you back."

Mordred sighed and slipped his hands on her hips. "I love you, Nimue," he murmured, nudging his nose against hers, "but you have made mindless mistakes. And now we must rectify them."

She pushed away from him. "What mistakes?" she snapped.

"Not killing the boy, for one," said Mordred. "Not killing the girl and not killing your sister. Need I go on?"

"I tried!" Nimue snarled. "They are protected! My magic didn't work on the stupid girl, and I needed the boy's blood to be fresh and living! I needed it *for you*. The boy was supposed to be the one to die when you returned, not Melara! It is not my fault the gods chose her over him!"

Nimue let out a sob. Melara had been her oldest and dearest friend. If she had known, she would have sent Melara far away.

Now she had to live with the guilt and shame. Even the fae she had housed had fled in anger over Melara's death.

"What have you done with Merlin?" Mordred asked.

Nimue stared at him, seething. "Merlin is trapped, dying a slow and painful death."

Mordred scoffed. "Is he?" He folded his arms across his chest and leaned against the table. "Or has he escaped and returned to the Otherworld with his grandmother?"

Nimue froze. "How do you know that?"

"You're not the only one who knows how to scry, my love. Mother taught me well."

"I needed my strength to kill Vivienne," Nimue said. "To get into Avalon!"

"And yet, you failed!" Mordred flew across the room, his face inches from hers. "You have always been careless and arrogant. It will be your downfall, Nimue."

Nimue growled at him and bared her teeth. "How dare you," she hissed. "You ungrateful bastard! I brought you back from the In-Between so you could be free and we could be together, and this is how you treat me?"

"Don't guilt me," Mordred snarled. "It won't work." He turned away from her and strode over to the table and picked up a small bottle. He popped the cork out and sniffed it. "It's no good."

"What isn't?"

"This tonic." He turned and tossed it to her. She caught it with her good hand. "We need more."

"I'm not strong enough to make it," she said quietly, sniffing it, and almost gagged.

"We'll stop by Mother's once you've rested a while. Then we shall head to Lothian."

"Do you not remember my and your mother's strained relationship?" Nimue said stiffly.

Mordred gathered the Treasures of Briton and stuffed them into a bag. "Of course I do," he said without looking at her. "Are you forgetting her soft spot for her only son?" He crossed the room, kissed her cheek, and went outside.

Nimue sighed and fell back into the bed.

CHAPTER
THIRTY-NINE

ANWIL

Anwil and Lancelot traveled quickly and stayed far from the main roads and villages. If they had to cross through a village, Anwil wore a cap over his hair and kept his head down. Posters of his face were plastered on road posts, and if anyone recognized him, it would call far too much attention. They hadn't stayed long in the village near Lancelot's house. Only long enough to pay the farmer for a horse. He thankfully didn't ask too many questions. Lancelot explained the village was used to his odd requests and that he was always good for payment, so they never pried.

Their journey was mostly quiet. Lancelot was on high alert, always searching their surroundings to make sure they weren't followed, and Anwil didn't wish to distract him. Although he was bursting at the seams with questions, he didn't ask them. Lancelot did take time to give him pointers on riding. Anwil wasn't a bad rider, but he wasn't particularly good either, not having much reason to ride on castle grounds. It was obvious Lancelot cared well for the horses, taking time to clean and brush them whenever they rested. Anwil found Lancelot talking to them as if they could reply more than once. Ariadne was the same way. She had learned to ride almost as soon as she could walk. Anwil remembered when they were little, Ariadne would be out at the stables or at the fields just watching them run. All the while, Anwil was in the library with his books. Perhaps he should have went with Ariadne a time or two, and then he may not have grown to be so useless.

After a few days, they came upon Glastonbury Tor, and Anwil breathed a sigh of relief. They were so close to Camelot. So close to home. But his relief did not last long as a piercing yell echoed through the air. Lancelot tore off, and Anwil followed.

They pushed their horses through the forest and marsh, down overgrown paths, and came to a halt at the lake, where Anwil's blood ran cold. The beach was bloody, and bodies were strewn about. Then he spotted bright red hair, the same as his. His blood froze at the sight of her laying on top of Gawaine, her arm bloody.

"Ari," he breathed. He jumped off his horse, his knee still sore, and he ran for her. Lancelot called after him, but he ignored him.

"Ari!" Anwil yelled, taking her shoulders.

To his relief, Ariadne looked up. Her eyes were red, and tear stains shone through the dirt on her face. Her eyes widened, but then she glared. She grabbed her sword and pushed herself to her feet, snarling at him.

"No!" she cried. "No. You won't fool me again! You killed them! You *killed* them! I'll kill you!" Ariadne lunged at him, but Lancelot blocked her before Anwil had time to react.

"Stay your hand, my lady!" Lancelot said. "What happened?"

"Who the fuck are you?" Ariadne growled, pulling her sword back. She went for Lancelot, but he easily blocked and disarmed her.

"Ari, stop!" Anwil threw his arms around his sister's neck. "Stop! It's me!"

Ariadne went rigid in his arms, panting. Anwil just held her tighter.

"Ari," Anwil said again. "Ari, it's me. It's me."

Ariadne broke. She fell to her knees, and Anwil went with her, holding her steady. She wrapped her arms tight around his waist and sobbed into his shoulder. Her armor poked and prodded at him, but he didn't care. He looked around the beach over her shoulder and saw Gawaine, Percival, and Lyrion. And then the Druids. His breath caught in his throat. This had to be a dream—a nightmare. They couldn't be gone. It wasn't possible.

"What happened?" Lancelot asked above him.

"Nimue," Brionna answered, holding her side and wincing. "And a man named Mordred, apparently."

Anwil curled his hands into fists. Nimue had taken far too many lives. If Anwil ever saw her again, he would kill her himself. They would pay. He would get better, he would train, and fight. No more hiding away in the library. He would join Ariadne on the training fields each morning. He lifted himself from Ariadne and wiped her tears, despite his own falling.

Ariadne sniffed and breathed another cry. "You're not dead," she whispered.

He shook his head. "No, I'm here."

Ariadne sobbed again. "They are," she said. "I should have—I shouldn't have—I got them killed. It's all my fault."

Anwil shook his head. "No," he whispered. "No. Nimue did this. She killed them, and she'll pay for it. I promise."

Lancelot gathered help from the monks rebuilding Glastonbury Abbey to help remove the bodies and load them on a cart to take back to Camelot. Ariadne hadn't said a word and barely responded when spoken to. Jabir said it was shock and that she would snap out of it soon. Anwil knew that when she snapped out of it, her anger would be incomparable. He felt it too. Anger, rage, grief, guilt. If he hadn't had gone off with Melara in disguise, none of this would have happened.

Gawaine, Percival, and Lyrion would not be dead. Lohengrin would still have a brother.

Anwil glanced at Lohengrin as they trudged the horses alongside the cart where they had laid six bodies. His face was pale and puffy. He, too, barely spoke. Anwil could only imagine the pain. If he lost Ariadne . . . He shook his head. He didn't wish to think on it.

The abbey was only half-built, but the monks had food to spare as the village close by had donated plenty. They ate in silence, most of them picking at the food while Mirah and Jabir tended to wounds. Brionna's ribs were broken, but the cut on her head was shallow. Jabir's leg wasn't broken, but he had a sprained ankle and a broken wrist. Lohengrin had mostly superficial wounds but sported many bruises. Nimue had loosed a spell that knocked them all off their feet, and Mordred showed inhuman strength and speed that he had bested them in mere seconds. They'd barely stood a chance. The Druids combined power hadn't been enough for Mordred's.

Lohengrin and Ariadne had gone off on their own, speaking in hushed tones just outside of earshot from the camp.

"I'm sorry." Mirah sat down next to Anwil, her own bowl of steaming stew in her hands. "I should have helped more."

Anwil shook his head. "Mirah," he said. "There was nothing to be done. Nimue and Mordred are too powerful. Besides, you're not a fighter." Mirah was too soft, but that's what Anwil liked best about her. She cared for everything, even the spiders and bugs that would sneak in with her herbs. Instead of killing them, she'd take them back outside, gently laying them in the grass.

"No, I'm not," said Mirah. "But I got a good punch in."

Anwil raised his eyebrows, and Mirah blushed. "I hated it." She rubbed at her elbow. "It was awful. All of it. As a healer, I'm used to blood, but to see the battle . . ." She shuddered and stared at her soup. "I'm sorry. Here I am complaining, and I'm the one who isn't injured. How are you?"

Anwil shrugged. "I don't know. I'm . . . I'm having a hard time . . . feeling everything. Nothing seems real." He couldn't tell her that he was a massive failure and not suited for the crown.

Mirah nodded. "Shock," she said. "Once we're home and you've had time to process, your emotions will flood back."

"Probably." Anwil pulled his knees to his chest. "I've been so focused on getting away from Nimue and coming home, I haven't thought on much else."

"That's normal. You've been trying to survive."

"How do you know this?" Anwil asked.

"Merlin's books," she explained. "He also studied human emotions. His notes are very detailed. You should read them. It might help." She trailed off as Lohengrin and Ariadne returned, their eyes red and puffy again. Ariadne plopped down next to Anwil and put her head on his shoulder as Lohengrin sat on her other side. They stayed there for a long while, eating

353

in silence until the monks filed out of the half-built abbey and bowed to them before beginning a hymn honoring the fallen. Lohengrin broke out into sobs again, covering his face with his hands. Silent tears fell down Anwil's face as he buried his face in his sister's hair.

CHAPTER FORTY

GUINEVERE

"What do we do with her?" Blanchefleur asked as Dindrane finished tying Ingride to the chair she had previously occupied.

"Leave her arse here, that's what," Dindrane grumbled, glaring daggers at Ingride.

"We have to be careful," said Guinevere. "If what she said was true, then we can't trust the guards at the moment."

"Horseshit," Dindrane snapped. "Those guards are loyal to Camelot and the crown. They can't be bought. My brother handpicked all of them."

"Still." Guinevere folded her arms across her chest. "Best not to alert anyone." She strode over to the window and peered down into the gardens. Gwent and Wessex men flooded the garden, but the Camelot guards held them back. She would have to completely redo security with Percival as soon as he returned. Find the weak spots.

"We won't get far." Blanchefleur peered over her shoulder.

"Neither will they," said Dindrane. "They're all about to have a rather rude awakening."

Guinevere watched as the guards attacked the Gwent and Wessex men. "So it begins," she whispered. Flashbacks erupted in her mind of the Battle of Camlann when Mordred sent his allies into the city. They hadn't made it far before they were overcome by Camelot's men. "Come, ladies."

Guinevere swept from the room, feeling a burst of energy. Dindrane and Blanchefleur followed her, locking Ingride in Guinevere's chambers behind them. They made their way down to the main level, which was absolute chaos. Camelot guards fought Gwent and Wessex men in the corridors. Dindrane quickly pulled Guinevere and Blanchefleur into one of the servants' doors before anyone noticed and slammed it shut behind her. It was dark in the hallway, but a light at the end of the hall opened into the throne room.

"You'll be a target, Guin," Dindrane said. "You'll have to hide."

Guinevere puffed her chest out. "I have never once in my life hidden from a fight," she said. "And I don't intend to now."

"Aye, well, best stick to the servants' halls anyway," Dindrane muttered, taking the lead down the hall.

They could already hear the fighting from the end of the hall, and Guinevere's heart pounded in her chest the closer they came, but she would not show her fear. Guinevere went through the doorway first and had to cover her nose from the stench of spilled blood. Gwent and Wessex men littered the blood-stained floor. Camelot guards walked about, checking on the dead or wounded. Constantine and Elyion had even taken up arms, and Lord Roland cleaned off his bloody sword with a cloth. He was the first to notice her.

"Guinevere!" he exclaimed. "Oh, thank the gods."

Constantine ran to her, eyes wide with fear. "Where is Yvanne?"

"I do not know," Guinevere said.

Constantine swore and ran from the room.

"Cerdic and Bors attempted an uprising," Lord Roland explained casually, as if it were a regular council meeting. "But of course, they failed. Caradoc has been apprehended, but Cerdic and Bors have yet to be captured. At least, to my knowledge."

"Thank you, Roland," said Guinevere. Her eyes traveled to Elyion, who sat at the Round Table, breathing hard. Guinevere went to him. "Are you all right, Elyion?"

"I'm too old for this." He let out a half-hearted chuckle. "But I'll be fine. Let's not do this again, though, eh?"

Guinevere squeezed his shoulder. "Guards," she said to the room. "Clean up the bodies and take any still living to the dungeons. Blanche, Dindrane, send down a few healers. We will not be cruel."

She beckoned for Roland to follow her, and he slid his sword into its scabbard, and they swept from the room. The action in the corridors was winding down. More Gwent and Wessex men lay about with Camelot guards still standing.

"You there!" Roland approached one guard. "Have you seen Princess Yvanne?"

"No, my lord," he said, winded. He dripped sweat under his helmet, and his tunic had specks of blood stains. "I did see Sir Malcolm run into the courtyard."

Roland and Guinevere hurried past him. Guinevere nearly dropped to her knees when they arrived at the courtyard steps. Cerdic and Bors had Yvanne bound, each with a dagger to her throat. Constantine was on his knees, held down by Gwent men. The Camelot guards that were in the courtyard were at an uneasy stalemate with the Gwent and Wessex soldiers. She did not see Sir Malcolm anywhere.

"I'm sad to say I am not shocked to see that you two are this stupid," Guinevere said, standing to her full height. "How do you think this will end? That you will be welcomed with open arms after you slaughter us? What do you think the people will do?" She nodded toward the crowd of subjects in the courtyard and hovering near the gates. "Our allies? Will they listen to you? Will they still honor the agreements?" Guinevere descended a few of the stairs. "Did you truly think you would rule over a grand kingdom?"

Bors scoffed. "I will not fall to your mind games, woman!" he yelled. "We've had enough of the Pendragons! Enough of your arrogance and twisted laws!"

"Bors," said Guinevere. "Did you know that Cerdic and Caradoc have not yet converted to Christianity, nor will they ever?"

"That matters not," Bors growled. "We have the same goal: to rid Briton of the Pendragons once and for all. You've all cheated your way to the throne for too long."

"And this *isn't* cheating?" Guinevere moved down another step.

Yvanne whimpered as Cerdic pushed the dagger into her neck. Constantine tried to jerk away from his captors, but they held him tight.

"Stay where you are," said Cerdic, eyeing her. "Or the princess dies."

Guinevere heeded his words. Cerdic was not one to bluff. "You kill her," she said, "and you'll have committed war crimes. Do you think you will not be held accountable? She is innocent. Let her go."

"I think not," said Bors. "Where's my wife?"

"In my chambers." Guinevere shrugged. "Enjoying the lovely view, I'm sure."

"Surrender, Guinevere," said Cerdic. "Now. We have the city."

Guinevere did a very un-queenly thing and snorted. "Do you truly believe that?" She snapped her fingers, and archers appeared from their hiding spots in the towers, along the gates, and behind her.

Sir Malcolm, an arrow nocked in his bow, aimed at Cerdic and descended the courtyard stairs. "Drop your weapons!" he yelled and put himself in front of Guinevere.

The Gwent and Wessex men looked around and hesitantly dropped their swords to the ground.

"No!" Cerdic slashed Yvanne's throat as Bors threw a dagger at Malcolm. Without thinking, Guinevere stepped out from behind Malcolm to run to Yvanne.

Constantine screamed as Yvanne fell, and Malcolm loosed his arrow, hitting Cerdic in the shoulder. Malcolm tried to grab Guinevere out of the way, but he was too late. The dagger caught her in the side. Pain exploded in her stomach, and she clutched at her wound and stumbled.

CHAPTER FORTY-ONE

ARIADNE

Ariadne screamed as she watched her mother fall. They had just arrived at Camelot to find the people carrying on about an uprising at the castle. They'd left the cart of monks behind and raced their horses into the city, coming through the gates just as Bors flung his dagger at Guinevere. It had all happened at once: Yvanne falling, Guinevere running into the dagger, Cerdic being hit with an arrow.

Ariadne jumped off her horse, sword drawn and running as fast as she could toward her mother. She barley hesitated as Bors saw her and came after her, heavy sword drawn. Ariadne saw red. She was too fast for him. He was too fat and out of breath to hold a proper fight. She gained the upper hand easily, and when he was on his knees, she swung her sword like a club and sliced through his neck. Blood sprayed over her as his head rolled to the ground. Another yell sounded and she looked up. Mirah was frantically tending to Guinevere, and Jabir and Anwil held a bloody Yvanne. Constantine, covered in blood and dirt, fell next to his daughter, a heart-piercing and shrill scream escaping from him. Anwil kissed Yvanne's forehead, her glossy eyes staring up at the sky, the last expression of a gasp on her face. Ariadne's grip on her sword shook. Her blood boiled.

The courtyard had broken out into a fight around her, but Ariadne only had eyes for Cerdic. She found him fighting Lord Roland at the top of the stairs. She stalked over to him, shoving her way through fights in the process and running up the stairs. He didn't see or hear her coming up behind him; he was too focused on Roland. Ariadne didn't bother to announce her presence before she shoved her sword through his back. Roland stumbled backward, careful to not be pierced with Ariadne's sword as well.

Cerdic froze, gasping.

"Long live the Pendragons," she whispered in his ear and slid her sword out. He fell to his knees, blood tricking from his mouth. Ariadne kicked him over and watched his body tumble down the steps. Her breath echoed in her ears as his body flopped over and over and landed on the dirt. She should be sickend at the sight, sickened that she cut Bors' head off without batting an eye, but all she felt was anger.

"Ari!" *Mirah.*

Ariadne ran toward Mirah's voice and dropped to her knees next to her mother. Blood soaked through her gown. Ariadne dropped her sword, the anger melting into desperation and fear.

Her mother gasped. "Ar—Ari—"

"Mother, hold on!" Ariadne grabbed her hand, tears streamed down her face, and looked to Mirah, who was holding a rag against Guinevere's side. "Mirah. Mirah, please!"

"I need to get her to the infirmary!" Mirah shouted.

"I'll take her," someone said above Ariadne.

Lancelot appeared, and Guinevere's eyes widened. Ariadne had forgotten all about him. He had stuck close to Anwil on the journey back to Camelot, but Ariadne didn't trust him. Ariadne didn't want him touching her mother, but Mirah pulled Ariadne away as Lancelot knelt.

"La-Lance?" Guinevere rasped.

"I've got you, Guin," he said gently and picked her up.

Ariadne followed Mirah and Lancelot to the infirmary, barely noticing what was happening around her.

They arrived at the infirmary, which was emptier than it had been in weeks, and Cassius immediately came to their aid. He cleared a table, and he and Mirah got to work. Lancelot laid Guinevere carefully on the table and backed up to let the two physicians do their work. He put a hand on Ariadne's shoulder and backed her up too to give them room. She shrugged his hand from her and he stepped back.

Her mother slipped in and out of consciousness, and Ariadne watched, silent tears running down her cheeks. This was all her fault. She should have stayed here, with her mother. She should have been with Anwil the night of the fire. She should have done more. She shouldn't have gone with the Druids' plans and gotten Gawaine, Percival, and Lyrion killed. And now her mother . . .

Ariadne let out a cry and crossed over to the table and took her mother's hand in her own. Guinevere was so pale, and her breathing was shallow. Mirah and Cassius worked to clean up the blood and sew the wound shut. Guinevere squeezed her hand, but her grip was weak.

"Oh no." Mirah's face drained of all color as she stared at Guinevere's wound.

"What?" Ariadne gasped. "What is it?"

Mirah didn't answer right away. She looked to Cassius, who frowned, the wrinkles pulling at his lips and eyes.

"Poison," he whispered. "There was poison on the blade."

The room felt empty of air. "You—You have an antidote, right?" When they said nothing, Ariadne repeated, "*Right?*"

"We'd have to know what the poison was," Mirah said, her voice barely above a whisper. "And there's . . . there's no time."

"No!" Ariadne growled. "No, I can't lose her too! No, you do something! Use your magic!"

Mirah looked heartbroken. "I can't, Ari." She started to sob just as Anwil came through the door, Yvanne's blood on his hands and shirt. He gasped, seeing Guinevere on the table. He hurried over, stopping next to Ariadne, looking over their mother and then up at the physicians.

"She'll be all right, yes?" he said, his voice shaking. "You can heal her?"

"Anwil."

Guinevere's whisper startled all of them. She weakly lifted a bloody hand, and Anwil took it, holding it to his face.

"My boy," Guinevere whispered. "I knew . . . I knew you were alive. You and . . . your sister. My darlings. My darlings . . ."

She took a gasping breath and let it out, her body going limp.

"No," Ariadne said through tears. "No. NO! Mother! MOTHER!"

Anwil shook beside her, and Ariadne laid her head on her mother's chest, her sobs echoing around the room.

"Come back," she cried. "Please. Come back. Please . . ."

But her mother didn't move. Anwil covered Ariadne, his own sobs shaking her as well. Guinevere couldn't be gone. She couldn't. She was their mother, their sturdy rock. Her time wasn't up! Not now!

After a long while, Mirah peeled Anwil and Ariadne off Guinevere, her own face streaked with tears and her eyes puffy. She took both of them in a tight embrace. "I'm so sorry," she whispered.

"It's not your fault," Anwil said, shaking his head. "You did all you could."

Mirah kissed his cheek and hugged Ariadne again. "I'm so sorry, Ari. I'm so sorry."

Ariadne laid her head on Mirah's shoulder. It wasn't Mirah's fault. It was Bors' and Cerdics'. And they were dead. Ariadne hoped they'd spend an eternity burning in Hell.

"Come," Lancelot said gently. "Let the healers work."

Ariadne let him lead her and Anwil out of the infirmary. Anwil took Ariadne's hand as they walked through the empty corridors. They were both covered in blood and dirt and sweat. Ariadne was hyperaware of her armor and the blood all over her. Her hair stuck to the sweat on the back of her neck. Her mind had gone numb, and she felt as if it were all a terrible dream. She hoped it was all a terrible dream, that she would wake up in her bed and find that it was all a terrible nightmare.

They arrived at the courtyard and found that the Gwent and Wessex men had surrendered. Servants were already helping to take the bodies away. When the people noticed Anwil's presence and the distraught looks on his and Ariadne's faces, they knew. And one by one, they knelt and bowed their heads.

CHAPTER
FORTY-TWO

ANWIL

F lowers, gifts, and other small memorials flooded the castle and courtyard over the next couple of weeks. There were so many that they lined the courtyard grass and along the steps, and the great hall was littered with them. People from the city and all over Briton came to pay their respects. Word of the uprising and deaths had traveled quickly. The Pendragons once again held a formidable reputation of strength and power. Any doubt from the last few months faded away, especially after word of Ariadne beheading King Bors and killing Lord Cerdic with barely a fight spread. Anwil was praised for escaping Nimue and returning the great Sir Lancelot to Camelot. If only they knew what he had actually done.

Anwil existed about in a daze, exhausted and drained. His knee had healed, but Cassius said it would most likely bother him for the rest of his life. There was so much to take care of. He was grateful for Lord Roland, who had taken over most of it. He couldn't find the concentration, no matter how much he tried. His mind kept seeing his mother, Yvanne, Lyrion, and Gawaine . . . and how much he wished he could close his eyes, travel back, and have them all alive again. But the more he thought about it, the more the panic rose in his chest, and he would need to leave the room, gasping for air.

He could barely look at Lohengrin. The guilt over his closest friend losing both his father and brother was too much. Anwil knew it was selfish, but he couldn't help it. They should have just left him to his fate and made Ariadne queen.

Ariadne was . . . angry. Angry at everything. And she took it out on the wooden dummies in the training yards or with Brionna. She'd ordered all Gwent and Wessex soldiers to be tried for treason, Queen Ingride among them, and Anwil didn't argue. Their trials were quick and swift. Lady Ilsa and a few other lower-ranking nobles were also tried and sentenced to death. Ilsa had begged and pleaded, even gotten on her knees, but the sentence stood.

Mirah and Jabir had washed and preserved Guinevere, Percival, Gawaine, Lyrion, and Yvanne. Their bodies rested in glass coffins in the throne room for people to pay their respects before the funeral was held. Anwil visited every night when

OF CROWNS AND LEGENDS

the castle went dark. They all looked as if they were sleeping, as if they could open their eyes at any moment and he would awaken from this nightmare.

One night, during the first snow, Ariadne joined him. Neither said anything. They didn't need to. They stood together for a long while, Ariadne's head on Anwil's shoulder, until they were both swaying on their feet and went to bed.

Anwil hadn't quite gotten used to sharing his bed with Yvanne before he was taken, but now, he found his bed too large, and he reached for her in his sleep.

The funeral was larger than Anwil's wedding. People packed the city and courtyard despite the freezing air, all wearing dark colors and black bands on their arms. But it was the quiet that disturbed Anwil the most. The city had never been so quiet. The hymns sung by the priests echoed in the wind as the coffins were carried to the tombs.

Anwil and Ariadne walked together directly behind Guinevere's, dressed in matching black. Ariadne's dress had a dove sewn into her skirt—her mother's personal sigil—and Anwil's gold dragon glinted against the black velvet of his tunic. Only the knights, kings, and Anwil and Ariadne entered the dark tomb, the stench of stale water and rot hitting his nose. Roland gave them a torch, and they lit the way.

Gawaine, Percival, and Lyrion were laid with the knights and Guinevere next to Arthur. Yvanne was given her own slot, carried by her father and his men. Constantine's sobs bounced off the stone-and-dirt walls. The ceiling was low, and Anwil swore the walls were closing in on him. But he stood steady as the knights slid the coffins into the freshly dug out graves.

Ariadne was the first to leave with a huff, and Anwil followed her out, grateful because he couldn't take the confined space any longer. He didn't want to see coffins anymore or feel the tightness of the walls. He couldn't.

Ariadne stopped near the tomb's entrance, and the people gathered closest had the tact to look distracted as they exited.

"We need to find her," Ariadne said through gritted teeth. "Find her and kill her."

Anwil squeezed her hand. "We will. And we won't stop until we do."

CHAPTER FORTY-THREE

MORDRED

Mordred glared at the quaint little cottage. If it had been anyone else's, he would have found it charming. A large garden, a small pond, and farm animals wound around the home, and chimes hung from the porch. A fluffy gray cat sat perched on the railing, flicking its tail at him and Nimue, and a murder of crows squawked from the roof. Ruins of a temple or manor were barely visible under the snow and paw prints were littered along the porch and small yard.

Mordred gritted his teeth. His mother should have been ruling Tintagel where she belonged, not hiding away in a fairy-tale cottage. He would right the wrongs done to her, him, and their people—what he had started all those years ago before falling to Arthur on the battlefield. He had been too naïve and impatient before. His own mistakes had cost him his life. But now, he would go about it better. He would be patient. He had to do this carefully. And cleverly.

Nimue's footsteps digging into the snow pulled him from his thoughts. She was pale, with dark circles under her eyes. Her hair was dull, and her skin showed the first signs of wrinkles. If they didn't heal her soon, she would fade. That was the first step. He needed her at her full power. She wrapped the cloak tighter around her shoulders as the icy wind swirled around them.

Mordred stepped up to the front door of the cottage and knocked. A dog barked from within. He only had to wait a moment before a woman open the door. Her long black hair was braided over her shoulder, and she wore a simple gray dress. Her eyes were still the priestess purple, and she stepped back with a hand pressed to her chest.

She gasped. "Mordred?"

"Hello, Mother."

ACKNOWLEDGEMENTS

There are so many people I want to thank for this story: First, to my high school Latin classmates, who got in trouble with me giggling about my book when we should have been paying attention to Mrs. Scarvel, you were my first readers. My mom and dad, of course, who said I had something good and I need to "quit changing things around and just finish!" My sister, Hannah, who put up with all my faire and book talk.

To my own knight, my husband, Tim, who helped me write the fight and joust scenes, who made sure the armor parts were correct, and who supports me unconditionally on my writing adventures, who listens to me on all the ups and downs of writing and publishing and never ever once told me to quit. Who says I will be famous millionaire author one day. I love you more than words can tell.

To Brie, who lit my spark after almost ten years of not writing, who told me that I needed to pick up the pen again and write this story, who was my critique partner and Snapchat buddy when I needed to work out plot holes and talk out ideas.

To my friends, Gretchen and Natalie. To my best friend, Candalyn, with whom I've shared so many adventures and stories, I say, WAFFLES HO!

To Randy, my fellow librarian and the real Lord Roland.

To Brittany, my Lady of the Lake, my friend, my sister, even though half the country separates us.

To those that modeled for my photoshoot, David, Megan, Josie, Melissa, Tony, Claudia, Richard, Allee, Mya, Aaron, Kait.

To Chad, who was my first ever official review and my most excited ARC reader.

To all of my friends who commented, liked, shared, and supported me on social media, who read the ARCs, who have become my found family. Thank you.

A special thank you to Chelsea at Enchanted Ink Publishing for the amazing copyedits, and for the "Hallelujah!" comment about coffee. Thank you to Stefanie at SeventhStar for the most magical book cover.

And to you, dear reader. Thank you.

ABOUT THE AUTHOR

Chelsea Banning is a writer, reader, performer, and lover of all things fantasy. She started writing at age fifteen and hasn't stopped since. She loves renaissance faires, camping, reading, and cosplay. She currently lives in NE Ohio, where she works as a librarian, with her husband, step-daughter, and dogs, Daenerys and Scooby.

Thank you for reading!

Sign up for my newsletter at www.chelseabanning.com for updates and more!

Follow me on social media and Patreon for updates and behind-the-scenes looks!

CHELSEA BANNING

Made in the USA
Monee, IL
17 December 2022

22134776R00229